TERMINATOR
SALVATION
THE OFFICIAL
MOVIE NOVELIZATION

TERMINATOR SALVATION

THE OFFICIAL MOVIE NOVELIZATION

ALAN DEAN FOSTER

Based on the motion picture written by

JOHN BRANCATO & MICHAEL FERRIS

TITAN BOOKS

Terminator Salvation: The Official Movie Novelization
ISBN: 9781848560857

Published by
Titan Books
A division of
Titan Publishing Group Ltd
144 Southwark St
London
SE1 0UP

First edition April 2009
10 9 8 7 6 5 4 3 2 1

Terminator Salvation: The Official Movie Novelization is a work of fiction.
Names, places and incidents either are products of the author's imagination or
are used fictitiously.

Visit our website:
www.titanbooks.com

Did you enjoy this book? We love to hear from our readers. Please email us
at readerfeedback@titanemail.com or write to us at Reader Feedback at the
above address.

To receive advance information, news, competitions, and exclusive Titan offers
online, please register as a member by clicking the "sign up" button on our
website: www.titanbooks.com

A CIP catalogue record for this title is available from the British Library.

Printed and bound in the United States.

For Brian Thomsen, who would have approved.
But who left much too soon.
In appreciation and friendship.

The future is not set.
I've been told I said that once.
Many years from now.
It was a warning.
That I was going to hell.
But if I fought hard enough,
I could escape.
I believed it for a lifetime.

— John Connor

CHAPTER ONE

Longview State Correctional Facility was no better or worse, no more architecturally attractive or depressing, than any other maximum security prison in the state of Texas, which meant that on the inmates' gauge of such wretched establishments it fell somewhere between dismal and butt-ugly.

Its residents, both short- and long-term, tended to be as hard and unforgiving as the land atop which their current place of residence had been raised. Few blue-collar criminals dared raise hand or head among the growling populace, whose professional pursuits tended to involve cracking heads as opposed to persuading them.

Or to put it another way, Longview was home to far more head-crackers than crackheads.

Among the former could be accounted a certain highly antisocial specimen named Marcus Wright. Regrettably, for much of his life Wright had been in the wrong. At the moment, he was sitting on a cot in a small piece of concrete hell staring at the wall opposite. The vision of flecking stone and cement had nothing particular to recommend it, but it beat gazing at any of the three men standing nearby. Two wore uniforms, the third did not.

No, he corrected himself. That wasn't quite true. All three wore uniforms. It was depressing for Wright to look at them because two stood on the other side of the welded iron bars that confined him in his current cage and the third could exit at any time. Society preferred to call his present, and increasingly transitory, home a "cell." Wright knew better. Both were four-letter words.

Two of the free individuals were guards. Armed and holding metal shackles, they kept a wary eye on the proceedings taking place on the other side of the bars. Their posture and expressions reflected the preoccupations of hard men who are fully conscious of the fact that any relaxation in the carrying-out of their daily routine could result in pain, injury, or death. They hadn't acquired their current positions within Longview because those of neurosurgeon and rocket scientist were unavailable.

It wasn't that they were ignorant: just that in their chosen line of work muscle and physical agility were more critical to continued survival than the mental kind. Not that this usually mattered. With few exceptions, their cranial capacity normally exceeded that of those they were expected to dominate.

Normally.

The third member of the triumvirate standing just inside the cell door defined himself through his words, though having attended to many present and former residents of the prison he too had inevitably been toughened by the experience. Over the years his recitation of the traditional biblical standards had devolved into a monotone tinged more by a lingering, bastard hope than actual expectation.

While the priest's optimism in the face of the brutality human beings could render unto one another had never been entirely quashed, it had been repeatedly squeezed and pummeled by a demoralizing range of harsh realism until it bore little resemblance to what one could expect to hear asserted on The Outside.

His faith was punch-drunk.

"Yea," he intoned mechanically, "though I walk through the valley of the shadow of death, I will fear no evil."

Stupid, Marcus Wright thought. *Stupid and redundant. Why would I be afraid of myself?* Wasn't he evil incarnate? Hadn't that asshole of a judge told him so, and hadn't he had it confirmed by a smarmy, quivering public? If that was their verdict on him, then it had to be true, didn't it? He'd long ago lost any desire to dispute society's judgment. That much he had in common with the concrete wall at which he was presently staring. Both of them were solid, impenetrable, blank-faced, and mute. If the wall could accept its fate in silence, so could he.

"...for thou art beside me."

The priest droned on. *Why couldn't the man just shut up?* Wright wondered silently to himself. Why would he, why would anyone, spend one minute longer in the bowels of this gray cesspool of decomposing humanity than they had to?

"Thy rod and thy staff comfort me."

Now that was a homily Wright felt he could get behind. *Give me a rod and a staff*, he thought with grim humor, *and then you better get out of my way. Give me a chance...*

One thing about hard polished floors and solid

enclosed corridors: they make for excellent acoustics. This can be unpleasant when someone is screaming incessantly, an activity not uncommon at Longview. The construction can also magnify ordinary footsteps, and this was the sound that caused Wright to give a cursory glance in the direction of the outside.

An instant later his full attention had shifted from the immovable wall to an approaching waist. His suddenly alert eyes proceeded to rove silently over everything both above and below that gently bobbing dividing line.

The guards looked, too. Visitants like Dr. Serena Kogan were rare in Longview. Her title was not what interested them, though Wright's reaction was more conflicted than they would have suspected. Long used to such blatant testosterone-fueled stares, Kogan ignored them.

Still in her thirties, she was unconventionally beautiful. Part of this was due to the nature of her work, which gave her an aspect of perfection that was partly the result of intense concentration. Uncharacteristically, desperation announced itself in the slight gauntness of her face and the tightness of her lips. It detracted from her beauty only slightly.

Halting outside his cell, she looked in and met Wright's gaze without flinching. The ensuing silence between them spoke, if not volumes, at least a word or two. He looked up at the priest.

"Leave." Emerging from the prisoner's mouth, it was plainly a command and not a request.

His State-supported visitor gestured hesitantly with the Bible he held.

"I'm not finished, son."

Wright's gaze shifted from wall to uninvited confessor. His stare was, arguably, more unyielding than the concrete. It was not necessary for him to respond—verbally.

As pragmatic as he was well-meaning, the priest got the message. As the heavy metal door was pulled back he did not even glance in the direction of the new arrival. He was lost in his own thoughts, which were not as comforting as he would have liked.

One of the guards managed to raise his gaze from the rest of Serena Kogan to her face long enough to give her a warning nod.

If you need us, me and my buddy are right here, his expression said, while the look on his colleague's face added, *Don't do anything to need us.*

As the cell door slid shut behind her, awkwardness substituted for a casual greeting. Disinterested at the best of times in casual chatter, Wright regarded her wordlessly. The silence between them threatened to grow as wide as the gap between their respective social positions.

"How are you?" she finally murmured.

In the troglodytic confines of the cell the query was at least as funny as the paramount punchline of a highly paid stand-up comedian.

"Ask me again in an hour," Wright replied coldly.

With the silence but not the unease broken, her attention wandered to the cell's small desk. It boasted little in the way of accoutrements save for a single tome: *Beyond Good and Evil.* Not exactly light reading, but she was pleased to see it.

"You got the book I sent."

Wright wasn't one to comment on the obvious. For all he mouthed in response he might have read the volume through, or he might have used the pages for toilet paper. His expression gave no clue. And they were both running out of options.

"I thought I'd try one last time." In the dim light of the cell her pale skin gleamed like the sun he could no longer see. "Beg, really."

No smile, no frown. Same monotone, same unreadable expression.

"You should've stayed in San Francisco," he muttered. "Situations reversed, I would have."

She stared at him a moment longer, then moved deliberately over to the desk. From the slim case she carried she removed a sheaf of neatly bound papers, set them on the battered, scored surface, and added a pen. Per entrance regulations, the pen had a soft tip. Her voice strengthened.

"By signing this consent form you'd be donating your body to a noble cause. You'd have a second chance, with your last act, to do something for humanity. It's an opportunity that's not offered to everyone in your position."

He looked up at her.

"You know what I did. I'm not looking for a second chance."

She hesitated, then picked up the pen and papers. Her slender hands were shaking, and not because of his nearness. Having corresponded with her, he knew at least part of the reason why.

"'Course, I'm not the only one with a death sentence, am I? Life's funny that way. You think by signing those papers I'm going to help cure your cancer, Dr. Kogan?"

She stiffened slightly.

"We're all going to die, Marcus. Sooner or later, everyone dies, every thing dies. People, plants, planets, stars—

everything. In the scheme of things my life, your life, none of them matter. We're here for a minute or two; we eat, laugh, and screw around, and then we're gone."

She snapped her fingers.

"Like that. I'm not worried about myself. I'm worried about the future of the human race."

He appeared to ponder her response, then nodded slowly.

"Like I should care about the future of the human race. Like anyone should. It produced me, didn't it?" He went silent for another moment, then declared, "Tell you what I'll do. I'll *sell* it to you. My body." He looked down at himself and the disgust in his voice was unmistakable. "This...."

It wasn't the final reply she had expected.

"'Sell' it? For what?"

He looked up at her again, meeting her gaze evenly. A glint of life had appeared amid the emptiness in his eyes. Or maybe it was just the angle of the overhead lights.

"A kiss."

Her lower jaw dropped slightly and she gaped at him.

"Are you trying to be funny?"

He shrugged diffidently.

"I'm not funny even when I try." Extending one arm, he indicated his surroundings. "Not much to joke about here. Well?" His other hand tapped his chest. "You want the merchandise or not?"

"You're kidding, aren't you?"

"Last guy thought I was kidding didn't have a chance to revise his opinion."

She swallowed. Her gut was riven with inoperable tumors. She had something to gain and absolutely nothing to lose. When you're dying, it's amazing how swiftly abstract notions like self-respect and dignity are reduced to useless platitudes. She set the pen and papers back on the desk, then turned back to him and nodded. Her arms dropped to her sides. She looked like a woman facing a firing squad.

For the first time since the priest had come and gone, Wright rose from the cot. Standing, he looked a lot taller, a lot bigger. The emotional as well as physical threat he represented extended out in all directions from his powerful frame. Just being in his vicinity was disturbing.

Outside the cell, the two veteran guards saw what was happening and immediately moved closer to the door. One gripped the handle in anticipation. But they had been told not to interfere unless it became absolutely necessary.

Wright moved closer to her. She held her ground. Slowly, taking his time, he leaned toward her. Over her. Before the guards could get inside he could reach up and snap her neck like a desiccated broomstick, and they both knew it.

Bending down, he kissed her.

His hands rose to hold the sides of her face as he held the contact. There was not a shred of sexual attraction, of romance, of tenderness, in the kiss. It was ugly and violating and psychologically—if not physically—brutal. While it continued her eyes were shut tight, and not with pleasure.

He held it for a long time.

Alternately repulsed and bemused, the guards looked on but made no move to intervene. Already they were imagining how they were going to tell the story to their cohorts. Later, over hot coffee and sweet pastries.

***

The unwieldy clinch continued until Wright had had enough. Maybe he simply grew bored. Or maybe he had sufficiently demonstrated what he could do if he wanted to. Letting go of her he stepped back, studying her face. Looking through her. When he finally spoke, his tone was atypically thoughtful.

"So that's what death tastes like."

Though she tried, her expression did not kill him. In any case, that was the State's responsibility.

Stepping past her, he picked the pen up off the desk. Without so much as a glance at the pages of extensive legalese, he signed where indicated. He could have misspelled his name, could have signed "George Washington," could have done any number of things to render the process legally invalid. Instead, he wrote "Marcus Wright" in clear, legible letters. A deal was a deal, and he felt he had gotten his money's worth.

Putting down the pen he turned to the corridor and turned his hands palm upwards, showing them to the guards. The one whose grip had never left the door handle now pulled the metal barrier wide while his partner hefted the leg shackles he was carrying. No explanation was necessary.

It was time.

Stepping out of the cell Wright stood stolidly, staring at the far wall of the corridor. It was a relief to be out of the cage. Even if it was just to be in the corridor. Even if it was for the last time. He did not move, nor offer any resistance as the guard methodically snapped the shackles shut around his ankles. Their weapons and training notwithstanding, he knew he could have taken both of them. They probably knew it too, just as all three of them knew that if he made any kind of hostile move he would never get out of the corridor alive, and that his demise would assuredly be less swift and probably more painful than the one that had been adjudicated by the State.

While his legs were being secured, Kogan was studying the papers. At once satisfied and relieved she tucked them carefully, almost reverentially, into her carry case. Only then did she exit the cell and stand to one side, gazing at the stone-faced Wright.

"You're doing something very noble."

He looked back at her. "I'm dying for my sins and letting you slice up my body until there's nothing left of me. Not that there'd be anybody to visit a grave if I was going to one. Yeah, I'm a regular hero."

"You don't understand. This is the beginning of something wonderful."

"No. It's the end of something miserable."

The guard who had put on the leg shackles made a final check of each before straightening. He and his colleague exchanged a glance. Then the other man nodded at the prisoner.

"Let's go. It's time."

Since there was no way to disguise the death chamber, and no reason to do so, no State had ever made the attempt. Pastel colors would have seemed out of place, any kind of décor beyond what was necessary and required would only be condescending. The room was spare, empty, as functional as a coal bin or a crankshaft.

There was a bulletproof glass partition. One side featured seats reserved for the invited: witnesses, the media, family members of the condemned's victims. The other side was reserved for death.

Many executions were attended only by those necessary to carry out the will of the people. Not Marcus Wright's. While not drawing the fervor of a seventeenth-century public beheading, it was the capital punishment equivalent of a full house.

Serena Kogan was among the spectators. Not because her presence was required, but because for reasons known only to herself she felt incumbent to be present.

Flanked by the ever-attentive guards, the prisoner shambled in on his own power. Too many had to be dragged, or sedated beforehand.

Not Wright.

Aided by the guards, the execution team took over. Guiding him firmly, they positioned him on his back on the gurney. As wrist and ankle shackles were removed, thick leather straps were buckled across his body and carefully tightened. At the moment of truth, powerful men who had been calm and even boastful beforehand had been known to fly into violent, uncontrollable convulsions. It was why the straps had been made strong enough to hold down a bucking steer.

As the team continued its silent, methodical work, Longview's warden spoke from where he was standing nearby. He did not say much. This was neither the time nor the place for idle chatter.

"Final words?"

Lying on the gurney as others labored silently and efficiently around him, Wright considered. He never had been very good with words. Maybe if he had been better with them than with his fists.... Too late for that now. Too late for any sort of recriminations. He would have shrugged, had the straps allowed it.

"I killed a man who didn't deserve it. Fair's fair. So let it rip."

In his years at Longview the warden had heard it all. It was not an eloquent farewell, but neither had the prisoner given in to hysteria. For that the warden was grateful. The process was no less distasteful for having become rare. It was always better when it was not messy.

A technician swabbed Wright's arm with alcohol. Turning his head to watch, he wondered about that. What, were they afraid he might get an infection? There was barely a twinge when the IV was inserted. The tech was very good at his job and the needle going in didn't hurt at all. Wright was unaccountably grateful.

His eyes began to move rapidly, taking in his surroundings and the rest of the chamber. Everything appeared suddenly new and heightened. The color of the technicians' coats. The blue of a guard's eyes. The intensity of the overhead lights. There was something else new, too. For the first time in the prisoner's eyes, fear.

Off to one side a technician adjusted a valve. Fluid began to flow through the tube that now ran into Wright's arm. The tube was plastic, the liquid transparent. It looked like water.

His eyes moved faster. Monitors showed that his heart rate had increased sharply, along with his breathing. There was no pain save the pain of realization. Along with the chemicals, he suddenly realized how badly he wanted to live. He wanted to fight back, needed to struggle. But he could not. The lethal cocktail was already taking hold, doing its work, shutting down system after system. Nervous, respiratory, circulatory, end of story.

He would have screamed but could not.

Overhead, the light was bright and white. Clean, cleansing. Faintly, as thoughts and mind and the remnants of consciousness slowly slipped away, he fought to compose a final, last thought. It was not about the things he had done that had led him to this place and this point in time. It was not of happier days, or of how his life had gone astray and might have been changed for the better. It was not of food or of sex or laughter or sorrow.

It was of that last kiss, and how he might have done it better.

CHAPTER TWO

Animals appear and thrive and then go extinct. Plants cover ground like a green blanket, retreat, and return with greater fecundity. Life expands, contracts, shatters and recovers, sometimes falling to the margins of survival.

But the Earth endures. No matter the number of species that swarm its surface or fall victim to flood, earthquake, plague, tectonic drift, or cosmic catastrophe, the planet continues its methodical swing around its unprepossessing yellow star. The waves of the ocean roll on, the molten iron at its core seethes and bubbles, winds fitful or steady continue to scour its surface. Ice forms and retreats at the poles, rains drench the equator, and heat shimmers above its deserts.

One such desert in the south-central part of the continent called North America was about to receive a momentary upsurge in heat that was not normal.

The missile came in low and fast on a trajectory designed to evade even the most advanced detection systems. The warhead it carried contained considerably more bang than would have been suspected at first glance. Guided by both its programming and its internal sacrificial intelligence elements, it skimmed along the surface so low that it was forced to dodge the occasional tree and still-standing power transmission tower.

Its target was a flat, burnt-out plain from which dozens of huge satellite dishes rose like shelf coral on a reef. The only sign of life in this technological forest of parabolic growths was a single bipedal figure. Marching at a steady, untiring pace among the dishes, it occasionally reached up to reposition the oversized rifle that was slung over one shoulder.

A sound drew its attention. Turning, searching the sky, it quickly focused on the incoming ordinance. Slipping the heavy weapon free, it aimed and fired with exceptional speed and precision. A shell struck one of the missile's fins, knocking it off-heading—but only for an instant. The weapon's internal self-governing guidance system instantly corrected course.

Even as the projectile inclined downward toward a patch of bare ground in the center of the expansive array, the guard was lining up his weapon to fire again. It was not at all concerned with what was about to happen to it.

The bunker-buster slammed into the earth with a thunderous *whoom!* The guard staggered, gathered himself, and prepared to aim his weapon again. Except that now there was only a hole in the ground to show where the missile had burrowed deep.

Then the world erupted in fire and sound as the warhead, having reached a preset depth, detonated.

Dirt and pulverized rock vomited skyward. Along with everything else in the immediate vicinity of the blast, the single guard was thrown helplessly skyward. He landed hard, rolled over, tried to rise, and sank back to the ground. Heat and flame had melted away skin to reveal the skull beneath. It should have shown white.

Instead, it gleamed.

Red eyes flickered.

Battling against the terrible damage it had sustained in the blast, the T-600 struggled to rise. Directives screamed for response. Servos whined and hydraulics pumped. But internal mechanics had been mortally impacted. That did not keep the Terminator from trying to stand.

Oblivious to the dogged determination of the severely impaired bipedal machine below, a flight of A-10 Warthogs roared past overhead, coming in low and slow. Unlovely and deadly, disdaining the sleek aerodynamics of much faster but less lethal aircraft, they began chewing up the ground in front of them with heavy cannon fire and rockets.

Instead of governmental insignia that had long since ceased to have meaning or validity, they were clad in a riot of colors and flurry of graffiti that reflected the tastes and attitudes of those who flew and serviced them: all of it wild, much of it obscene.

Popping up out of the ground, a single anti-aircraft weapon tracked, took aim, and fired. Striking one of the Warthogs behind its armor and hitting the vulnerable rear-mounted engines, it blew the Resistance fighter out of the sky. Before it could zero in on a second attacker, another aircraft hit it with a guided bomb that left only a smoking crater where the defensive weapon had once stood.

As the Warthogs whirled and danced overhead to provide cover, a flurry of helicopters appeared. Touching down, they began to disgorge squads of Resistance fighters clad in a mismatched array of uniforms, hunting gear, and civilian clothes. The attackers were armed with a hodgepodge of unusually hefty weapons that were as varied as the mix of military and civilian choppers that had transported them. Not one of the assault group would have passed muster in a proper military parade. On the other hand, all of them were alive.

One of the helicopter's landing skids set down directly on the skull of the T-600 that had been patrolling the dish array, crushing the metal and pressing it deep into the ground. Reacting automatically to the proximate presence of human feet, the crippled killing machine still struggled to strike back. Its critically damaged servos whined loudly.

A narrow metal tube made contact with the red-eyed skull: the barrel of a rifle. A single large-caliber shot blew half the glistening cerebellum off, sending it flying and bouncing to one side. Exposed to the light, internal circuitry flared, fizzled, and went dark.

John Connor regarded the lifeless T-600, waiting to make certain it was good and dead. The damn things had a dangerous habit of simulating death and then leaping up to bite you in the ass. This one, though, was good and demised. He lifted his gaze as another Warthog sputtered past overhead, trailing smoke. He did not look around as the weary but determined figure of Captain Jericho approached.

"Are you Connor?"

Grunting something unintelligible, Connor looked up.

"*The* John Connor?" Even as he addressed the other man, Jericho was keeping a wary eye on their immediate surroundings. "The guy who, according to the plan, was supposed to land his unit on the ridgeline and hump it in?"

Connor's gaze met the captain's.

"The plan was no good."

Jericho looked as though he was about to say something else, but he was interrupted by the arrival of Connor's unit. Spilling out of a nearby chopper, they assembled behind their leader and focused their attention on him.

"Trouble?" The grizzled trooper who spoke shifted his gaze from Connor to the captain.

Connor let his eyes linger a moment longer on Jericho. Over the last several years of fighting, the term "chain of command" had been transformed into an expletive that had more in common with the traditional SNAFU than with actual military procedure.

"No, no trouble. Let's go."

Jericho watched as Connor's team joined the others in racing to the rim of the gaping breach the first missile had opened in the ground. There was plenty he still wanted to say. Wisely, he said nothing.

Leaning over to peer cautiously into the cavernous maw, one of Connor's men declared with assurance if not eloquence, "That is one big-ass hole in the ground."

"Wonder what's down there?" His neighbor nudged him, just enough to unsettle but not unbalance his companion.

The other man snorted. "Want to bet we're gonna find out?"

General Olsen was young for his rank and older than his years. Unrelenting combat had aged him. To save one soldier's life he would throw procedure out the window. Now, in concert with his troops, he too found himself peering down into a darkness than was as metaphorical as it was literal.

"Make no mistake, men. We don't have a goddamn clue what's waiting for us down there. Hell, for sure. But what kind of hell we don't know and we need to find out." He glanced back. "So I need a volunteer—"

He broke off as a shape went shooting past him, seemed to hang in the air above the pit for a long second, and then went arcing downward. Like a spider's silken support strand, a single braid of climbing cable trailed from Connor's harness, glistening in the desert sunlight.

Away from the edge of the abyss, one of his men kept a watchful eye on the link where the other end of the cable had been secured to a twisted, seared hunk of aircraft debris.

Unable to decide whether to curse or cheer at Connor's unhesitating initiative, Olsen settled for waving at the clusters of men who stood gawking at the younger man's rapid descent into darkness.

"All right, single file! Everyone after Connor! Let's go, go *go!*"

Swinging slightly at the end of the cable, Connor could not hear the general. Pulling a flare from his service belt and igniting it, he tossed it outward. It sank into blackness, revealing only fleetingly the extent of the underground labyrinth that marched off in all directions. The subterranean facility was enormous. Like the others, he had expected it to be sizable, but this was far beyond anything they had been led to expect.

He hung quietly at the end of his tether, not making a sound, waiting for his fellow spider-soldiers to join him.

Jet swings gave them access to the side corridors. One by one, individual teams fanned out into the depths of the vast complex.

The human infection is coming, Connor thought with satisfaction as he led his men into one flooded tunnel. Waist-deep in water, he took his usual position at point. Other team leaders preferred to stay in the rear or move forward only when surrounded by their troops. Not Connor. He looked forward to leading the way physic-ally as well as tactically. It was a decision that had taught him something early on: Soldiers are far more likely to follow a leader who actually leads.

Weapons at the ready, David and Tunney hung close behind. As they advanced, David was muttering under his breath. Connor knew why but said nothing. David didn't mind dirt, wasn't afraid of action, would take on half a dozen enemy all by himself without bothering to call for backup—but he couldn't swim. Not normally a cause for concern in the southwestern deserts, and yet here he was up to his collywobbles in water.

Tunney flanked David, and Connor suspected it was all he could do to restrain himself from commenting on his partner's obvious discomfort.

The burrower bomb had done its work well. Ceilings had collapsed throughout the tunnel, unattended flames ate at advanced instrumentation, and the distinctive red lighting typical of Skynet environments flickered unsteadily. Connor would have been perfectly happy to see it all wink out, turn black and lifeless. If that happened, he and his men had come equipped with adequate illumination of their own.

The percussive chorale of distant gunfire echoed

faintly through the corridor they were probing. Evidently some of the other squads were encountering more than just dim lighting and broken plumbing.

Something stirred the water behind them, and it wasn't a consequence of collapsing infrastructure. By the time the T-1 was half out of the water both David and Tunney were whirling on it. It was David who got off the necessary burst. Shards of metal and carbon fiber splinters went flying as the would-be assassin was blown apart.

"Hey bro, I thought it was my turn." With the muzzle of his own weapon, Tunney nudged a floating scrap of Terminator.

David shrugged. "Gotta be faster than that, Ton. I'm going for a new high score. But I'll sit back and watch while you take out the next two."

His partner grinned tightly. "'Preciate it, bro. Anyway, if you're going for T-1s, you're not even in the game."

"Over here." Connor interrupted, calling to them from just up ahead. Instantly the two soldiers were all business again.

Shouldering his weapon, Connor used both hands to tug on the large handle of a heavy door set in the tunnel wall. It refused to budge. Another man might have put a foot on the door to gain leverage or asked his companions to assist. Having better things to do and insufficient time in which to do them, Connor instead removed a brick of C-4 from his backpack, followed it with ignition cord and a detonator. In his hands the complete explosive package came together like a pizza in Naples. Clustering nearby, his team looked on in admiration.

"Don't lose any fingers there, Chief." Nervousness was apparent in the voice of one of the younger soldiers as he watched Connor's fingers fly. A far more relaxed David glanced back at the concerned speaker.

"Shit, Connor's been a Class A terrorist his whole life. How many fingers is he missing? Right—none. Only thing getting blasted here is that door." Turning, he started wading back the way they had come. "Might want to put a little distance between you and the show. Otherwise you might lose face."

As soon as everyone had cleared, Connor set the timer and sprinted to join them. Time passed with interminable slowness before another soldier could not keep from whispering.

"I know how experienced he is, but it's sopping down here and mayb...."

The thunder of the C-4 was magnified by the narrowness of the corridor. The effect was not unlike hearing a dozen trumpets sound off all at once—with the listener crammed inside one of the instruments.

Several of the soldiers flinched. Not Connor or his two backups, Tunney and David. The explosion was just one more peroration in an interminable concert scored for instruments that consisted of expressively volatile compounds. Even before the air had cleared, Connor was leading them forward.

The room they entered was large and filled with smoke. While the haze was already dispersing, it was still difficult to see. Difficult enough so that Connor slipped on something and nearly fell. Looking down, he expected to see more water. Instead, the liquid underfoot was dark and sticky. For an instant he held onto the hope that it might be machine oil. But the color was wrong, too red.

The blood was reasonably fresh.

New sounds distracted him. For the first time since he and his squad had entered the complex they heard voices other than their own. The strongest of them was subdued, the weakest barely audible. Moans and pleas. Reaching down to his belt, he pulled and ignited another flare and lobbed it forward. It lit up the still diffusing mix of smoke, debris, evaporating liquid— and cages.

The voices were coming from multiple knots of humanity who had been packed with inhuman lack of concern into numerous holding pens. As Connor and his men drew close, hands extended toward them. His gaze flicked over pleading faces, gaunt bodies.

Some of the internees were in the last stages of exhaustion or starvation.

Tunney surveyed the unfortunate detainees with a jaundiced eye. As he contemplated a situation that, based on experience, made no sense, movement at the far end of the room caused him and his companions to hastily raise their weapons.

Almost as quickly, they relaxed. David even smiled. A larger compliment of their colleagues had broken into the chamber from another corridor.

Pushing his way through the internment area, Connor forced himself to ignore the pleading and extended hands. He was making his way toward a set of illuminated screens that fronted compact consoles. The latter, thankfully, were still functioning—but for how much longer it was impossible to tell. One thing he did know—they'd better work quickly. Hefting his communicator, he spoke into the pickup.

"Olsen, objective located. There's something else you have to see." Putting up the hand unit, he moved to the computation complex.

The general arrived soon after. Taking one glance at the glowing, living complex, he turned and barked a name.

"Barbarossa!"

Immediately, the team's lead technician hurried to join the two men. Soldiers moved around them, sealing the location. The tech halted, stunned by what he was seeing.

"Come on, man," Olsen prodded him. "We don't know how much time we're going to have here. Get to work." Nodding silently and slightly dazed, the tech drew his battlefield laptop and began fumbling with a handful of cables. Down here they didn't dare risk broadcasting their presence or any attempt at entry by trying for an over-the-air hookup.

"Spread out," Olsen told his troops. "Secure the perimeter." He pointed. "I've got a big gap over here. We're busy and I'm not in the mood for any surprises." Turning back to the silently watching Connor, he lowered his voice. "Why didn't we know about this?"

The tech chief interrupted him.

"I'm in. Looks like the central server cluster. I think it's still intact." Like a wasp assaulting a termite hive, he tore into the protective programming to expose still active links, circuitry diagrammatics, relays. Some of it was like nothing they had ever seen before, incredibly advanced and distressingly incomprehensible. Some of it was familiar.

Enough of it was familiar.

Overall, the hack was accomplished with admirable

speed. Imagery soon filled the brightly lit screen directly opposite the three men. There were no pictures, no accompanying music. No video and no shout-outs. It was all code and schematics, cold and disciplined. Sometimes it read right to left, sometimes top to bottom. Over time, the techs had learned how to interpret Skynet-speak.

So had Connor.

If you're going to understand an enemy, you have to know how to speak its language.

"Here we go." Barbarossa muttered as a flood of information began to spill across the screen. "Seems that these people here were to be taken to the northern sector for some kind of R and D project." His fingers danced across the portable keyboard in front of him. "There's more."

Something on the screen caught Connor's attention.

Olsen turned. "Hardy! Front and center!"

Connor ignored the general, his attention focused on the screen and the tech chief.

"Wait. Go back."

Barbarossa hesitated, realized who had made the appeal, and immediately complied. Connor's eyes widened as the section he had requested reappeared and was played back more slowly. David crowded close to his commander for a better look.

"Jesus, Connor," he muttered, "it's just like you said it would be."

"No." Connor exhaled sharply. "It's not. It's worse." He nodded at the tech. "Okay, I've seen what I needed to see. Resume."

Noticing that Connor was paying attention to the readouts rather than the prisoners, the impatient Olsen turned back to him.

"Sir." Staring wide-eyed at the screen, Barbarossa's voice was almost inaudible as he tried to understand what he was seeing. "Sir...."

Olsen had moved closer to the other man.

"Connor, this isn't your business. Get your nose out of there." He jerked his head to his right, in the direction of the pleading prisoners. "Let's cut these sorry bastards loose."

Intent on the information that was pouring across the screen in front of him, Barbarossa finally managed to raise his voice even as his fingers continued to race over his laptop's keyboard. Pausing the info flow, he glanced back at the general.

"I've found something else, sir. Looks like intel on our people."

Olsen nodded dourly. Such a discovery was hardly surprising.

"This isn't the time or the place to try extended analysis. Just send *everything* you find on to Command. Let them break it all down. We can't do anything from here."

Another pair of techs came forward and began compiling a temp surface feed utilizing the officer's computer. With a number of satellite dishes on the surface still intact it was just a matter of locating a live contact within the cluster, hacking the feed, and taking over the uplink.

Those soldiers not engaged in freeing and assisting the prisoners or guarding the entrances crowded around to watch. Most of them couldn't follow the procedure. Tech wasn't their business—killing was. But it raised morale to see how efficiently the tech team was going about its work.

Olsen barked into his radio.

"Jericho! Come in!" The only response was static. Not good, the general knew. "Jericho," he repeated. "Shit."

The room shook. Not an earthquake. At least, not one that had been propagated by a tired Earth. Olsen snapped into his radio again.

"Jericho, what's the damn ruckus up there?" The response was more static, which was soon drowned out by a second, louder roar that reverberated through the entire chamber. Dust and dirt sifted down from the ceiling; a slow earthy rain. The shouts from the remaining imprisoned grew frantic, the looks on the faces of the soldiers strained.

"Jericho, come in!" Olsen's fingers tightened on his communicator.

Jericho didn't come in. Neither did any of the captain's colleagues. The communicator's locked frequency was as silent as the grave. *A bad simile*, the general thought, especially considering his present subterranean location. As he had done on previous occasions, he found himself turning for advice to one particular squad leader. Unlike Jericho, he was not reluctant to do so. Like any good administrator, good soldiers are able to suborn their egos to necessity.

"Connor, get your ass topside and remind those men they need to answer me when I call, even if they're dead. Connor!"

Solemn-faced as ever, Connor acknowledged the order and headed for the hatchway he and his men had blasted wide. Olsen followed him with his eyes for a moment, then gestured toward the holding pens as he turned back to his immediate subordinates.

"Let's cut these people loose. Seeing them like this

makes my stomach turn. Listening to them hurts my heart." Nodding agreement, the small circle of officers and noncoms that had clustered around him dispersed to see to the opening of the last cells.

By this time the world was supposed to be swarming with inventions designed to make life easier, Connor thought to himself as he worked the hand-held ascender that was taking him up the cable. Jet packs and synthetic food. Colonies on Mars and rejuvenated oceans. Computers that could be controlled by thought.

Those things had not come to pass because of one unfortunate oversight: Machines that could be controlled by thought had indeed come to pass.

The problem was that they were thinking for themselves, not for their creators, and their thoughts had turned out to be not at all nice.

A tremor ran through the ground as he reached the surface. He hesitated there until he was able to identify the source of the deep-throated rumble.

Passing almost directly overhead, a huge Skynet Transporter thundered past. Part of it was open construction, allowing him to see that the interior was crammed with more human prisoners. The ones who had been dumped in the top of the container were crushing the life out of the poor beggars trapped at the bottom.

On the other hand, he mused as he pulled himself out of the hole, *those on the bottom might be the lucky ones.*

Though he doubted there was anything he could do for them, he knew he had to try. Had to keep trying, until there was no more try and no more life left in him.

It was his destiny.

Scanning the battlefield and the remnants of the

Skynet satellite array, his gaze settled on an apparently intact chopper idling nearby. Whatever it was, its original mission was about to be changed. Hefting his gear, he raced toward it and clambered inside. A glance showed the big Skynet Transport picking up speed as it angled northward.

"They've got human prisoners on board that thing!" he yelled as he pulled himself into the cockpit. "Get after it! If your weapons systems are operational maybe we can...."

He broke off. The chopper's weapons might be operational, but its pilots were not. Both slumped dead in their seats, a single hole in their respective foreheads. Telltale Terminator work. A hasty look around indicated that whichever machine had killed them had moved on in search of other organics to exterminate.

The Transport full of hapless prisoners was nearly out of sight. One reason Connor was still alive was because he had learned to move fast. Linger too long over a notion and the machines, which were subject to no such hesitation, would splinter your skull before you could conclude your thought.

Working fast, he unbuckled the dead pilot from his harness, dragged him backward, and laid him gently if not reverently in the chopper's hold. The steady *whup-whup* of the idling rotors rose to a whine as he threw himself into the now vacant seat and took control.

While the pilots had been coldly executed, the craft had been left untouched. No minion of Skynet would harm another machine, even a non-sentient one, without cause. Connor himself had seen tanks and other heavy vehicles from which their human occupants had been extracted left unharmed on the field.

The chopper was responsive, undamaged, and full of fuel. It rose obediently at his touch. Trailing the by now almost out-of-sight Transport, he accelerated in pursuit.

Far below, the work of Olsen and his troops was slowed as liberated prisoners threw themselves into the arms of their rescuers. Soldiers tried to comfort them as best they could while continuing to break locks and wrench open oddly welded cage doors.

Behind the sob-filled commotion, Barbarossa continued to probe the server cluster they had hacked. Frowning at something on the main monitor, he once again paused the flow of information. As he looked closer at what he had found, his thoughts surged back and forth between a steady flux of technical analysis and a serious attack of *whatthehell*.

"I've found something else, sir," he called out. Seconds later Olsen was looking over the tech's shoulder.

"What've you got, man?"

"I'm not quite sure, sir, but it's readable." His fingers flashed over the keyboard before him.

Buried within the reddish illumination that lit the chamber, a deeper crimson began to glow. An edgy drone unlike any human alarm began to rise above the continued wailing and crying of the freed prisoners.

Away from the techs and the civilian babble, Tunney looked at his friend David. Their eyes met. Having served together and been in the field a long time, their senses had grown battlefield sharp. Unlike the techs they were unable to interpret the flow of information that continued to stream across the multiple monitors. Unlike the techs, they also knew that the flashing

lights and keening whine that now enveloped them
portended no good.

High above but insufficiently far away, Connor was
banking the commandeered chopper when a few square
miles of southwestern desert heaved upward, seemed to
hang in the air a moment, and then collapsed back upon
itself. Gouts of flame shot from depths unmeasured, volcanic eruptions of dirt and smoke, and a shockwave that
sent the chopper careening off its axis. Hard though
Connor fought to maintain control, the blast was of
such magnitude that puny human muscles were helpless
against it.

It was a miracle that he managed any kind of landing.
Striking the ground at an angle sheared the rotors, sending potentially lethal metal blades screaming in all
directions.

The engine died but Connor did not. Arms, legs,
head—he was far more intact than the machine that had
cushioned him from the crash. Staggering out of the harness and the now mangled helicopter, he found himself
gaping at a gigantic depression that marked the limits of
the obliterated subterranean Skynet facility.

It was all gone, entirely destroyed. A very good
thing—except that his entire company, from command-
ing officers down to the lowest-ranking member of his
own squad, were also gone. Friends, fellow fighters—
there was nothing left.

Well, not quite nothing.

A grotesque mass of mangled metal, the T-600 he had
put out of commission earlier, slammed into him from
behind. Behind what remained of the battered skull,
emotionless eyes glowed a deep, burning red.

His arm slashed, a surprised and dazed Connor stumbled clear. As single-minded of purpose as all of its brethren, the T-600 came lurching after him. Pulling his sidearm, Connor took aim and fired several times. He might as well have been throwing spitwads. The small-caliber shells pinged harmlessly off the T-600's face, and Connor was unable to hit either of the eyes.

If the machine had been intact, Connor knew he would already be dead. But while they were both hurt, the machine was more badly damaged than the man. Staggering backward and trying to keep clear of the crippled killing device, Connor banged into something else unyielding: the downed chopper. Protruding from the nose, its mini-gatling gun drooped downward, but was still attached to its swivel mount.

Reaching into the cockpit, he fumbled at the controls, working from practice and relying on memory. Equally unbalanced, the Terminator lunged at him. Connor jerked to one side and the stabbing claw-hand just missed his face.

Recovering, the T-600 re-triangulated its apparently helpless target and came forward again. As it did so, the human used his other hand to swing the barrel of the gatling hard around. The muzzle slammed into the Terminator's faux human jaws as Connor yelled and activated the trigger.

A shriek of metal-piercing rounds blew the T-600's head into a hundred pieces of scrap metal. Breathing hard, Connor slumped back against the side of the chopper. Small flames from ignited circuitry flared from the neck of the decapitated machine—Terminator terminated.

When the voice reached him the shock of it was nearly as great as the reappearance of the T-600. But this was a recognizably human voice. The source was the helicopter's radio. Garbled at first, the transmission gradually became fully intelligible as the operator at the other end worked hard to clear the frequency.

"Bravo Ten, come in," the exhausted Connor was able to make out. "Bravo Ten, this is HQ. Anyone there? Respond, come back."

Reaching inside the cockpit, he located the compact mike, brought it to his lips, and switched it on. What should he say after what he had just been through and had just witnessed? What *could* he say?

"Here," he gasped.

There was a pause at the other end, as if the caller was trying to derive whole reams of information from the one-word response.

"Who is this?" the mike finally crackled afresh.

"Connor."

"John Connor?"

"No. Lucy Mae Connor."

That prompted another pause, followed by a query voiced in a stronger, no-nonsense tone.

"Is the target destroyed?" When Connor didn't respond, the voice tried again, more forcefully. "Connor! You're in a hot zone! You have no time. Acknowledge. Do you copy? I repeat—is the target destroyed?"

Gathering himself, Connor gasped out a one-word reply.

"Affirmative."

The radio voice turned from demanding to anxious.

"You have a location on General Olsen? We can't raise him."

This time Connor took a deep breath before replying.

"Olsen's dead."

A longer pause.

"Proceed to ex-fil point. We'll send pickup. How many survivors are there?"

Straightening, Connor regarded the new valley that had appeared where formerly there had been flat desert and a few low, scrub-covered hills. Still settling dust continued to obscure the view. The vast satellite array, the rest of the Skynet center, all the poor, pitiful human prisoners, every one of his comrades—dead and buried as the ages. Remembering that he was isolated only physically, he lifted the mike once again.

"One."

The voice on the radio came back much subdued.

"Repeat—please."

"One!" Connor snapped.

Perhaps surprisingly, nothing further was heard from the mike. After waiting to make sure the connection had been cut, Connor put it down, straightened, and started limping away from the chopper. Not because he had a destination in mind—he wasn't even sure exactly where he was. Not because he feared a resurgence of the T-600 he had finally and definitively put down. He started walking because, if nothing else, he desired to put the scene of colossal devastation and destruction as far behind him as he possibly could.

If he was lucky, he mused as he trudged toward an increasingly stormy horizon, maybe he would find a lizard. In the world in which he now found himself, any companion not made of metal and circuitry was one to be cherished.

***

The storm brought darkness to the desert sooner that it would otherwise have arrived. Frequent flashes of lightning illuminated the scorched and shredded fragments of the day's reckoning: bits of bone, limbs both human and metal that had been divorced from their owners' bodies, pieces of machine that had served humans, pieces of machine that had been motivated by their own ruthless and uncompromising drive. Among the organic and metallic debris, nothing moved save clouds and bursts of torrential rain.

Even the birds and insects had fled.

Amid the destruction, a patch of mud stirred. Wormlike shapes emerged from the sodden earth and thrust skyward. Not snakes, not centipedes—human fingers. The fingers were attached to a hand, the hand to a wrist, the wrist to....

A shape arose, cloaked in mud and dripping fragments of debris. Eyes opened, vitreous but not glowing. Dazed by the reality of itself, arms at its sides, the figure tilted back its head to stare at the storming night. Driving rain lashed mud and dirt from face and ribs, limbs and torso. The shape was that of a man.

Naked and in shock, Marcus Wright parted his jaws wide and howled at the sky.

Shivering slightly, Wright wrapped his arms around his naked chest and lowered his gaze to the tormented earth on which he stood. Then he noticed the crashed chopper. Slowly, cautiously, he started toward it. Leaning into the ruined aircraft, a disoriented and bewildered Wright found himself gazing upon the dead body of one of the pilots, a bullet hole punched neatly through his helmet.

Wet, cold, confused, and very, very alone, he could only stand, stare—and wonder.

CHAPTER THREE

Connor thought he might have heard an owl, but it could just as easily have been ground sundered by distant lightning. His hearing wasn't working too well and his vision was dimmed by exhaustion. He was tired and hungry, but at least dehydration hadn't been a problem. As the storm had moved on, it had left in its wake dozens of desert pools overflowing with fresh water. He badly wanted to take a bath, but experience dictated otherwise.

In his present debilitated condition, confronting even a damaged Terminator could be dangerous. Encountering one while floating stark naked in fresh water would be fatal.

He didn't know how the big chopper found him and he didn't much care. Once he had established to his satisfaction that it was actually crewed by his own kind and was not a Skynet decoy, he hustled out from behind the rocks he had been using for cover and forced himself to travel the rest of the distance to the waiting vehicle on the run. By the time he reached the idling Chinook, someone inside had slung the door open.

Gazing inside, he found himself face to face with a pair of startled troopers. To their credit, they didn't panic at his sudden appearance. Turning in his seat, the pilot looked back and noted the new arrival.

"RTB?" he asked, his voice indicating that he figured he already knew the survivor's desired destination.

Connor surprised him.

"Take me to Command," he snapped.

The pilot hesitated. "Sir?"

"Command. Now."

Another moment's hesitation, and then the man nodded.

"Roger—rerouting."

They were in the air a long time. Improvising out of necessity and working with concentrated biofuels, bio-engineers and airframe techs had improved the range of such transports. They had been forced to do so since countless airfields had been rendered untenable by the forces of Skynet.

Hitting heavy weather as soon as they crossed the coast, the storm made it impossible to see land in any direction. For all Connor knew there might have been an entire archipelago underneath the 'copter. If so, it was submerged beneath a steady succession of enormous swells the likes of which Connor had never encountered, not even in recordings of old weather broadcasts.

He could only guess at how long they had been fighting through the storm while over water when the co-pilot called out to the noncom who had been staring at Connor for the better part of an hour. There had been little chatter between the passenger and soldiers, which suited Connor fine. He was exhausted, needed the rest, and was in no mood for casual chitchat. Occasionally one of the soldiers on board looked at him as if to say something, but thought better of it. Connor was clearly preoccupied.

Forward movement ceased as the Chinook slowed to a hover. One of the chopper crew pulled back the door and the interior of the craft was assailed by wind, rain, and intermittent illumination courtesy of frequent flashes of lightning. Peering out and down, a dubious Connor could just make out crashing waves not too far below. From up front, one of the pilots called back to him.

"Request denied. Command doesn't want to give up their physical position. They're allowing radio comm only."

Connor eyed the enormous waves.

"Are they down there?"

The pilot shook his head.

"Doesn't matter. Request has been denied, sir."

The passenger looked thoughtful. Then he rose.

"Open the ramp. Tell them I need divers for a lock-in. Now."

After a moment's hesitation the pilot nodded and turned back to his console. Walking to the rear of the chopper, Connor waited tensely until the rear-loading ramp was lowered. The additional opening only made the chopper more unstable and it began to rock even more violently in the howling wind.

Taking a deep breath and murmuring something under his breath that he hoped neither of the soldiers could hear, John Connor took a short run down the length of the metal platform and sailed off into the darkness.

For several minutes he was, oddly enough, able to relax. Leaning his head back and thrusting out his legs, he let himself be drawn up, up, and then down first one and then two huge swells. It would be different if they started to break over him instead of simply passing beneath. His concerns about having to body surf in the middle of the ocean soon proved unfounded. A dark low shape became visible nearby—a sub.

Moments later he was swarmed by a clutch of divers.

Cold and soaking wet, he was escorted into the sub with the same grim-faced determination that had been shown to him during the long flight on the chopper. Sailors treated him with an odd mixture of wariness and admiration.

He was immediately given warm towels, food and water, and a soft cot to lie on. He dried himself off and did his best to make himself at least semi-presentable given the limited resources that had been provided. Not that he much cared what anyone in Command might think of his appearance, but retaining a modicum of personal pride was an important element in sustaining one's humanity.

He had just finished cleaning himself up when they came for him.

The sub was enormous, a modified Los Angeles-class self-contained underwater community. Big as it was, though, he could tell when they sat him down in a chair on the bridge that a lot of the electronics surrounding him were hastily cobbled-together add-ons. Where the interior hull was not covered with information-rich monitors it was wallpapered with printouts, charts, and complex lists.

In addition to the members of the crew, the bridge conference table was occupied by several Very Senior Officers. While Connor recognized some of their insignia, others sported motifs in styles and languages that were as foreign to him as their wearers. It dawned on him that many of the generals and admirals from the world's surviving armed forces were crowded into the same room.

As he was brought in, several of them glanced in his direction. Most ignored him. Armed sailors and marines had been watching him ever since he had been brought onto the bridge. Several of them were more nervous than Connor would have liked.

There was one empty seat at the table, near the center. Turning, a standing four-star general started toward it. His attention was focused not on the table and his fellow officers, but on Connor. The name patch over his breast pocket read "ASHDOWN." The general did not otherwise introduce himself, nor did he extend a hand in the prisoner's direction. His speech was clipped, gruff, and left no doubt as to the nature of his opinion of the new arrival.

"Soldier, you put everyone in this tub in jeopardy with that little frogman stunt of yours."

Connor said nothing.

When the general halted beside the table, the other officers rose. Ashdown slapped a file down on the synthetic wood.

"Take a seat." He paused, glanced at the file, then up at the newcomer. "John Connor. Prophesied leader of the Resistance. Let's get something straight. I've been a soldier for a very long time, and soldiers don't put much weight in prophecy." With a shrug, Connor walked over to join the gathering of officers.

Showing unexpected speed, Ashdown pulled his sidearm and jammed the muzzle in Connor's face. The newcomer didn't flinch.

"At least, I don't when one can rewrite the future in

a heartbeat," Ashdown murmured from behind the service revolver. "We on the same page?"

"Yes sir." Connor spoke calmly, evenly. "We're on the same page."

Ashdown hesitated a moment longer, then smiled thinly and put the gun down on the table.

"Good. Good. This Command is well aware of your exploits and your valor in the field. We've all heard your broadcasts. And I, personally, appreciate everything you've been doing for the cause." He stopped momentarily, and the smile vanished. "So tell us, soldier—what the hell are you doing *here*?"

Before replying, Connor took his time concluding his study of the bridge, taking in the makeshift electronics, the dedicated but worn crew, the chatting officers. He was less than impressed. His eyes met those of the general as he offered a terse explanation.

"We've been able to determine that Skynet is taking human prisoners for R and D. They're dissecting them. Replicating human tissue for the new model Terminator. I saw the schematics. Based on my knowledge of..." he hesitated, "based on what I know, that's ten years too early. If the new model goes on line now, this war is over."

Ashdown nodded, let his gaze meet the expectant gazes of his fellow senior officers.

"A new genesis of Terminator."

Connor was feeling better. It appeared that he wasn't going to have to explain everything from scratch.

"Cybergenic infiltration unit. Titanium combat chasis. Nuclear fuel cell, fully armored, very tough."

"Yes," Ashdown agreed readily, "and also the machine that tried to kill your mother, Sarah." Connor stared at him. Ashdown didn't miss a beat. "Pescadero State Mental Institution. Escaped. Connor, crazy isn't going to win this war. Soldiers like you and I are. Don't give the new model another thought. It's not going to be a problem because it's never going to go into production."

Connor frowned. "How do you know that?"

Ashdown's grin returned. "You think you're the only one who knows things in advance? You'll be briefed on a need-to-know basis."

"Okay—how about right now? I need to know. My men died down in that hole. So I need to know. Why did we launch that attack? Why did we go down there? And most importantly, what did we *find* down there?" His expression twisted. "I would've asked the survivors myself—except I couldn't find any survivors."

Ashdown considered before finally replying.

"Hope. We found hope." He gestured to one of the other generals. In addition to his insignia in Cyrillic, the other officer wore a second identification patch with the name Losenko. Connor eyed him with interest. The older man's face was as gnarled as an old Siberian Spruce. Here was a man who plainly had spent time in the lower ranks. Someone who would talk straight with a lower-ranking officer—and shoot him point-blank if he thought the other man represented a threat.

"We found a solution that can end this war once and for all." As Connor stared at him, he turned and gestured to a waiting aide. The man nodded and turned to manipulate hidden controls. A nearby screen flashed to life. Though he was familiar with the subject matter, the initial images were new to Connor and he straightened slightly, taking in every detail of the portrayed new model.

"We know the machines use short-wave transmitters to communicate among themselves. Thanks to your assault, intelligence has isolated a hidden channel riding beneath the primary." He was looking hard at Connor. "This secondary channel allows for direct control of the machines. It permits anything—or anyone—broadcasting on it to override the usual communications."

On the screen, a line of code was isolated and highlighted. It was not impressive, but what it represented was. Ashdown picked up from the Russian.

"Skynet is a machine. And like every machine it has an 'Off' switch. Thanks to you and your troops, we now have that switch in our possession. We're going to shut them down and bomb them back to the Stone Age."

While he had taken it all in, Connor's thoughts remained focused elsewhere.

"What about the human prisoners?"

Ashdown's brow furrowed as he replied.

"What about them? You questioning my humanity? When the time comes, I'll do the right thing."

Their eyes locked and held. Finally Connor nodded, tersely.

"Okay, our intel people have found this signal. They've analyzed it. They think they know what it does. Which leads to the next question: *does* it work? Or are our tech teams just spitting theory?"

"Will it work?" Ashdown glanced down at the file on the table. "Yes. Has it been field tested? No."

A quick surge of adrenaline pulsed through Connor.

"I'll do it. I'll test it. Give it to me."

Ashdown eyed him a moment longer, then looked across at Losenko. The Russian pursed his lower lip as he contemplated the man who had dived from a helicopter into open, storming ocean in hopes that they would allow him to join them.

"Mr. Connor and his tech comm unit have an excellent record. Assuming enough of them survived, I think we should allow him this opportunity."

"All right." Looking past the table, General Ashdown directed his words to the soldiers who had brought Connor in. "Take him topside. Prepare for lockout." His gaze fell once more on the visitor. "If we get this right, the war is over, Connor." His expression tightened. "Good luck, soldier. We mount our offensive in four days." Turning, he headed for the far end of the bridge. The other senior officers rose to accompany him.

Only Losenko remained. Removing a small portable drive from a shirt pocket, the Russian handed it over.

"These are the codes for the signal. I have all confidence that your technical people can put together the appropriate instrumentation to propagate it. Good luck."

Pocketing the drive, Connor nodded.

"Why four days?"

"A 'kill' list was intercepted from Skynet. It says matter-of-factly that everyone in this room will be dead by week's end. You were number two on the list." He turned to rejoin his fellow officers.

"Who's number one?" Connor called after him.

Losenko looked back and shrugged, more indifferent than bemused.

"Some unknown. A civilian named Kyle Reese."

The infirmary was crowded—the infirmary was always crowded. Doctors and nurses, general services technicians, soldiers and supply personnel surged back and forth like the tide, according to whether wounded were incoming or those that had been adequately treated were being moved out. It was a routine that, while far from comfortable, had at least become familiar.

Then John Connor walked in.

Initial feelings of relief and even joy turned rapidly to sorrow as one by one those present realized that he was alone. Hopes that there might be surviving wounded elsewhere vanished with his continuing silence. Had there been other survivors of the mass assault on the Skynet VLA, he would by now have said so.

Approaching the new arrival, a lieutenant with "BARNES" stitched across his shirt spoke for everyone in the room when he inquired softly, "My brother didn't make it, did he?"

Connor put a hand on the man's shoulder. He knew Barnes, just as he knew everyone who was permanently assigned to the base.

"I'm sorry."

Pain flushed the noncom's face. In lieu of tears he replied, fighting to keep a rising quiver out of his voice.

"If he died fighting with you, he died well."

Connor nodded, dropped his hand, and pushed on. There was nothing more to be said and nothing else he could do.

In her work among the wounded and the dying, Kate Connor had become entirely too conversant with the persistence of bloodstains. She had long ago given up trying to keep her scrubs spotless. No one expected it of her and, at several months pregnant, she had neither the energy nor the inclination to try. She had rather more important issues to focus on.

Like the man washing his face at the sink.

Raising his head, Connor stared at his face in the mirror. Both of them were used, beaten up, slightly cracked. Lifting his hands, he wiped at the beads of liquid on his skin. Kate came up behind him.

"Do you want to talk about him, John? You haven't said anything about him." He looked over at her. "About Kyle."

Turning, he nodded toward the doorway.

"He's out there, somewhere. Alone, I would imagine. And Skynet is hunting him." He toweled off his face. She was with him, but he was still alone. His gaze met hers.

"This isn't the future my mother told me about."

Moving to a nearby desk, he sat down and activated the laptop in front of him. The portable drive that had been given to him by the Russian general protruded from one side. Pulling up a chair, Kate sat down beside him. She didn't have to look at the screen to know what he was studying so intently. They had discussed it earlier.

"What about the signal? Have the tech people come to any conclusions?"

He shook his head, irritated not at her but at the uncertainty that surrounded what he was viewing.

"No one knows if it'll work. I don't know about this, Kate. It doesn't seem like the sort of backdoor vulnerability Skynet would overlook. Still, if it goes back to the original programming...." His voice trailed away momentarily. "I'll know more when I get the chance to test it out. In the field. For real."

She put a comforting arm across his shoulders.

"Why don't we start out with something small. Something we know. I'll have our people capture a Hydrobot." She nodded to her left. "They're always patrolling the river outside the base perimeter. We'll bring one in for testing."

He considered, then nodded his approval.

"Yes, but we have to be careful. We can't risk Skynet learning that we've found this code. If it does, it'll take immediate steps to close off the vulnerability. Whatever we test this on, we have to destroy." He went silent, looking past the laptop. An old picture rested there, carefully positioned upright. Reaching out, he picked up the photo of his mother.

"What is it, John?"

"Something's changed. Something I can't put my finger on. And in this future, I don't know that we can win this war."

"If you saved us once, in another future, then you can save us in this one."

Doubt colored his response. "This signal has to work. It may be the only way to save Kyle—my father. We're outnumbered by machines working around the clock. They never have to pause, they never have to pull back and regroup, they never rest. We don't have a lot of time, Kate. Either we win this and win it soon, or it's over. For all of us. Kyle won't be alive for me to send him back to my mother."

She drew him closer. "Then we fight to the end. We fight for what's to come." Leaning over, she kissed him on the cheek. "We fight for the future." Smiling, she reached out, took his hand, and placed it on her stomach. "We fight for *our* future."

CHAPTER FOUR

Not only was there nothing in San Francisco like the country he was presently traversing, there was nothing like it in any of Marcus Wright's memories. *It might well be a fit landscape of hell,* he thought to himself as he strode numbly onward. If it was heaven, then the priests and pastors he had briefly known as a child were even further off the mark than he had always suspected.

What place in either afterlife the wreckage of a crashed 747 occupied was a physical and philosophical conundrum he couldn't even begin to fathom. The metal hulk was empty, deserted, giving no sign anyone had ever been in it or near it. Striding past, he wondered if this piece of limbo had been raised up exclusively for him. Since regaining consciousness (or whatever it was that he was experiencing) he had not seen any indication that the space he was presently exploring was home to so much as another human being.

Much later, his foot kicked aside something that caught the subdued sunlight. It was a shard of reflective red plastic. Kneeling, he wiped away the sand that half buried it. For his efforts he was rewarded with the sight of a highway reflector. Brushing away more sand and grit exposed pavement and a yellow dividing line.

Incongruous though it might be in the complete absence
of any vehicles, it did provide him with something he
had so far been lacking.

A direction.

More hours of walking found him gaining instead of
losing strength. That made no sense, but since nothing
else seemed to make any sense he saw no reason to
question the contradiction. He accepted it just as he
accepted the sight of the nearly obliterated hillside sign
that was just intact enough to proclaim "HOLLY-
WOOD." From his vantage point he had a good portion of the city spread out before him.

Or rather, what had been the city.

Like the metropolis it had once been, the ruins
stretched out as far as he could see, the promontory of
the Palos Verdes Peninsula looming like a buff shadow in
the distance. Of life there were still no signs. In the
entire vast vista of destruction, not even the dust moved.

It took him a while to work his way downtown. There
he hoped to find potable water, though so far all he had
encountered was wreckage and devastation in close-up,
from obliterated storefronts to the dinosaurian hulks of
cars and trucks, some of which had crumbling skeletons
slumped at the wheels.

Something moved in the distance, walking. Though
several hundred yards away, there was no mistaking the
human shape of the lone figure. Disbelief gave way to a
ray of hope. Cupping one hand to his mouth, he yelled.

"Hey!"

The figure turned toward him. It was humanoid—but
not human. No human could have supported the oversized machine gun it started to aim. As a shell-shocked
Wright gaped at it dumbly, a grim-faced youth

appeared as if from nowhere and slammed into him.

They tumbled together behind a heavy forklift as a hail of heavy-caliber shells tore into the pavement where Wright had been standing a moment earlier. How they missed him he could not understand. Rising to the fore, half-forgotten instincts took over. Rolling deeper into cover, he found himself face to face with the teen. When the boy spoke, he did not sound young.

"Come with me if you want to live."

More slugs ripped the air around the forklift as the figure that had trained its weapon on Wright started toward them. Red eyes flickered; scanning, seeking, looking to exterminate. The teen led Wright back around the corner of one crumbling structure. They were out of sight of their attacker and out of range. For the moment.

Facing his young companion, Wright jerked his head back in the direction from which they had come.

"What the hell is...?"

Despite the difference in their ages and the disparity in size, the teen did not hesitate. His open hand clamped across Wright's mouth, shutting off the older man's query. In an earlier time and place the blatant physical imposition would have caused Wright to rip the youth's head clean off. Under the present circumstances, however, he was too confused to do more than accept the gesture.

Pointing in the direction of the bipedal creature that had fired at them, the teen then gestured at his own ear. Only when Wright nodded that he understood did the youth lower his hand from the stranger's mouth.

Time passed: not much of it, and all of it fraught with tension. Advancing toward them, their pursuer was barely visible, and inclined its head in their direction.

The muzzle of its rapid-fire weapon rose. That was when the teen slammed his arm down on something metallic protruding from the side of the building against which he and Wright had been pressed.

The wire that looped around the stalker's right foot was not thick, but it *was* unbreakable. Machine and machine gun were turned upside-down as the contracting cable yanked it completely off the ground. Frustrated but not disoriented, it struggled violently at this unexpected interruption of its pursuit.

Not waiting around for the machine to free itself, the teen grabbed Wright's arm and led him down the alley where they had taken cover.

There was barely enough room at the top of the mound of rubble that blocked the entrance to the ruined factory for the youth to wriggle through. Wright had a harder time, having to rely more on brute force to make his way to the other side. Standing at the base of a disintegrating stairwell, the youth gestured impatiently for Wright to follow. Too stunned to argue, the older man complied wordlessly.

On the street outside, the stymied T-600 fired twice at the cable that had wrapped around its right foot. Most shells missed the gleaming, slender target. Those that struck it glanced off. Responding to the overriding resolve of its pursuit programming, it proceeded to shoot off the restraining foot. Thus freed, it slammed into the pavement below with enough force and weight to buckle the old concrete.

Proceeding to right itself, it limped toward the entrance to the factory.

***

By the time he and his guide reached the roof of the building, Wright thought he ought to be out of breath. That he was not he attributed to the inevitable surge of adrenalin that always accompanied being shot at.

Halting, the teen flashed a succession of hand signals across the flat surface. A second figure emerged from the shadows. Slight of build and grimy of appearance, the little girl was clad in layers of salvaged clothing, child-sized cowboy boots, and an old police hat with a flipped-back brim. A single metal star gleamed on the front of the hat, above eyes that were preternaturally hard. With brown hair that exploded wire-like from beneath this singular chapeau, she looked to be about nine or ten.

In response to the older boy's gestures she turned toward what looked like an old railcar wheel assembly. The enormous hunk of rusting metal sat on the edge of the rooftop where at one time it might have handled cargo deliveries. Having long since eroded away, a portion of the underlying structure had been replaced with a series of shims and props.

As she leaned over the edge of the building, the girl was intent on something below. When the moment suited her, she shoved hard against a pole that was centered on the mass of shims. They promptly gave way, followed immediately by several tons of abandoned industrial manufacture. The noise this all made when it struck the street far below was eminently satisfying.

Hurrying to the edge, Wright peered over and down, and drew back as a burst of automatic fire erupted from below. When none of the shells whizzed in his direction, he took a second look. Pinned beneath the mass of metal, the exposed gun arm of the crushed machine was still firing, but wildly and seemingly without control. It continued to do so until the weapon's magazine ran out.

Shaking his head, he straightened and turned to his youthful savior.

"What the hell was that?"

Stone-face, the teen shook his head curtly. He had the build and look of a lone wolf.

"You first. Who are you?"

Ignoring him, Wright shifted his attention to the little girl.

"What was that?"

Taking a step forward, the youth partially interposed himself between the ingenuous stranger and the girl.

"She doesn't talk, but you need to. Who are you?" His voice did not change. All the emphasis it required was provided by the gun he drew and aimed. Wright regarded it as dispassionately as he did the question.

"I'm—Marcus."

This concise response was inadequate to reassure the teen.

"Why are you wearing a Resistance uniform when you're obviously not a member of the Resistance?"

Wright glanced down at himself, then back up at the youth.

"I—needed clothes. The dead guy I took it off didn't."

Still wary, the teen began rifling the pockets of the older man's jacket with one hand while keeping the pistol trained on him with the other.

"Well, if you're one of those crazies whose brains turned to oatmeal from radiation poisoning, jump off this roof right now 'cause I'm not letting you get us killed." He continued fishing through the jacket pockets and continued coming up empty.

Wright stared blankly back at him. Everything that had happened, everything that was happening, was happening too quickly, giving him no time to analyze, no time to digest—only to react.

"I—I don't know what happened to me," he explained sincerely.

His honesty was insufficient for the teen.

"Nice handle on reality, roadkill." He licked his lips. "Where's your *food*?"

Wright mumbled a response. "Roadkill?"

"That's what you're gonna be, you don't start waking up to certain *facts*. Like who's looking to smoke you and who isn't."

Wright's memory might have been shocked and his perception stunned, but there was nothing wrong with a lifetime of instinctive reactions. In a single swift, smooth motion he reached out, grabbed the teen's wrist, twisted him around, relieved him of the gun, and shoved. Barely aware of what had taken place, the teen abruptly found himself lying on his back on the rooftop with the muzzle of the gun positioned frighteningly close to his face.

Nearby, the now terrified girl had retreated several steps.

Wright gazed down at the prone teenager. The boy was shaking, and Wright knew exactly what he was feeling. Because there had been a time, long ago, when he had all too often found himself in similar situations.

"You want to rip a guy off, make him empty his own pockets. If you do it yourself, you get too close, it gives him a chance to turn things on you. Never get closer than two arm-lengths to whoever you're locking down." Taking no notice of whatever the teen might chose to do, Wright turned slightly to one side, popped the clip out of the gun, pocketed it, and tossed the weapon onto the teen's chest.

"You point a gun at someone, you better be ready to pull the trigger." He stared down at the youth, who stared back a long moment before finally nodding.

"Right," the teen muttered.

Reaching down, Wright extended an open hand. As he picked up the gun that had been stripped from his grasp the teen regarded the powerful fingers warily, but decided to accept the offer. The stranger, helping him stand, all but lifted him off the ground.

"Now I'm gonna ask you one more time." Wright indicated the edge of the building. "What the hell was that?"

Back on familiar ground, some of the teen's former boldness returned.

"Terminator. T-600. It kills. And once it locks on to you it won't stop—ever. Until you're dead."

Lifting his gaze, Wright surveyed the surrounding devastation, letting his eyes roam across the ravaged Los Angeles basin as far as heat and haze would allow.

"What day is it?" When the boy looked at him as if he really was crazy, Wright revised his question. "What year?"

"2018," the kid replied.

Wright stared at the panorama of destruction.

"What happened here? To—everything."

"Judgment Day happened." The teen was eyeing him curiously. "Are you just stupid, or...?"

He didn't finish, probably deciding that the "or" really

wasn't important when all that mattered anymore was surviving to the next day.

Wright rubbed the back of his head, as if the thought itself was painful.

"Gotta get out of here." He muttered to the teen. "Away from this area."

The younger man's shrug seemed to suggest that geographical designations like "away" no longer held much in the way of relevance.

"Can't go on foot, that's for sure. Machines will cut you down. If you expect to get anywhere you're gonna need speed."

Something, at last, that made sense.

"I need a car."

"Good luck." The teen squinted over at him.

"You're serious, aren't you? Well, it's your funeral. Moving car is just a bigger target." He gestured ahead, toward the nearby hills. "Last time I was up that way I saw a few of 'em by Griffith Observatory that didn't get incinerated. You can try. None of 'em run, though."

"Take me there."

Coming to a halt, the youth was ready with another acid response when the girl suddenly stopped as if shot and dropped to the ground.

"Get down!" he yelled at the stranger. "And when you're down, *don't move*. Act dead—or you will be."

Wright complied. Lying motionless, he was starting to feel like a fool when a low rumble became audible. It rose quickly in volume if not pitch. Not daring to raise his head, he caught a glimpse in the broken windows of a nearby building of something in motion. It was enormous, purposeful, and now almost directly overhead.

***

As the airship moved with lethal deliberation through the canyons of the ruined city, it scanned its surroundings with an assortment of sensitive instrumentation. Seeking sound or movement, it passed by the three inert figures splayed on the ground without reacting.

Wright winced slightly as a nearby still-standing tower crumbled from the effects of the airship's vibration.

The three humans stayed motionless even after the giant machine's last aural twitch had receded into the distance. Taking his cue from his younger but far more knowledgeable companions, Wright didn't rise until they did. The teen explained before Wright could ask his question.

"HK—Hunter-Killer. Can't stop that with an improvised spring trap." He nodded forward. "We should keep moving."

As they resumed their march Wright glanced toward the girl.

"How'd she know? That it was coming."

The youngster looked uncertain.

"Not sure. Just glad she does. Better than talking. She's got a sixth sense or something about the machines. She's kept me alive plenty." He lengthened his stride. "We're too exposed here. Pick it up."

Wright matched the teen's pace effortlessly.

"You know my name now. Who are you?"

"What's it matter?" The teen dodged around the scorched wreck of a city bus. "You had my gun. Why didn't you shoot me?"

"Why would I have done that? I don't shoot people just because...." A memory came rushing back.

A bad one. Wright's voice trailed away without finishing the declaration.

The teen frowned at him, appeared to hesitate, came to a decision.

"My name's Kyle Reese. Come on. Let's go."

It had been dark outside for a while by the time the tech crew and their heavily armed escort arrived. Water dripped from the tarp-wrapped object they were carrying. When they finally laid it down on the place that had been cleared for it, the display table groaned under the weight. Beneath the tarp, extremities akin to limbs were thrashing uselessly. Connor was still careful not to get too close.

Carefully pulling back the tarp, the tech chief revealed an intact Hydrobot. Superbly if inhumanly engineered to operate in the water, on dry land it struggled to carry out its programmed functions. It was unable to prevent the silent soldiers from securing it to the tabletop. The tech chief eyed it with grim approval.

"We fried its transmitter and backup, so it can't call any of its pals. But it can still receive."

Connor nodded. He had been briefed on what to expect. His gaze was intent as he scrutinized the small, crudely cobbled-together transmitter that rested on a nearby bench.

"Turn it on. You got it?"

The tech nodded. "Give me the strap." Holding the device, the senior technician flipped a switch. A soft hum came from the transmitter's battery. The setup was far from state-of-the-art, but it functioned.

Proof that both the transmitter's circuitry and programming were working was provided by the Hydrobot.

It spasmed once, then went inert on the table. Connor pointed out to the tech that while the single red light in the center of the machine's head faded to an ember, it did not wink out entirely.

The chief technician nodded. "The code signal creates a disrupt. It's not a permanent turn-off or we'd simply send out the broadcast and shut down all the machines."

Connor grunted. "So it's more of a 'pause' than an 'off' switch."

"I'm afraid so," the tech told him. "And the signal has to be continuous in order to sustain the effect. Any interruption and…." He flipped the switch back.

The Hydrobot immediately jerked back to life, beating violently but futilely at the tabletop and its bonds. Locking eyes with Connor, it snapped viciously in his direction. He studied it dispassionately, like a defiant mouse that had suddenly managed to turn the tables on its would-be trap. The tech switched the transmitter back on and the machine was once again immobilized.

"While the signal is being broadcast, it can be traced. It gives away your location. But it works." He eyed the dormant Hydrobot with unconcealed loathing. "And while it's working, you can walk right up to any machine and blow it to bits."

"I'd rather have a full-time 'off' switch," Connor muttered.

"We all would." The tech was sympathetic. "But if this is the best we can come up with based on the information that was acquired in the course of the attack on the Skynet VLA, I know plenty of people in the field who'll be glad to have it."

"Speaking of people in the field, John…."

Turning, he saw that Kate had been watching from the other doorway. Entering, she smiled gently.

"Have you forgotten? It's time for your radio broadcast to the survivors."

He spoke more curtly than he intended. "There's no time. Not tonight."

She put a hand on his shoulder. "There are people left out there. Not just those in the Resistance. People out on farms, scattered in the mountains, hiding in the desert. Trying to keep it together in national forests and city subways and on small boats at sea." Her fingers contracted gently against him. "They need to hear a voice. Your voice."

She hesitated briefly, then added the unavoidable coda. "You know who's out there, John."

Looking back at her, he didn't have to ask who she was referring to.

"All right. What I've got in mind is going to take some time, anyway." Turning, he saw that the chief technician and the entire tech crew were waiting on his orders. He indicated the motionless Hydrobot.

"Destroy this thing. See if you can rig up a more portable version of that transmitter. We're going to try it out on something bigger. We have to, otherwise we're just spinning our wheels."

"That sounds more like something a machine would say, sir," declared one of the watching soldiers. Everyone who heard it chuckled at the quip.

The clandestine radio room the two of them entered was unoccupied except for the technician on duty. *Waiting for me*, Connor thought. Waiting for encouragement, for hope. Wanting to supply both, he knew he could offer only words. Broadcast via hidden, surreptitiously maintained towers, the Resistance base's encrypted signal would be decrypted only at the final points of transmission—an assortment of battered but still functioning translators scattered across the continent. Each had been rigged to self-destruct in the event of its discovery by the machines.

Every month, more were lost. Every month, the voice of the Resistance grew fainter, its area of coverage smaller. But they would keep talking, right up to the end. *Whichever end the end turned out to be*, he thought.

He settled himself in the chair facing the microphone. Off to his left, the busy technician was intent on his equipment. Checking not only to see that everything was functioning and that the carrier wave was sufficiently strong, but also that it was not being traced. Only when he was satisfied with both did he turn to the waiting Connor and give him a silent thumbs-up.

Connor nodded and leaned slightly toward the mike. He could feel Kate's eyes on him; watching, waiting, expectant. Though he had performed such broadcasts many times before, the words never came easily to him.

What could he say that had not already been said? What more could he do to exhort those who continued to resist, to encourage those who were still fighting back?

What could he say to Kyle?

He stared at the radio for a moment longer and then leaned toward the microphone.

"I hope he's listening to this," he muttered, before beginning his transmission.

"We've been fighting for a long time. We've all lost so very much. So many of our loved ones are gone. But you are not alone. There are pockets of Resistance all around the planet. We are at the brink...."

CHAPTER FIVE

Where once it had resounded to the laughter and awed exclamations of excited children getting their first close-up glimpses of the stars and the planets, the old observatory now sat silent and ruined. Little of its distinctive green dome remained. Destroyed displays and weather-damaged exhibits lay broken and battered with scant regard for the knowledge they represented.

The pages of indifferently strewn books rustled fitfully in the wind, their words seeming to drift away to rejoin the vanished spirits of those who had originally set them down.

Marching steadily downslope and across the cracked and shattered parking lot without regard to the priorities or interests of either men or machines, the uninhibited chaparral vegetation that had been cleared for the construction of the observatory was now reclaiming its ancient territory. Trees thrust upward through weakened asphalt, while vines, creepers, and incongruously flowered bushes assailed crumbling walls or pushed their way through windows devoid of glass.

For all the destruction, the place was not quite deserted.

While the war with the machines had cost much of mankind access to electricity, fire had never left him.

Around the makeshift pit filled with carefully piled kindling and a couple of chair legs had been gathered the remnants of a devastated civilization: several useless televisions, a couple of radios, a microwave oven suitable for storing if not preparing food. Into this dovetailed detritus came three tired figures. Though their discrepancy in size and shape suggested they might as well have represented three separate species, they were in fact all of the same.

A species that was, at present, not doing very well at all.

Wright studied the debris. "Where are the cars?"

"You don't want to go out after dark," Reese told him. "Hunter-Killers have infrared and who knows what else. They hunt even better at night." He stepped over a line of crushed metal and plastic. "We can make a run for it in the morning."

Settling down beside a scorched depression that had obviously been used as a firepit, he began the work of starting a small blaze. Returning from rummaging through a bigger heap of broken furniture and other unidentifiable detritus, Star passed him a double handful of meat—also unidentifiable.

Wright looked on. In his time he had done plenty of scavenging of his own.

"So what's dinner?"

Reese nodded at the unappetizing bounty.

"Two-day old coyote." He paused to let that sink in. "Better than three-day old coyote." Pausing again, he added, "There's enough for everyone."

Wright smiled. "Thanks."

"You're welcome. Sorry, but we're fresh out of mustard. And everything else."

Looking to occupy himself as the youth started

cooking the single mass of meat, Wright's gaze settled on the shotgun. Searching the surrounding debris, he found a decent length of intact cord. When he reached for the gun, the teen tensed visibly. Smiling without having to say "take it easy," Wright positioned the holster around his shoulder.

"Grab it."

Reese frowned at him. "What?"

"Grab it."

Letting the meat sizzle on its stick, Reese leaned over sharply and clutched the shotgun. But he couldn't pull it away—the new cord kept it connected to the older man.

"Magic." Wright smiled at the youngster. "Got it?"

Reese's uncertainty turned to understanding. He almost, but not quite, smiled back.

"Got it. Thanks."

Wright passed the gun, holster, and cord back to its owner. Reese glanced at it thoughtfully. His expression suggested that the stranger was still a stranger. Just—a little less strange, now.

As he turned away from the children and the incipient supper, a spark of interest flared in Wright as he examined the collection of decrepit electronics. Working his way through the pile, he picked up a radio and tried several of the controls. One produced an agonized scraping sound. Holding it at arm's length, he studied it closely.

"Does this radio work? Looks like it's in better shape than anything else."

Reese shook his head. "It's broken. My dad tried to fix it. But we could never get it to work." He shrugged. "Better broken anyway. Don't want to make too much noise."

Turning it over in his hands, Wright studied the fasteners, then pried open the back cover. Reese was watching him closely.

"If all this stuff is busted," Wright asked, "how do you know what's going on in the world?"

The teen looked away. Wright transferred his gaze to the girl. Very little in his life had touched him the way her brief gaze now did before she returned her attention to the ground. That was when it struck him that they didn't answer his question because they could not. They had no idea what was happening anywhere except in the immediate vicinity of their little observatory camp. They were well and truly alone.

He was the adult. It was incumbent on him to comfort them, he knew. To bolster their confidence. To reassure them now that he, a grown-up, was here, he would look after them and that everything was going to be all right. Instead of that, when he picked up the radio again he said what was actually on his mind.

"Girl. Phone. Get me a phone. Bring it here."

Marcus Wright had never been a believer in fairy tales. At least, not the ones with happy endings.

The teen hesitated, then turned and gestured at the girl. She indicated her understanding, rose, and trotted off. Maybe the gesture was some kind of private code they had devised between them. Maybe it was gang slang for this piece of hell. Wright didn't care. All that mattered was that they had both reacted positively.

In addition to not believing in fairy tales, Wright had never been one to waste time. He had no intention of waiting for the hoped-for phone. In the girl's absence he started probing the guts of the radio. His fingers were tough and strong, but they were also capable of more delicate work. In their time they had done plenty of damage—sometimes to inanimate objects, sometimes to those who protested, too often to those who had simply had the bad luck to find themselves on the wrong side of one of his all too frequent bad moods. They could also fix things.

"What's her name?" He struggled with the uncooperative device, but carefully. What he wanted to do was expose the radio's guts without damaging any of the internal components that might still be intact and functional.

He saw Reese looking on as he manipulated the radio's components.

"I call her Star. When I found her, she didn't know her real name. She was all alone under the stars. I'd ask her, and she'd just turn off." He shrugged. "She loved that hat of hers so much, I just...." His voice trailed away for a moment. "Maybe Star is her real name. I dunno. I just know that she responds to it. What else am I supposed to call her?"

Wright's fingers slowed as he took a moment to once more regard the surrounding wasteland in which he now inexplicably found himself.

"How do you do it? How do you wake up every day to—this?"

Reese took a moment to consider the question—no doubt because he had never actually contemplated it before.

"Just know it's important that I do." His voice was devoid of ego or bravado, his expression even. "Beats the alternative."

In his largely misbegotten life Wright had associated with men and women who considered themselves tough, even dangerous. None surpassed the resoluteness or conviction he sensed in this slim teen. It stood in stark contrast to his own youth.

He was still working with the radio's insides when Star returned. The phone she offered him could have been newer and in better condition, but he was glad to have it nonetheless. Lining up his thoughts, he found that he was glad of something to do. Something to focus on besides his unrelievedly depressing environs and the unexplained process that had dumped him here.

"Thanks, Star. I could use another hand. Think you can help me out a little?"

She looked at Reese, who nodded approvingly. Eyes wide and attentive, she turned back to him.

"Here, hold this." Wright handed her the back panel of the radio that, thanks to careful work, he had managed to remove in one piece. As he probed deeper into the electronic guts, he took no notice of the little girl's increasingly worshipful stare.

"Where is everyone?" he murmured as he carefully removed the ends of several cords and began rewiring the radio's interior.

"They're gone," Reese told him simply.

"Why are *you* still here?"

"Star and me, we're the Resistance."

Wright forced himself not to smile as he regarded the boy and the girl.

"You and her are the Resistance?"

Reese nodded assertively. "L.A. branch."

"Resisting what?"

The teen's gaze narrowed while he studied the enigmatic stranger, as if wondering if perhaps he had escaped from the moon. Or more likely some half-destroyed mental hospital.

"It's not funny. The machines. Skynet."

"Just the two of you?"

"Yeah."

Using his free hand Wright pointed to the red band that encircled his arm.

"Then why don't you have one of these?"

"I haven't earned it yet," the youth shot back pointedly.

Wright nodded. "Your parents? Are they Resistance? Did they feed you that crap?"

"They're dead." Reese spoke coolly, as if discussing the obvious. "Death follows you very closely in this world. It sucks. But you get used to it. You get used to whatever you have to get used to in order to survive." He glanced meaningfully at Star. "Some handle it better than others. Some just handle it differently."

Wright understood completely.

"Pain can be controlled. You just disconnect it. Along with whatever else is necessary. It's better that way."

Wright flipped the radio's "on" switch and was rewarded with—nothing. He was disappointed but not surprised.

"Dammit. Okay...." He handed Star the opened device. Colorful wires trailed from its interior like the intestines of some ancient hard-shelled sea creature. "Hang onto this."

Childlike curiosity prompted her to study the inside of the radio while he searched through the surrounding debris. Finding a microwave oven, he used the knife Star gave him to unscrew the back and began sorting through the components. Finding the parts he wanted and yanking them free, he strode back to where Star was holding the radio and took it from her. What he really needed was a soldering iron and a crimper. Though the circumstances were radically different, what he was doing was not so very different from similar exercises he had engaged in before.

Sitting down, he resumed working on the radio's interior.

"Just like hot-wiring a Mustang," he murmured contemplatively. "Used to be able to do it in under eight seconds. Beemers took longer, 'vettes kind of in-between."

Reese didn't understand. "Is that good?"

This time Wright did reply, though without looking up from or pausing in his work.

"Owners didn't care much for it." Concluding the rewiring, he started to bring one color against another, then paused to smile softly at the girl. "You want to see some magic, Star?" She stared back at him. "Don't look at me like that. Make yourself useful. Press the button." He held out the radio. "This one here. See if you can make it come alive."

The radio was cheap and its speaker crummy, but the static that crackled from it as he adjusted the tuner was as welcome as any music any of them had ever heard.

The girl's mouth and eyes widened as she stared at the device. The look she then turned on Wright was so penetrating and adoring that he was forced to turn away. Caught in her stare of childlike wonder, he had for just an instant forgotten who he was. That was not only dangerous, it was unwarranted.

Wright advanced the dial one tiny increment at a time, not wanting to chance skipping over the faintest, most distant signal.

Static. More static. Nothing but static.

Wright saw the youth's expression fall, watched his shoulders slump. He was just as disappointed as the lanky teen, but there was nothing he could do about it. In a life that had been filled with disappointment the silence of the radio was just one more. Used to dealing with disillusionment, he would handle this latest bout as stolidly as he had all that had preceded it.

As for the kid, well, he had obviously learned how to cope with worse. He would deal with this, or he wouldn't. Either way, Wright figured, it wasn't his problem.

Reaching the end of the dial, his expression set, he starting turning the knob back. As if in his careful search he might somehow have missed something. Static, rising and falling. The music of nothingness and nowhere.

Unexpectedly, a scratchy voice emerged from the speaker. Stunned, Wright nearly forgot to stop turning the knob. Doing his best to fine-tune the reception, he had to settle for turning up the volume. The distant words remained faint but intelligible.

"...the effective range of their main weapon is less than 100 meters. Your best plan is to outrun them."

Weak as the reception was, the speaker's assurance still came through clearly. Without really knowing what was going on or what had happened to the world he once knew, Wright found himself drawn to the spokesman's voice. You could tell a lot about someone not only from how they carried themselves but from how they carried their vowels.

"This guy sounds like he knows what he's talking about. Who is it?"

Equally fascinated by the confident transmission, Reese could only stare at the radio and shake his head.

"I don't know."

As for Star, she did not care about the words that were being spoken. She did not begin to understand everything that was being said.

What mattered to the nine-year old was that somewhere, someplace, there were still others.

It had become an intermittent but highly anticipated ritual. Scattered across what remained of the western United States and parts of northern Mexico, groups of survivors gathered together to listen to the unscheduled broadcasts on motley assortments of cobbled-together radios and amateur receivers. No dearly lamented sports play-by-play, no important political speech, no jocular social commentary or international reportage was ever listened to with the rapt attention that the still-living paid to those sporadic transmissions. Knobs were turned, wires pressed together, components coddled, speakers constantly cleaned as the often intermittent, sometimes scratchy, but always mesmerizing voice of John Connor resounded through crumbling buildings, desert canyons, dense forests, and shattered lives.

"If you can't outrun them," declared the by now familiar voice as it spoke from its unidentified location, "you have one or two options."

Somewhere in Utah, a group of bedraggled citizens huddled closer around a campfire, listening intently.

"The T-600s are large and pack a lot of firepower, but they're a primitive design." Connor's voice hissed from the remnants of a radio.

* * *

In a cave in New Mexico, the senior male present stretched skyward a hand holding a makeshift antennae, fighting for every iota of improvement in the sound his family's scavenged equipment was receiving.

"The small of the back and the shoulder joints are vulnerable to light weapons fire. As a last resort, ventilation requirements leave the motor cortex partially exposed at the back of the neck. A knife to this area will slow them down. But not for long."

Sitting in front of the broadcast unit in the outpost, Connor halted. Many times he had delivered the irregular evening address. Many times he had fought to find the right things to say. He was not a comfortable speaker, not a natural orator. He did not intuitively know how to reassure people, how to comfort them, how to offer hope. Practice alone had made him better at it.

Practice, and necessity. Still, there were times when he just came to a dead end; out of words, out of thoughts, out of encouragement.

It was at such times that a comforting hand on his shoulder was of more help than volumes of instruction on public speaking. Seeing Kate smiling down at him enabled him to resume transmitting.

"Each and every one of you...." he continued.

Huddled around a fire near the ruins of the observatory, two determined children and one very mystified adult found themselves captivated by the broadcast.

"...above all, *stay alive*," the voice on the radio emphasized. "You have no idea how important you are—how important you will become, each and every one of you."

***

Connor paused to look up at his wife. A more personal note had begun to creep into his voice and he deliberately forced it down.

"Humans have a strength that cannot be measured by mechanical means, by the machines that struggle to understand us. Join us. Get to a safe area to avoid detection. Look for our symbol. Make yourself known. We will find you," he murmured into the pickup. Swallowing and regaining full control of his emotions, he rushed to conclude the broadcast.

"I promise—we *will* win. But you, me, everyone, we all need to keep fighting. My name is John Connor. If you're listening to this, *you* are the Resistance."

Static returned, but this time the listeners did not mind. The broadcast had proved that there was more out there than devastation. More than silent, inhuman, hunting mechanisms. There were people. People who were fighting back, instead of living like the rodents and roaches they had so long disparaged. There was—hope.

Reese turned to meet Wright's contemplative gaze.

"John Connor." His expression and voice overflowing with unrestrained admiration, he peered over at the radio. Star was watching him intently. "I don't know how—but we gotta find this guy."

Off to the side the technician was checking to make sure the evening's transmission was not being traced. Connor slumped back in the chair, rubbing at his eyes.

"Was it good?"

Kate Connor squeezed his shoulder and nodded.

"It was good, John. It's always good. The words don't

really matter. It's hearing the conviction in your voice that gives people reason to have faith in something."

He nodded, reached up and pressed his hand over hers. How many were still out there, hanging on? Of those, how many had access to working receivers? Was Kate right and his irregular sermons were doing some good? It was impossible to know. Was it just possible, just maybe, one of those out there listening and trying to survive was his own father?

That too, was impossible to know.

CHAPTER SIX

Voices in his head, fire in his face. Tubes in his arms. They all liquefied together in a seething, clinging, stinking swamp of confused memories. Pain was present, too, but that did not unsettle him half so much as the melting, merging visions. Pain was something he had lived with most of his life. Pain he could deal with.

Not this.

He was being restrained, held down. Rousing himself, he tried to fight back. He would not be interned now. Or was it interred? The memories...he struggled, kicked, struck out violently.

Sat up.

His heart was pounding and his breath was coming in short, deep gasps, like the breathing of someone who had just finished a long sprint. He had been dreaming—but of what? Reality, nightmare, actual memory—he could not tell, could not sort imagination from truth. Even as he tried to pin down details they were slipping away from his recall.

He wasn't alone in his dreaming. In the first light of dawn he saw an uneasy, softly moaning Kyle Reese sleeping sitting up, with his back against a collapsing wall. The girl Star had somehow managed to find a position that allowed her to sleep with her legs sprawled across the teen and her head on Wright's shin. He looked at her for a long moment and as he did so, the worst of the dreaming faded away.

Reaching down, he gently eased her head off his leg, then rose and strode off into the darkness without waking either of them.

He had always preferred sunrise to the rest of the day. Before the sun was fully up the world seemed so clean, so fresh, so decent. So full of the possibilities that always seemed to lie just beyond his reach. It was the one time of the day when he could be alone without fear of the troubles that so often had seemed to follow him. He had frequently felt that was where he was best suited to live: in that narrow sliver of time before night became day. Sadly, it never lasted as long as he wished.

Surrounded by junk, trash, and debris, he set about trying to make something out of it. Of all the ruined vehicles in the observatory parking lot, the jeep was not in the best shape. But it was a jeep, and painted in camouflage. As he worked, he found better and more familiar tools than Star's scavenged knife. Each new tool saw his work proceed faster.

The pile he was assembling alongside the waiting jeep grew steadily. Batteries, wires still flaunting their insulation, spark plugs that looked as if, given the right encouragement, they might still spark, an air filter that was less dirty than others, a fuel filter so clean it must have come from somewhere other than L.A.... Some of his finds stayed on the parts mountain while others found their way into the heart of the 4x4.

The sun was well up by the time he felt he had put together something under the hood of the jeep that might pass for an engine. Finding a battery that still had juice was hardest of all, given how long the automotive graveyard had been in existence. Satisfied that he had done the best he could with the materials available, he carried the battery over to the jeep and began bolting it onto the waiting support plate.

The necessary connections were almost complete when the bent and rusted prop that had been holding up the hood finally gave way. He yanked his arm back sharply, but the falling metal still scraped his withdrawing arm. Blood appeared against the skin, seeping. He stared at it as if seeing it for the first time, ignoring the return of his old companion.

Pain.

Off to his right, something moved. Reaching into one of her many pockets, the girl fumbled a moment before removing a single band-aid. On it was imprinted the image of a white cartoon dog with a black nose and a contented smile. What was the character's name? Wright tried to remember as she carefully applied the child's bandage to the fresh wound. It was far from broad enough to cover the slash and blood continued to ooze from around the adhesive's edge.

Stepping back, she eyed her handiwork with all the dignity and professional gratification of a surgeon who had just closed up a patient's exposed spine.

He ought to say something, he realized. "Thank you" would probably be appropriate. They locked eyes for an instant. Then he carefully lifted up the jeep's hood, fashioned a new temporary prop, and resumed installing the battery.

How much Reese had observed of what had just transpired between himself and the girl Wright didn't know, and didn't care. But there was suspicion and uncertainty in the teen's manner as he approached the jeep. For a while he said nothing; just stood and watched as the older man connected wires and cables. Eventually curiosity overcame any attempt at appearing disinterested.

"You get it working?"

Wright spoke without taking his head out from under the hood.

"Almost. Won't know 'til I try. Parts seem to work okay separately. Next we'll see how well they work together. At least the gas in the tank hasn't turned to varnish." He indicated the assembled wrecks. "Managed to siphon enough to fill 'er up."

Turning, Reese gazed off into the distance.

"We should head east. Into the desert. That's the best place to get away from the machines. If we're lucky, we might run into some real Resistance fighters." Long-suppressed excitement crept unbidden into his voice. "Maybe they'll give me something to fight the machines with besides spring traps."

Wright was tightening a bolt deep within the engine compartment. It wouldn't do to get the jeep up and running only to have some vital part fall out halfway to his destination. He doubted a call to the Automobile Club would bring much in the way of a response. If there still was an Automobile Club. If he had anything to call with.

"I'm heading north."

That didn't sound good, Reese decided. Not just the "north" part. The "I'm" part. He immediately protested.

"No—why—you can't. That was one of the first places the machines took over. Machines control the whole Northern Sector. It's Skynet Central. You can't get in there. Why would you even want to try?"

Something went *clang* under the hood and Wright cursed. The expletive was short and pungent. Reese twitched while Star looked on in continued and blissful ignorance.

"I've got to find someone," Wright finally responded.

It was enough to solidify Reese's suspicions. Not "we"—"I". He glanced at Star, whose expression was as open as ever, then turned back to the preoccupied stranger whose face still had not emerged from the depths of the jeep's engine compartment.

"I don't know where you came from or what you do or much of anything else about you, but I do know that there's obviously still a lot you don't know about Skynet. How it works, how the machines work—all kinds of stuff. Stuff that if you don't know can get you dead. It's too dangerous for us, for anyone, to go there."

"What about the 'L.A. Branch' of the Resistance? Who'll fight the machines here if you leave?"

Reese hesitated, uncertain if the older man was being serious, having fun at his expense, or a mix of both, and decided to take him at his word. He turned to Star.

"Come on, man. We need to get out of L.A." He nodded at Wright, then indicated the jeep. "If you can actually make that thing go, that is."

The girl wasn't waiting. Clambering over the side of the vehicle, she settled herself into the passenger seat and waited. Ignoring her, Wright continued to tinker with the engine. Something coughed under the hood and sputtered to life. Half expecting it to die at any moment, he was more than a little surprised when it did not. In fact, the longer the engine ran, the smoother it sounded.

No telling how long it had been sitting busted and unmoving, he told himself.

Alone in the idling jeep, Star studied the profusion of knobs on the dash. Since no one told her not to do otherwise, she began playing with them, twisting and turning one at a time. None of them did anything until she pressed a button slightly to the right of the steering column.

That there was a CD in the player was not exactly a revelation. That the unit functioned was considerably more of a surprise. A startled Star gaped at it in amazement. Reese both looked and listened in awe.

"What is this?"

Coming around from the front of the 4x4, Wright gazed at the indicator lights on the in-dash entertainment unit.

"A CD player."

"No, no," Reese corrected him impatiently, "the music."

Wright's thoughts were ping-ponging back and forth between the inexplicable present and a less-than-inspiring past.

"Doesn't matter. Something my brother used to listen to. 'Us and Them', by Pink Floyd."

And what about me, he wondered silently. *What's happened to the world? What kind of wall am I another brick in?*

The music was bringing back too many memories. Reaching in, he switched it off. When the girl gave him a cross look, he motioned impatiently for her to exit.

"Come on," he prompted her, "let's go." She didn't

move, confused both by his words and his suddenly abrupt tone. He clarified his meaning for her. "Get out."

Her eyes never left him as she slowly climbed over the far side of the jeep. At least, that was how he felt. He could not meet the wide-eyed girlish gaze.

Reese gaped at him, unwilling to countenance what he was hearing. Despite the doubts he had been feeling, the stranger's words still left him in shock.

"You're leaving?"

Ignoring the teen, Wright dropped the hood, made sure it latched shut.

"You're just gonna leave?"

Reese continued as the stranger carefully collected the tools he had scavenged and put them in the back of the jeep. By this time he was crowding the older man. Wright tolerated this invasion of his space even as he ignored the increasingly accusatory teen.

"We saved your life."

Reese wanted to grab Wright, to shake him and make him look into his eyes. It was a good thing he didn't.

"You're going to leave us here?"

Realization suddenly dawned and he stepped back.

"I get it. I understand. We'd just hold you back, right? Slow you down. You can move faster without us. It'll be easier for you alone." Somehow he kept in check the anger that had been building within him.

"You know one of the differences between us and the machines? We bury our dead. They don't bother." Taking the bewildered Star by the hand he started to back away from the now silent stranger, eyeing him as if he carried some incurable communicable disease.

"Go on—you go kill yourself. You're not the first one

to leave. But no one's coming to bury you anyway." He spat at the ground. "Star and me, we've got better things to do."

Wright just nodded. In his life he had been insulted by experts and disrespected by masters. The teen's feeble efforts had no effect on him.

What did have an effect was the expression on the girl's face. It had shifted from hurt and confusion to one of sheer terror. Remembering what Reese had told him, Wright instantly began scanning the immediate vicinity. So did the teen. Their search was unnecessary, as a moment later the source of Star's alarm dropped down on them from above.

Compact, utilitarian, and extremely advanced, the small flying machine buzzed rapidly past the jeep before rising back into the sky and preparing itself for a second pass.

"Aerostat!" Reese was yelling even as he ran toward the jeep. As he did so, the ruddy light of a scanning laser was taking the measure of him from head to toe. The light was harmless—except for what it implied. The Aerostat would be transmitting even as it was evaluating.

Wright didn't wait for further explication. Picking up the girl, he vaulted the side of the idling jeep to land in the passenger seat. He did this only because the driver's seat was already occupied by Reese. The teen fumbled with the shift, managed to get the vehicle in reverse and moving away from the steep slope that rimmed that section of the parking lot.

Wright had other ideas. Reaching over the seat, he threw the jeep into drive.

"Go!"

* * *

Reese wanted to argue but was already mature enough to realize this was neither the time nor the place. Gritting his teeth, he floored the accelerator. Responding with welcome agility, the jeep obediently shot forward, jumped the curb, crashed through the remnants of some decorative border brush gone wild, and plunged down the embankment on the other side.

Once committed, the teen kept his foot on the accelerator and both hands on the wheel. At any moment he expected the vehicle to slew sideways and crash, go airborne and crash, or hit something unyielding and crash. He was mentally prepared for almost anything except keeping the battered jeep going straight downhill.

"Aerostat must've heard the music!" he yelled back without shifting his attention from the hillside down which they were careening. His hands gripped the wheel so tightly they were beginning to turn white.

"What about your gun?" Wright shouted at him.

"You've still got the clip!" With a boulder the size of a bulldozer looming in their path, he swung the wheel to the left. By some miracle of gravity the jeep did not roll and continued banging its way down the mountainside.

Wright dealt with the confusion calmly. Among the innumerable emotions he was not heir to was mad panic. Searching the pile of tools he had dumped in back, he picked up an X-shaped tire lug wrench. While not exactly aerodynamic, it had the virtue of being as throwable as it was solid.

Opening the door on his side, he leaned out, took aim, and threw the tool. The speed and force with which it spun through the air aft of the jeep gave it the heft and appearance of some crazed ninja-throwing star as customized by a local auto repair shop. Amazingly, it smashed socket-on into the trailing Aerostat. Bits and pieces of the machine went flying.

Some of them must have been important, because seconds later the independently guided Skynet tracking device crashed into the ground. This resulted in an eruption of many more bits and pieces as well as a termination of the pursuit.

Leaning over the back seat, Star gawked in wide-eyed delight at the grounding of their pursuer. It had not been destroyed, but it was definitely grounded. Wright swallowed as he contemplated the unexpected efficacy of his throw. He remembered being adept at such destructive labors, but not quite this adept.

Though visibly relieved to be rid of the machine that had been on their tail, Reese was less sanguine about their chances.

"Too late. It would've transmitted our location to its friends within the first minute."

Wright tried to take the teen's knowledgeable assessment into account.

"We're still going. Maybe they'll find their damaged buddy but by that time they won't know where we are."

Glancing over, Reese studied the stranger's face.

"You really don't know anything about Skynet's capabilities, do you? They'll know exactly where we are—we're in Los Angeles. That'll be enough to get them started looking for us."

After a moment's thought, Wright leaned forward, reached out, and pulled hard on the emergency brake handle. Reese yelped as the jeep skidded into a half turn before finally coming to a stop. Simultaneously delighting and surprising Wright, the engine continued to run, if not exactly purr. Youth and man locked eyes.

"Then if the idea is to stay alive, I'm driving," Wright informed the teen quietly.

"How's it feel?"

Connor asked Barnes the question as he examined the heavy but sufficiently portable transmitter that had been strapped to the other man's back. Another soldier was responsible for transporting the batteries that would power it while yet another carried the collapsing broadcast antenna. Still, when they were in the field and on the move, it was possible that Barnes would have to handle the entire one-piece setup by himself. The man's answer was pretty much the same as Connor had come to expect from any soldier of the Resistance.

"The awkwardness is worse than the weight, but I'll manage."

Connor had received that same response from tired men and women who had at one time or another been confronted with an absence of food, a shortage of ammunition, or an approaching squadron of T-600s. Each time, they had managed. Each time, they had persevered. *They would continue to do so,* he told himself grimly, *until Skynet and the last of its minions had been wiped from the face of the Earth.*

They had no choice.

A tech came toward him as he was speaking with Kate. "Just got word, sir." She fiddled with the closed-channel communicator that had been fitted over her left ear. In another life, she might have been a model. Dirt, war, and the sight of too much death had aged her prematurely. But there was no sign in her voice of the depression or despair that might have been expected to afflict someone so young and attractive.

"We've got significant enemy movement north of L.A. Report's not sure of type and quantity, but it's definitely something bigger than isolated Ts or scouting Aerostats."

Connor considered the possibilities. "Are any of our people operating in that area today? Search and rescue, or maybe a scavenger pickup team?"

The tech conveyed the query and waited for a response before replying.

"No one on the ground. Two A-10s in the air— Williams and Mirhadi. But they're ninety miles away and on routine patrol. Too far to provoke this kind of reaction."

Kate's attention shifted from the communications tech back to her husband.

"Looks like some civilians decided to try and get out. I don't know what else would rouse this kind of activity in what's been a dead zone for so long."

Connor nodded in agreement, looked at the tech.

"Let's help them out. Since they're not occupied machine-busting at the moment, send our birds over to the flare-up. If some unidentifieds are making trouble, they would probably welcome a little cover. And our people can guide them to a safe area." Leaning toward his wife, he gave her a parting kiss as he and Barnes headed out.

"Okay." She turned back to the tech. "Get on it."

CHAPTER SEVEN

Even when it was new, the secondary road through the desert outside Los Angeles had never carried a lot of traffic. Now it constituted the first leg of a journey north for a single weather-beaten jeep.

At least, Wright thought to himself as he scanned both the pavement ahead and the scrub-covered hills off to his left, *traffic wasn't going to be a problem.*

A glance at the passenger seat and in back revealed that his two companions were still asleep. He did not think of them as children. That identifier implied an innocence that was no longer present in this world. Competence existed exclusive of chronological age. He would far rather embark on the trip ahead in the company of a knowledgeable and experienced teen and a brave nine-year old than some fat fool of a forty-something.

In his short, brutish life he had known far too many of the latter.

Save for the comforting grumble of the jeep, the silence on the old highway was pervasive. Tough and resilient, the desert scrub appeared to have survived better than the largely transplanted and imported landscaping of Los Angeles.

Occasionally he thought he caught glimpses of movement among the stones, succulents, and cacti. Rats, mice, rabbits, ever-opportunistic coyotes and cats gone feral. He smiled to himself. Small mammals had survived the age of dinosaurs by fleeing to burrows. Perhaps humankind would survive the age of machines the same way. Something dark and winged soaring overhead drew his gaze upward.

He was not at all surprised that among the surviving species of birds, buzzards seemed to be doing particularly well.

If the 7-Eleven that hove into view was a mirage, it was a pleasingly solid one. Though for all that was left of it, it might as well have been vapor. Torn and battered, its windows and front broken out, with its filling island twisted as if by a tornado, it appeared to have been ravaged as much by the weather and human refugees as by Skynet.

Bent and rusted as they were, the presence of the gas pumps prompted him to glance down at the jeep's dash. He was not surprised to see that the fuel gauge indicator was flirting with a large letter E. Determination would still get him to San Francisco—but another tankful of fuel would sure be a big help.

At the moment, he was not ashamed to admit that he needed the expertise of someone much younger than himself who knew about their present surroundings. Reaching over, he elbowed the sleeping teen awake. Reese muttered something unintelligible, but when his eyes opened, they opened fast. He was instantly awake, his awareness ignited like the flame on a gas stove.

Slowing further as he drew closer to the station turnoff, Wright indicated the silent structure.

"Looks dead. What do you think?"

Leaning out the side of the jeep, Reese squinted at the building. Excitement replacing exhaustion, he pointed to a symbol that had been spray painted on one wall. More than anything, it resembled a crude double helix.

"Hey...that's it." The youth pointed. "That's the insignia of the Resistance. It means this place has recently been visited by its soldiers and found to be clean. Looks deserted, too. It should be all right to get out here—at least for as long as it takes to pick up what we can. Pull over." Reaching into the back seat, he nudged the jeep's smallest passenger.

"Star, wake up! We've found a store."

Sitting up, the girl rubbed at her eyes, and looked at Reese as if to say, *What kind of store?*

Settling back down in the front passenger seat, the teen studied the ruins absorbedly, dividing his attention between the relic and the now alert and attentive little girl in back.

"It's kind of a mess, but it looks like a mini-mart." At this her eyes widened hopefully. He had to smile at her reaction.

"Don't get too excited," he told her. "You know what these places are like inside. We went through plenty of 'em back in L.A." He eyed the gaping, windowless front speculatively. "Maybe we'll be lucky this time, maybe not." He turned back to the older man. "Come on. You drive like a grandmother."

His initial reaction after they parked the jeep and finally got inside was "not." Star's expression showed how her heart sank as she joined the two men in inspecting the rows of broken, crumpled shelves. The mini-mart's interior had been ravaged and scavenged with a thoroughness fit to satisfy the most scrupulous barbarian. The store had been cleaned out. There wasn't a paper clip to be had, much less anything edible. A long-silent freezer contained a single empty carton of milk.

Wright wondered why whoever had drained the contents had chosen to place the empty container back in the silent freezer. A choice made out of reason, respect, or madness?

Following close on his heels, Reese suddenly froze. Star wasn't the only one whose senses had been sharpened by years spent surviving in the shell of the Southern California megalopolis.

"Someone's here."

He had barely uttered the exclamation when half a dozen figures suddenly materialized from different corners of the store.

Wright froze in his turn. They had guns. Not that this would stop him if he felt compelled to defend himself, but while the scruffy shapes wielding the weapons were clearly on edge, their trigger fingers were relaxed. Had their anxiety exceeded their curiosity, they would have fired without bothering to emerge from hiding. That they hadn't done so indicated that their preference was to talk—at least initially.

Of course they would, he told himself. In this world all human life was precious, because it meant one more individual alive to rage against the machine.

That didn't mean every survivor welcomed every other one with open arms. Survival still trumped friendship. Confirming this belief, the man Wright took to be the leader of the group kept his shotgun trained on the intruders.

At the first appearance of weapons Reese had stepped in front of Star to shield her. He too had singled out the same man as the group leader.

"We saw your sign," the teen ventured by way of a hello.

"The old lady put up the sign. Not me. We can't help you." The shotgun's muzzle gestured toward the pump island outside where Wright had parked the jeep. "Wherever you're headed, you need to keep on going."

Stepping forward, an elderly woman regarded the trio of arrivals a moment before finally nodding and turning to the much younger man holding the weapon.

"Ease off, Len. They're okay." Her shoulder-length hair had turned white as marble.

Licking his lips uncertainly, the shotgun wielder gestured with the end of the weapon again, this time singling out Reese and Star.

"These two might be. Ain't seen a machine yet that tried to imitate a kid." Cagey and alert, his eyes flicked back to the silently staring Wright. "But what about him?"

"We don't want to cause trouble." Wright kept his tone even and unthreatening. "We just need fuel."

The man laughed bitterly. "Don't we all. How about some steak and ice cream while we're wishing?" His gaze narrowed. "The dark season is coming. We only have enough for ourselves."

Wright stared back at him calmly. "Why? You planning on taking a long vacation some time soon?"

Tensing, the other man took a step toward Wright, only to be stopped by the exasperated elder.

"Len, put the gun down. You really think I'm going to let you send these children away starving?"

He looked at her sharply. "Virginia, we're running out of food."

Spreading his hands, Reese pleaded their case.

"We're not asking for much. Maybe one meal and some gas for our jeep, then we'll leave. We don't want to stay. We're trying to reach the Resistance."

For the second time since they had entered the store, Len let out a burst of sharp, acrid laughter.

"The *Resistance*? What a joke! There is no 'Resistance'. There's only talk and wishful thinking. You can't fight the machines. All anyone with any sense can do is try to stay out of their way." He gestured at their teetering surroundings. "Why do you think this place is still standing?"

"Because the machines haven't gotten around to it yet," Wright opined quietly.

Len glared at him. "No! It's because we don't make trouble. We don't shout our presence. We keep our heads down and they ignore us."

"You keep your head down," Reese told him. "They'll come for you eventually. I've seen this before. They don't ignore you. They don't ignore anybody. What they do is set priorities. Pick their targets according to the possible threat they might pose, starting with any they consider potentially dangerous to them. Once those've been wiped out they start working their way down their list. No one escapes notice. No one gets left alive. They want us *all* dead." In spite of Reese's youth, it was easy to see which of the two men was the more mature.

"They want you dead. Whether you 'make trouble' for them or not. Maybe you can hang on here for a while longer yet, but they'll get around to you eventually."

Len was not about to have the agenda that had led to his continuing survival misrepresented by a garrulous teenager.

"We help you, maybe they will."

Wright spoke up. "So give us some gas and we'll get out of your hair."

While the men had argued, the older woman had walked over to peer down at the silent Star.

"No one's going anywhere," she declared with resolve, "until this one has had something to eat." Kneeling, she reached out to touch the girl's cheek. Star did not flinch.

"Look how young you are." The woman shook her head sorrowfully. "I had a granddaughter about your age. Before—everything. The world we've left to you, poor thing—I'm so very sorry for that. People acted without thinking. Not for the first time, but until now things always turned out all right. This time—I just don't know." She rose and smiled encouragingly. "Come on, let's feed you. Unless, of course, you're not hungry."

Star nodded violently.

"I thought so." Moving to a part of the store nearer the back, the woman called Virginia pushed aside an empty metal rack. Bending, she curled her fingers around a handle that had been painted to resemble the rest of the floor and pulled. A wooden hatch cover rose on sturdy hinges.

While Wright remained aloof, waiting, Reese could not help himself. Straining to see down into the opening, he was able to make out piles of packaged and canned food, vacuum-sealed loaves of bread, a startling variety of canned beverages that ran the liquid gamut from beer to soda to water, even some bundles of semi-fresh vegetables.

Len noted these actions with ill-concealed displeasure.

"We haven't finished evaluating this bunch. We still don't know who they are, where they come from, what they're doing here, or how they managed to get hold of a functioning jeep." He indicated the open hatch. "What are you doing?"

Virginia did not bother to look in his direction. Kneeling and bending down, she began pulling an assortment of provisions from the subterranean store-room. Reese eyed the apparently unending stream eagerly. He hadn't seen so much food in one place since—well, he couldn't remember *when* he had seen so much food. Plainly, living outside a major city and beyond Skynet's immediate ken had its advantages.

"I'm using a mother's intuition." The older woman looked back at the disapproving Len. "Now put your paranoia away and come welcome our guests."

Though she neither looked nor sounded like Reese's conception of a survivalist leader, it was obvious who was in charge here. Around the interior perimeter of the ruined mini-mart weapons were lowered, including Len's. Hands came off stocks and triggers. Several of those present helped themselves to bottles and settled down to drink.

Gesturing at the assortment of food she had laid out on the floor, Virginia smiled at the newcomers.

"Help yourselves."

While a famished Reese and Star dove unhesitatingly into a pile of goodies the likes of which had vanished from their memories, Wright held back and continued to regard the older woman. In welcoming him and the children unconditionally she was revealing a pair of character traits that had been more or less entirely absent from his life. Trust, and kindness. Being as unfamiliar with such ordinary human touchstones as he was with the cultural norms of central Africa, he hung back, uncertain how to react to an offer for which nothing was expected in return.

Marking his hesitation, she put some food into a weathered basket and brought it to him. He eyed the packages. Some were familiar to him, some utterly strange. He shook his head "no." Lowering the basket, she tried another tack.

"Are you all right, son?"

Len's gaze narrowed. "What are you doing?"

"Life is lived moment by moment, Len. Choice by choice. It signifies what it means to be human."

Lifting up his gun, he pointed it again. Not at Wright this time, or at Reese. At her.

"I can't let you do this, Virginia. This is *our* food. *Our* fuel. It's not your choice to make."

Ignoring him, she turned back to the stolid Wright.

"You look so cold. We have a stock of spare clothing. I think some of it will fit you. Do you want a sweater?" Again he shook his head. This time not because he intended to further refuse the offering of food, but because he found himself distracted. His attention had been drawn to Star.

She had paused her feverish eating. Holding a sandwich halfway to her mouth, she had tensed visibly. Her eyes were wide. It was a posture and response Wright had seen before. Out of the corner of an eye he saw that

Reese had noticed it too and was already racing for a far corner of the floor. He beat Wright to the spot by half a second.

A loud *crack* sounded. The bottle Len had been drinking from exploded in his hand. Startled, he gawked at the glass shards and the precious drink that was now dripping from his open palm. Blood oozed from his neck where some of the glass had struck.

The roof exploded.

The digits that plunged through the resultant opening were large, powerful, and metallic. Clamping around a stunned Virginia, they pulled her out through the newly made hole in the roof. Racing for the front door, one of the other survivors screamed at Wright in passing.

"*Damn you!* You brought them here!"

Bashing its way through the rapidly disintegrating ceiling, a second mechanical claw missed the accuser but snatched up another survivor.

Wright didn't have to tell Reese and Star to run. They were already sprinting madly for the store front. Around them was chaos and confusion as the remaining survivors scattered in search of an exit, any exit, while the pair of probing claws sought additional prey.

As they burst free of the mini-mart's confines, Reese and Wright looked back to see the attacker. Star did not—she just kept running.

"Harvester!" Reese exclaimed without breaking stride.

A mechanical marvel, the machine was many times the size of a human being. Powerful arms and legs sprouted from its body together with an assortment of sensors. Only some of these observed their surroundings by seeing via the normal visual spectrum. Others looked to be attuned to seeing in the infrared, still others in the ultraviolet. Gleaming limbs of dark metal held Virginia and the other snared survivor in an unyielding jointed grasp.

People were screaming and scattering in all directions. Many rushed toward a parking area packed with vehicles, some of which had been laboriously cleaned up and restored. Flanked by the children, Wright headed straight for the painstakingly repaired jeep. They did not reach it—which was fortunate. Looming over the crumpled roof of the store on girder-like legs, the towering Harvester let loose a massive discharge that turned the jeep into an eye-blinding fireball. Wright and his young companions were forced back toward the mini-mart.

While he easily shook off the effects of the blast, the concussion had been too much for Star. Dismissing an odd and unfamiliar surge of emotion, he bent and picked her up. With a curt nod in the direction of a slowly accelerating camper, he led Reese toward it in hopes of intercepting the departing vehicle.

Len cut them off, though not intentionally. A fleeing Saab sideswiped him. He must have hit the fender and hood just right, because he rolled clear with no apparent injury. Reaching the camper, he yanked open the passenger-side door and jumped inside.

The fleeing vehicle did not escape the attention of the Harvester. One shot reduced both the camper shell and the pickup on which it had been riding to flaming scrap. Having gained a head start, it looked to Wright as if the Saab and its occupants might make their escape. The Harvester's range, however, was the equal of its precision. Blown high into the air, the Saab tumbled end over end to slam into the remnants of the metal canopy that partly shaded the single line of gas pumps.

Still carrying Star, he and Reese took cover behind an intact corner of the mini-mart's auto service bay. Glancing inside, he spotted a pair of unoccupied and possibly functional vehicles: a tanker and a battered heavy-lift tow truck that had been kitted out to fight the machines. Loading the unmoving Star into the truck's front seat, Wright pretzeled himself under the dash and began the process of hot-wiring the vehicle. A hand on his shoulder made him pause and look back.

Meeting the older man's gaze, Reese shook his head and used both hands to diagram a mushroom shape in the air while blowing out his cheeks. While Wright knew he might not be the brightest man on the planet, neither was he stupid. The teen's meaning was as clear as it was correct: based on the action they had just observed and had barely managed to avoid, climbing into a car and attempting to speed away might not be the best strategy for avoiding the Harvester's attention.

Then what? he thought furiously.

The big machine saved him the pain of having to think. Short bursts from its secondary weapon began to collapse the walls of the service bay. Years of dust and accumulated grime blossomed out to form impenetrable clouds as the Harvester pondered how best to remove them from the truck.

Glancing sharply at Reese, Wright mouthed the words, "Trust me" and brought wires together beneath the truck's dash. The engine growled, stalled, growled again, and rumbled to life. Throwing himself into the driver's seat as Reese slid in on the other side and shielded Star, Wright slammed the truck in gear—into reverse.

Ramming the tanker, the heavy truck strained for traction. Looking back, with one hand on the wheel and a foot jamming the accelerator into the floor, Wright saw that two-thirds of his plan was working. Pushing back the tanker had slammed it into the legs of the Harvester and brought the collecting machine to a temporary stop. As a result of being smashed by the tow truck, the tanker was spilling gasoline from several ruptures in its steel body.

It might as well have been spilling milk. In the absence of the hoped-for sparks, the pungent fuel was simply pooling up on the floor of the service bay. The angle at which the Harvester had been pinned prevented it from bringing its weapons to bear, but that was unlikely to last forever. As he was trying to decide what to do next, a hand tapped him on the arm. A small hand.

Now awake, a silent Star was proffering an emergency highway flare.

Taking it, he ignited the warning device, took aim, tossed it back and out the door of the truck, and floored the accelerator. As the tow truck streaked out of the service bay, the flare landed in the nearest stream of gas and flared back in the direction of the tanker. Seeing the truck flee, the Harvester raised the muzzle of its main cannon and took aim.

The result when the line of fire reached the immobilized tanker was most satisfying.

The explosion was even bigger than Wright had hoped. As flames balled skyward behind him, he gunned the tow truck away from the mini-mart and headed for the highway. He didn't smile at Reese, and the teen did not smile back, but the feeling of appreciation was clearly mutual.

Then the Harvester plowed through the wall of flames that had engulfed the service bay and started after them.

It fired—and missed. Since the beginning of the assault on the mini-mart this was the first shot unleashed from its primary weapon that had failed to strike its intended target. The failing might have been due to the machine having suffered some slight damage from the tanker explosion and the resulting flames. Or it could have been due to the hasty evasive action taken by Wright. More likely the miss was due to the fact that the Harvester's legs were still locked, entwined, and in several spots melted to the remnants of the tanker.

But while the machine's mobility and ability to follow were seriously compromised, that of its component parts were not.

Reese had seen them in action on the streets of greater Los Angeles, and for his new friend's benefit he identified the two-wheeled machines that dropped clear of the larger machine's body as Moto-Terminators. Capable of speeds far in excess of anything the Harvester could achieve, they hit the ground and shot after the fleeing tow truck.

Like the rest of the old highway, the section Wright was speeding along was littered with dead and abandoned cars. Now, instead of driving to avoid them, he deliberately slammed the truck's reinforced steel front bumper into as many as he felt he could safely impact. As pieces of abandoned vehicle went flying and bouncing down the road in the truck's wake, the noise inside the cab was deafening. Neither Reese nor Star complained.

It was a clever effort—and a useless one. Steered by senses far more responsive than those of any human driver, the pursuing Motos deftly maneuvered around the careening debris without ever slowing down. The distance between truck and hunters closed rapidly.

Wright grew aware that Reese was yelling at him, screaming to make himself heard above the metal carnage that was fueling the truck's wake. He could have argued with the teen's declared intent, but there were two reasons why he did not. One, someone had to drive the truck. And two, he didn't have any better ideas.

Climbing out the rear window of the cab, Reese carefully made his way to the rear of the rocking, swaying vehicle. The first sizable object he saw that wasn't bolted down was a barrel of oil. Several kicks with both feet sent it flying off the back of the truck. Bursting on contact with the road, it sent a wide spill of black liquid slashing across the highway. The first of the two Motos managed to avoid the rapidly spreading pool. The second did not. Striking the slick, it spun wildly out of control.

Continuing to accelerate, the other machine was working to try and cut off the truck's line of flight. Frantically searching the vehicle's bed, Reese found a toolbox, opened it, and began throwing everything he could find at the red-eyed machine. Screwdrivers, nails, a file—all bounced harmlessly off the machine's outer shell, until a heavy mallet landed just ahead of the front wheel. Unable even with its superb mechanical reflexes to react in time, the Moto hit the bouncing mallet, skewed to the left, and disappeared beneath the heavy tow truck's right front wheel. The truck bounced as first the front wheel and then the rear one ran over the machine.

Having recovered from its spin-out, the second Moto had rejoined the chase and was once more closing in on the fleeing vehicle and its fragile organic occupants. Righting itself, the one that had gone down and been run over by the truck quickly recovered to rejoin its companion as though nothing had happened.

Fresh out of everything that was easily heavable, a frustrated Reese rummaged through the truck bed until his attention was caught by the main cable release. Slamming both hands down on the appropriate lever, he sent the heavy towing hook airborne off the back of the rocking vehicle as the now unrestrained cable began to unspool. Sparks and shards of asphalt flew as the steel S-shape struck the road and began bouncing and jimmying wildly behind the truck.

Then the flying hook caught onto the frame of the nearest Moto and locked tight.

Finding itself fixed securely to the truck, which was sliding and shimmying unpredictably as Wright fought to avoid the pursuers, the Moto went fishtailing in all directions. Similarly, being forced to drag the unexpected weight made the task of controlling the truck increasingly difficult. As it lurched from side to side, skewing all over the road and occasionally onto the flanking dirt shoulders, Reese found it increasingly difficult to maintain his own balance. When one especially violent jolt sent him tumbling, he grabbed for balance onto the nearest projection.

This happened to be another of the tow control levers. A motor engaged and began to reel in the errant cable—as well the homicidal machine to which it was presently affixed.

Struggling to bring its front weapons to bear on the

source of this continuing annoyance, the Moto made repeated attempts to blast free from the restraining line.

Up in the cab, Wright had had about enough of trying to dodge the pursuing Motos. While he was perfectly willing to play defense when the situation required, after a while his natural instincts took over. It was time to go on the attack. Especially since they were now rocketing along a winding canyon road where room to maneuver was restricted by a steep slope on one side and a reinforced embankment on the other.

Sitting in the passenger seat, Star took it all in without mouthing a word.

Slowing slightly, he let the second Moto catch up until it was speeding along parallel to the truck. A hard wrench of the wheel trapped the Moto between the truck and the embankment, crushing it against the restraining wall. This untenable situation persisted until the barrier finally gave way. The hunting machine was fast and agile, but it could not fly. A brief fountaining of water showed where it struck the river that was churning through the canyon below.

Wright felt a lot better for about three seconds. That was the total amount of time that elapsed between his looking down at the river and returning his gaze to the road ahead. Looming immediately in front of them was a bridge spanning the river that had swallowed the Moto. Sitting in the center of the bridge and blocking the road completely was a hovering Hunter-Killer. As he was trying both to absorb what he was seeing and figure out a way to cope with it, the waiting HK fired.

Able to rely more on brutal force than precision, since its directive did not include trying to take humans alive, its aim was not as precise as that of the Harvester. As Wright slammed on the brakes and cranked the wheel, the blast blew apart the road directly in front of the tow truck. As it spun wildly, centrifugal force sent the still-hooked Moto swinging around in a wide arc. Smashing into the blockading Hunter-Killer, the smaller machine erupted in a burst of flame and ignited munitions.

The force of the explosion was strong enough to buckle the narrow bridge. As Wright fought for control, the truck started sliding into the gorge.

"Hold on!" he yelled.

Screaming, yelling, and unable to grab onto anything to halt their fall, first Star and then Reese were sent tumbling out of the truck. Their plunge was halted by a pair of hands. Unfortunately, they were hands of metal. Scorched and dented but far from incapacitated, the trailing Harvester had caught up to the confrontation in time to pluck both children out of the air. Unyielding digits deposited both of them into a waiting Transporter.

That was enough for Wright. Grabbing an axe, he took a short run, jumped, and managed to grab hold of the hovering Transport. Reese and Star were clearly visible within the human-proof enclosure. Bringing the axe up, he started to swing it around when the nearby Harvester swept him off the vehicle's roof. Apparently deciding that this particular specimen was especially valuable, it prepared to deposit him into the Transport's forward section.

"Marcus!" Reese yelled from inside the holding basket.

"Get back!" He raised the axe again.

A new presence marked by a double scream caused it to pause. The source of the sound was a pair of A-10 Warthogs that came roaring across the top of the river gorge. Recognizing the appearance of this greater threat, the Hunter-Killer ascended skyward on its impellers and immediately took off in pursuit of the two aircraft. Moments later another HK arrived on the scene, followed by a third.

"Williams—Harvester's got a friendly pinned to that Transport. HK's coming in to finish him off—get in there." Connor barked into the radio. Kate and Barnes stood next to him in the control room, while the control operators worked with calm efficiency around them. Connor's mission for his two A-10 pilots—Williams and Mihradi—helping a few civilians through a dead zone had in the past few minutes become deadly serious.

A female voice came through on the radio.

"Got it, sir. Closing in—2,000 meters. Locking on—"

Above the gorge, the sky was suddenly filled with bursts of cannon fire as the two pilots found themselves unexpectedly outnumbered and outgunned. That didn't keep the second pilot from blasting apart the HK that was pursuing the Harvester.

"Good hit, Williams. You nailed it."

Barnes clenched his fist in silent victory as Mihradi's message came through. He glanced over at Connor who was already working through the next move. He leaned in toward the radio, speaking intently.

"Mihradi, take out the Transport's main engine—"

"What about the prisoners?" As if anticipating the pilot's concerns, Connor barely paused in his instructions.

"It'll auto-land on passive thrusters—and we can get 'em out."

The pilot's voice was crisp and clear.

"Affirm, coming in 200 feet off the deck."

The lead pilot banked sharply, dove, and shredded the rear half of the Harvester that was holding a large human prisoner.

Hit multiple times and losing power, it still retained control of its captive. The towering machine reached toward the slowly accelerating Transport for support.

The effort came to naught as an internal blast destroyed the Harvester's processing unit. Still holding tight to its prey, the machine plunged over the side of the canyon and toward the river below. The man fought his dying captor all the way down, when they landed in the river, and as they sunk toward the bottom of the fast-moving watercourse.

"HK's on our six!"

As they heard Williams' voice the three Resistance fighters watched the monitors intently as the red blip that represented the HK closed in on the two Resistance A-10s.

"It's got a lock on you—break off!" Connor yelled into the radio.

"No! He's down; he's down." Williams' shout came through as one of the green blips disappeared from the monitor.

High above, caught in an unexpectedly ferocious crossfire, one A-10 disintegrated in a shower of metal and composite splinters. As the second plane banked and attempted to get away from the overwhelming firepower of the swarming HKs, it took a hit that blew away one engine.

***

"Evasive maneuvers—now!" Connor ordered and his knuckles turned white as they gripped the table. But his voice remained steady.

The same couldn't be said of the pilot.

"It's all over me. Can't shake it." Her words were taut as if Williams was gritting her teeth when she spoke. "Engine's out! I got half speed only!"

Connor's response was instant and his voice turned urgent.

"Eject, Williams! Eject!"

Swept away by the fast-moving river, the dead Harvester finally lost its grip on its single human prisoner. Kicking free, Wright struggled toward the surface. He broke through the white water overhead long after the average swimmer would have blacked out from lack of oxygen. Long, deep breaths filled his lungs—as he saw the second A-10, trailing flame, come plunging directly toward him.

Arching his back, he dove and kicked as hard as he could for the bottom he had just escaped. He moved fast underwater—faster even than he remembered being able to—but not fast enough to escape the pile of metal that landed almost on top of him. The river quickly quenched the flames that were pouring from the fatally damaged aircraft. It also dragged the plane and the man who had been trapped beneath it swiftly downstream.

He had no idea how long he had been underwater or how far from the destroyed bridge he had been carried. Of the downed A-10 there was no sign. Coughing up river, barely conscious, wondering how he had survived,

Wright grew aware that half of him was still submerged in the eddy that had deposited him on the sandy shore. He told himself firmly that answers to such questions could come later.

For the moment, being alive was enough.

Feeling that if a sudden rush of water came downstream and caught him he would not have the strength to fight it, he knew he had to get completely out of the river. Rolling over, he lay on his back exhausted, trying to recover some sense along with his wind.

This won't do, he told himself. Out in the open and lying flat on the riverbank, the sun would dehydrate him quickly. Furthermore, sprawled helplessly he was completely exposed to the eyes of any patrolling machine. With a groan, he rolled over again and worked to get up onto his knees. That accomplished, he took a deep breath, stood, swayed for a moment, and steadied himself.

Since he had fallen into the river it stood to reason that any Terminators looking for him would begin by searching there. Checking the position of the sun, he headed inland in a northward direction and away from the water.

The wall of sand and loose scree that fronted the waterway was not easy to climb, but it did have one unexpected benefit. As he ascended, loose sand and gravel slipped downward to fill in and obscure his footsteps. He would leave no trail. Having no local destination in mind but retaining his northern bearing, he angled toward the only structure in the vicinity. If nothing else, it might offer some shade.

As it developed, the half-collapsed high voltage transmission tower not only offered shade, but a surprise.

It was impossible to miss the parachute that was hanging from one of the tower's twisted cross-supports. The lightweight material fluttered slightly in what passed for a breeze. No doubt the chute had been deployed from one of the two downed fighter aircraft. As he drew nearer he saw that something was dangling from the lower end of the chute, at the terminus of the multiple nylon lines.

It was a body, sagging limp in its shroud.

The body proceeded to address him.

"Hey!" It was a feeble salutation, but certainly far more than Wright had expected to hear. The weakness of the shout notwithstanding, he determined that the suspended pilot was possessed either of an unusually high voice or a different set of chromosomes. Walking over to the ruined structure and peering upward, he saw that it was the latter supposition that was accurate.

"*Hey!*" Her second shout was slightly more vigorous than its predecessor. "Gimme a hand, will you?"

Standing on the sandy surface staring up at her, Wright studied the warped metal spire for a moment, chose an angle of ascent, and went up it like a gibbon. The speed and agility with which he reached her side took her by surprise. Took him by surprise, too, but then as a kid he had always been adept at tree climbing. He studied the surrounding landscape.

"Nice view." Turning to examine the snarl of chute lines he started wrenching and pulling, trying to untangle her.

"Name's Williams. Blair Williams."

"Marcus Wright." He continued wrestling with the lines. They were not cooperating. Standing atop the transmission tower he knew he was almost as out in the open as he had been lying on the beach, and he didn't like the exposure. Hanging helpless in the straps of her ejection pack, the Resistance pilot was an even more obvious target.

Their thoughts and concerns coincided.

"I like to think I'm a tidy person, Marcus," she told him, "but this is no place to waste time on neatness." She nodded toward the ground. "How about we cut to the conclusion? I've got a knife."

He stopped wrestling with the frustrating knot of ropes. "Where?"

"Back of my left boot. Ankle sheath."

Her right foot was hanging over emptiness. Holding onto a section of metal with one hand, he leaned out and flailed at the indicated limb with his other hand.

"Can't reach it."

"Hang on." Dangling from the lines, she began to rock back and forth, building up momentum without regard to whether or not it might cause her to spill out of the harness. Wright waited, waited, and then timed his reach perfectly, locking his hand around her boot. Probing fingers released the catch on the sheath and he pulled the knife free. It was bigger than he expected; long, sharp, and with one edge lined with jagged teeth.

Sitting back on his perch, he eyed it admiringly. For the first time since regaining consciousness he had come into contact with a memory that was pleasing. In a life devoid of friends, knives had always been there for him, ready and willing to do whatever he wanted them to do. Sometimes too often.

He shook off the worthless reverie. "Nice knife."

Something in his voice, maybe, or something in his expression caused her to keep her response short.

"Thanks. *My* knife."

Without comment, he began sawing at the thickest part of the tangle. He was halfway through when he realized that with nothing to hold her back she was going to take a hard tumble when he cut through the last cords. The sand below the crumpled tower was thick and soft, but it was still a substantial drop. Turning slightly, he extended his left arm toward her.

"Take my hand."

She nodded, and had to swing briefly again to reach him. Gripping her right hand firmly with his left, he resumed slicing at the cords. He didn't have to cut the last one—unable to hold her weight by itself, it snapped with a soft *pop*. Dropping a couple of feet, she came to a sudden stop and found herself dangling high above the ground. Though she was not small, he held her easily with his one arm.

Bending down as much as he could without releasing his grip, he swung her like a toy until she could grab one of the metal struts. Their eyes met and locked for several seconds.

"You can let go now," she told him softly. He released her hand, and together they made their way back to the ground. He watched her with admiration. Most of the women he had known couldn't climb worth a damn. Those who could were usually responding to unusual motivation, such as the shouts of pursuing police to stop where they were.

She was dusting herself off as Wright started walking away. His attention was focused not on her, but on a specific point in the distance. One he could not see, but seemed to know was there.

"That thing the machines put the people in—where is it going?"

Still checking her gear, she glanced up at him.

"The meat Transport? I don't know. Nobody does. There are all kinds of theories. Nobody talks about it much. Doesn't make for pleasant dinner conversation."

He nodded, and promptly started off in the direction he had last seen the machine traveling. She gaped at him.

"Where the hell are you going?"

He spoke without looking back. "After it. They took my—friends."

She shook her head. What part of the sky had this doofus—an admittedly very strong doofus—dropped from?

"I hate to break it to you, but if you've got friends on that thing, they're as good as dead. The machines don't swap prisoners. When they lose fighters, they just build new ones." He was still walking, forcing her to shout after him. "You'll be dead too if you keep going in that direction!"

This time he did look back. His tone was stone cold.

"I've been dead for a while now. I'm getting good at it."

She jogged after him until she caught up. Part of her said just to let him go. You couldn't stop a fool from going on a fool's errand, especially one as determined as this idiot seemed to be. On the other hand, every live person was one more who could raise a weapon against Skynet. If there was anything the war had taught even the most cynical, it was that every human life was worth preserving. Having seen that common sense had no effect on her rescuer, she switched to persuasion.

"You can't do anything for your friends on your own. You're making a noble gesture that will end in your death—and there are easier ways to commit suicide."

Reaching out, she put a hand on his arm. "Come with me back to my base. It might take some time to hoof it, but there'll be others out looking for me. We might be able to help your friends—though I'll be honest and say I doubt it. If the regular military doesn't have any ideas, Connor might know a way."

The mention of that name stopped Wright in his tracks.

"Connor? The man on the radio? I just heard him speak. He was—positive."

She smiled encouragingly. "That's Connor, all right. He puts out a regular regional broadcast, same as every base commander. Goes with the job. But Connor's not like 'every' base commander—leastwise that's what I've been told. He knows as much about the machines as anyone."

Though still gazing longingly at the horizon, Wright found himself forced to temper desire with reality.

"Where is your base? You said we might be able to walk there."

She relaxed, relieved to have gotten through to him.

"Should be one or two days hike. If nobody picks us up in the interim, I'm pretty sure I can get us back. I've flown over this part of the country plenty of times." Digging into a pocket of her flight suit, she pulled out a compass. Like so much of the equipment humans had been reduced to using since the rise of Skynet, the compass was functional but low-tech.

Still he hesitated. "Are you sure you know which way to go?"

She smiled reassuringly. "The base is there. You coming?" Her smile twisted. "It's got a great view."

CHAPTER EIGHT

The interior of the Skynet Transport was an accurate reflection not only of machine design but of their disdain for humankind. It was dark, cramped, and uncomfortable, providing just enough room and air to keep its captives alive. Not unlike the cages humans had once used to smuggle endangered animals from one country to another in the service of the lucrative and illegal exotic pet trade.

Trying to hang onto the little bit of space he had managed to carve out by dint of mild pushing and shoving, Kyle Reese did not feel like he was going to be made into a Skynet pet. While he had no idea why the machines had taken them alive, he doubted it was to fete him and Star and their fellow prisoners with candy and ice cream. The brief thought of ice cream, which he remembered clearly but had not tasted in years, did nothing to soothe either his mood or the hunger that was once again rising in his gut.

They were not alone in the belly of the Transport, though nearly all the other captives were adults. Conversation was muted and conducted in a variety of languages. Around them the steady whirr and hum of the machine was interrupted only by an occasional clank. He had already decided that the Transport was not equipped with the most advanced machine mind. There was no reason why it should be, since it was essentially a semi-sentient truck.

Where there was a way in, there had to be a way out. Looking around, searching every corner and ignoring the other captives, he began hunting for one.

A tiny sniffle broke his concentration and caused him to look down at the little girl who was curled up against him.

"Don't cry, Star. We'll get out of this. We've gotten out of worse." Then he noticed the reason for the uncharacteristic sob. "You've lost your hat." She nodded, staring up at him.

He had to smile to himself. That was Star. Imprisoned by the machines, being hauled off to who-knew-what ruthless, inhuman fate, and she was worried about her hat.

"Don't worry. I'll find it." It was an unfounded but necessary boast. He had no idea where it might be. Most likely it was lying at the bottom of the river beneath the shattered bridge where they had been captured. The machines wouldn't have kept it. The only human artifacts that interested them were devices that could be studied with an eye toward improving themselves or weapons that could be used against them. But his pointless promise served its purpose. She stopped crying.

Most of their fellow captives were strangers, but not all. He noticed one white-haired woman who was actually smiling across at him. It was Virginia, the woman from the now eradicated convenience store who had taken them in and generously given them food. How she could smile under such mournful circumstances was something of a wonder in itself. She was the type of person, he decided, who if being roasted in hell would find it in her heart to comment favorably on the clement temperature.

Hell being, he reminded himself gloomily, a distinct possibility, since while no one knew what the machines had in store for them it was unlikely to be nice.

One stocky, swarthy man had draped an arm protectively around the shoulders of a woman who was likely his wife. He was holding her hand with the other.

"Don't worry. We'll be okay," he was murmuring in soft Spanish.

While still alert, the woman was plainly in danger of withdrawing from reality. Her eyes were vacant, indifferent.

"What's going to happen? What are these things going to do to us? I'm afraid we're going to die. I don't want to die."

"Don't worry." His hand squeezed hers tightly. "No matter what, I'm not going to let you out of my sight."

Seated nearby, a man clad in a tattered Resistance uniform was studying the unadorned ceiling and muttering to himself in French.

"*Il ne devrait pas être beaucoup plus long.*"

Still clinging tightly to his wife, the Hispanic blinked at him. "What did you say?"

Meeting the other man's gaze, the solemn-faced fighter switched to English.

"I was saying that it should not be much longer. Until we reach—wherever it is we are going."

"What makes you think that?"

"Because the machines know we need food and water, and it makes no sense to take us alive if they do not intend to keep us that way." He hesitated. "Until we have fulfilled whatever purpose they have in mind for us, at least."

Seated across from the Frenchman, a wide-eyed Angeleno in his thirties had his arms wrapped around his knees and was rocking slowly back and forth.

"It doesn't matter. We're all going to die. They're going to kill us all."

"No they're not." Though misplaced and entirely unjustifiable, Virginia's quiet confidence was something to admire. Much to his surprise, Reese was sufficiently motivated to agree with her. He hugged Star a little closer.

"That's right, Virginia. They're not going to kill us." He looked down at Star. "I won't let them."

The despondent speaker who had given voice to his gloom sneered at Reese. "Smart-ass kid like you will be first."

"It is like this gentleman said." Virginia indicated the French fighter. "If they simply wanted to kill us they would have done so already. There would be no reason to take us prisoner."

Someone else in the chamber muttered, "Maybe they want to study us. Open us up and look for vulnerabilities."

While potentially accurate, that was quite possibly the worst thing anyone could have said. It turned quiet inside the Transport for a long time. Eventually taking it upon herself to break the oppressive silence, Virginia leaned toward the silent Star.

"You feel like a story? I know some good stories."

Refusing to be mollified, even indirectly, a heretofore silent young Chinese woman spoke up. Her voice rose just above a whisper, as if she was imparting an accepted fact instead of just speculating.

"They're just keeping us in here until the war is over. It's not true about the machines killing us. They're just keeping us in here until the war is over."

Another man spoke up. "I've heard what they do. It's worse than just killing you."

The depressed man who had challenged Reese turned toward him.

"Why's that? What's worse than being killed?"

He raised his voice slightly. His eyes were haunted.

"I've heard what they do with prisoners. I heard the machines tear your skin off your body while you're still alive, slide it over a metal skeleton so you can't tell who's human and who's a machine."

Ever positive, Virginia refused to accept the nightmare scenario.

"If that was true, there'd be no survivors to escape and tell that story."

The Frenchman was shaking his head. "What I would not give for a tomato. And a sip of a decent shiraz."

The woman who held a different theory crawled back to her space.

"I don't know if one is true or the other. It's just what I heard."

This time the man who had voiced the terrible possibility voided his frustration on her instead of Reese.

"What difference does it make? So they intend to kill us, or dissect us, or make us slaves. What does the method matter if the end is the same?" He let his gaze roam around the interior of their traveling prison. "What we should be doing instead of thinking about how we're going to die is trying to come up with a way to save ourselves. Look at us. We're in a cattle car. We're on the way to the slaughterhouse!"

While Virginia was hopeful, she was also practical. "What can we do right now? We're trapped in here."

The man's voice rose to a snarl.

"See what toaster's piloting this plane and take it over."

"And crash us into the ground?" Reese shot back. "Besides, what would you suggest we do? Hold a gun to the onboard computer and threaten to blow its circuits out? We don't have any weapons anyway." He leaned back against the inner wall of the compartment, one arm draped loosely over his right knee. "No. I'm with you when it comes to trying a breakout, but not while we're an unknown number of feet above the ground. We hold tight, wait until we land, and then look for the right spot and time to make a move."

"Yeah, that'll work," the man growled. "Wait until we land and they dump us in a pot, or whatever." His hands bunched into fists. "I'm not waiting around for whatever the machines got in store for me. I'm fighting back now." He let his gaze sweep the compartment. "Who's with me?"

The gauntlet he threw down was allowed to lie where it fell as his challenge was met by a deafening silence from the rest of the downcast prisoners. He kicked at the unyielding floor, unable to scuff the smoothly machined surface.

"Cowards."

Ignoring him, Reese shifted Star against him. Having moved to join them, Virginia took one of the little girl's hands in her own. "I'm going to tell you a story. Guaranteed to make you smile. Okay?"

Staring up at her, Star nodded.

But she did not smile back.

***

It was raining hard and Wright was cold again. The downpour didn't seem to bother Williams. Or maybe she was just one of those stoic types who like to pretend they are immune to whatever the world cared to throw at them, be it bad weather, harsh language, or explosive projectiles. He had known many people like that and thought it a foolish way to go through life. Marcus Wright had never seen much point in trying to deny reality.

They had arrived at a racing arena of some sort, and clearly it had been a long time since anyone had taken a victory lap around the old racetrack. With humankind locked in a battle for its very survival against the machines, the devotion—even in another era—of so much time and effort to something so superfluous seemed not merely wasteful but obscene. Wright didn't care whether the track had been home to pointlessly circling horses, deceived dogs, or supercharged engines masquerading as cars. What mattered now was that it offered the promise of shelter from the elements, which was more valuable than anything it had ever hawked when performing its intended function.

The first overhang they encountered was not large, but it was intact and kept off the rain. Moving as far in away from the weather as the structure would allow, Williams regarded their surroundings with satisfaction. They should be safe here for a while. Though the machines were immune to the rain, they preferred not to operate during strong downpours. Heavy rain complicated electronic perception of their surroundings and occasionally interfered with bipedal movement. Even the most powerful machines preferred to operate on a stable surface rather than mud.

"Looks like a good place to camp for the night."
Williams took a last glance at the compass before flip-
ping it shut and slipping it back into her suit pocket. "I
think if we can maintain the same pace as today, we can
make it to my base by tomorrow night."

Wright's attention remained focused on their surroundings. The track was a useful place to stay because the
open area fronting their shelter would allow them to see
anything that was approaching while it was still a good
distance off. Personally, except for the chill, he was
enjoying the rain. In a world gone mad it was a familiar
and insofar as he could determine unaffected companion
from the past.

Turning away from the wind- and water-swept track,
he watched as Williams slipped the pack off her back.
She was moving slowly, deliberately. Using both hands
she lowered her service belt to the ground. Eschewing
comment, he took note of the holster and the oversized
pistol it held. That was when he saw the dark stain that
had soaked part of her flight suit. She winced as she
dragged off the underjacket. As his eyes roved over her,
his gaze settled on the gash above her arm. Something
gleamed there that was not exposed flesh. In addition to
dried blood he saw glints of metal. Evidently not all of
her downed aircraft had been washed away by the river.
Some of it was still stuck in her shoulder. The wound
continued to seep blood, but not copiously. It was not a
lethal injury, but it must have been a painful one.

His lips tightened. He ought to have asked how she
was feeling. But in the course of the entire long after-
noon's march, she hadn't said a word about the
presence of the shrapnel.

He moved nearer, studying th

"You're hurt."

She waved him away.

"I can take care of myself. You
something we can burn to keep warm.

He gestured out into the deluge.

"Why not ask for steak and lobster while you

"I didn't say it'd be easy. Look under the granda
It seems pretty much in one piece. It ought to stay dr
under there, at least in spots."

He nodded, staring at the rain and wondering why he
wasn't shivering.

"I think I've been cold all day."

Her reply was mocking.

"That's why they call it a nuclear winter, Marcus. Or
did you think this was 'normal' weather for this part of
the world?"

"I didn't realize how much it had changed," he
murmured.

"Everything's changed. Now those of us who are left
have to find a way to change it back." When he didn't
move but continued to stand and stare, she added a
terse reminder. "Fire?"

"Oh. Right."

He headed back out into the storm.

Once she was sure he was out of sight she began peeling down the top of her flight suit to completely expose
the wound. The sight was not pretty, but she was up on
all her shots and not too worried about infection. That
confidence wouldn't last if she left the shrapnel in
place, though. A pouch on her service belt yielded
gauze and hydrogen peroxide. Basic therapy, but it

to do. The corner drugstore was closed.

ng her teeth, she used a small probe to dig out
of metal. She could only extract those she could
Anything smaller or in too deep would just have to
y where it was for the time being. When she had the
ash as clean as she thought she could manage she
dosed a gauze pad with peroxide, gritted her teeth, and
slapped it over the wound.

The rain would have drowned out any noise she
wanted to make, and there were no machines about in
any case. Still, she didn't utter a sound. Because there
was someone present who would have sneered had she
whimpered.

Blair Williams.

Nothing organic survived in the ruins of the long abandoned racetrack. No food, no fried chicken bones, not
even a ketchup-stained hot dog wrapper. Such edible
debris had long since been cleaned up by the planet's
other organic survivors: dogs and cats, buzzards and
crows, pigeons and rats and the ubiquitous insects.

Wright came across discarded beer and soda cans
from which any remaining liquid had long since been
drained or evaporated. There was nothing left to tell
that the oval facility had once played host to thousands
of screaming, cheering, blissfully happy human beings.
Now the place was being reclaimed by the land and by
the elements.

Williams' assumption had been correct. Where the
overhanging roof remained intact, it was dry beneath.
He set about the business of ripping up anything made
of wood, from railings to posts. Another man would
have needed a saw, or at least a sledge, to do the job.

Wright managed with his bare hands.

Williams' shoulder was throbbing. Picking small shards of metal out of her flesh wasn't the activity she would have chosen to begin a relaxing evening, but nothing vital had been cut and none of the wounds seemed to go deep. After letting the peroxide-soaked pad sit for a while, she pulled it off, tossed it aside, and dressed the wound as best she could with the limited materials she had available. She still wasn't certain that she had removed every last fragment. There were likely to be microscopic particles still embedded in the muscle. But the arm rotated freely, she experienced no loss of strength, and that would have to do for now. When she got back to base, one of the doctors could take a closer look at the injury with better equipment.

Pulling up the flightsuit, she searched through her medical kit until she found a makeshift foil pack. From the patchy contents she selected a painkiller and an antibiotic—one pill each. She could have taken two, but given the difficulty of obtaining fresh supplies it was vital to ration such medication. Rainwater helped her to swallow both with ease.

She had just downed the second pill when an unannounced voice rose above the drum-tap of falling rain.

"What've you got there?"

There were three of them. Disheveled and indifferent to their appearance, worn down by a world that seemed bent on annihilating them, sullen of demeanor, they were one of thousands of such bands of independent-minded survivors whose only interest lay in the preservation of self. Such men (and sometimes women) banded and traveled together not out of love or family or friendship but for mutual support. The trio's unexpected emergence from the storm was troubling; the fact that each of them was armed made it more so.

"Name's Turnbull." The speaker nodded toward the foil packet she was still holding. "Antibiotics? Painkillers? Narcotics? Not easy to come by the hard stuff these days."

Williams studied each of them carefully; measuring, appraising, calculating the most rational response.

"I don't have much, but you're welcome to take what you need."

One of the other men looked over at Turnbull.

"Hear that? We're welcome to take what we need. And we gonna." He squinted out at the sodden racetrack. "Be good to get out of the stinkin' rain for a while."

"We've been watching you," another of the men said.

Williams could not keep from sneaking a glance in the direction of her service belt. The belt was where she had left it—but the holster was empty. Smiling, the third member of the group held up the Desert Eagle it had formerly contained.

"Looking for this? Nice gun." He examined the huge pistol thoughtfully. "Kinda big for such a pretty lady." His eyes glittered in the faint light. "Name's Carnahan. I'm thinking you shouldn't have to haul so much extra weight around. There's easier ways to get exercise. Better ways."

Despite the pounding rain Wright saw them clearly from a distance as he approached the temporary shelter. Holding the heavy load of firewood, he quickly evaluated the unforeseen state of affairs. He had already delayed his trek northward and altered his course once in order to help the pilot. His fight was with the machines that had taken his friends, not with other humans he did not even know.

Probably they wouldn't kill her. There would be no reason to. They would tend to their business and move on, leaving her to make it the rest of the way back to her base. Meanwhile he could easily avoid a confront-ation he had not sought. They were no threat to him. They didn't even know he was there.

Searching with increasing desperation for an escape route, Williams was not finding one. The men were armed and had spread out, blocking the way to the racecourse. Thoughts of appealing to their better nature faded swiftly as she realized that this trio had none. All she could do was play for time while hoping that some other possibility presented itself.

"Come on, guys. Machines are the enemy. Skynet is who we have to join together to defeat. We're all on the same side and we're all equal in this fight for the future."

Carnahan pursed his lower lip, feigning thoughtfulness.

"Not exactly. See, I've got two friends on my side and you've got none, so we're not really equal. In any fight." He smiled again, as unpleasantly as the first time. "'Course, nobody has to fight. Not that we're against it. We can do this any way you want."

Stiffening, she moved her right leg back, raised her left arm, and dropped into a fighting stance.

"You want to fight, I can do that with or without a plane. It's good that you've got friends. You'll need someone to carry you after I'm done with you." Opening her extended left hand, she gestured with her fingers, taunting him to make a move.

None of the three would have qualified for a university scholarship, had there been any functioning universities remaining. Having survived by stealth and brute force, neither were they prepared to risk health and limb for the sake of false pride. Instead of accepting her challenge, Carnahan raised the muzzle of the Eagle and took aim at her head (no point in wasting the rest, he had already decided). A minor point of macho conceit failed and he had to use both hands to hold the heavy pistol level.

"She's a firecracker, ain't she?" He leered at Blair. "Want to have some fun? Let's have some fun—you and me."

She nodded once toward the wavering weapon.

"You might want to chamber a round. Or do you think a pilot is stupid enough to wear a loaded sidearm in a cockpit where it might go off accidentally?"

On close study and subject to the rules of logic neither of her statements would hold up. However, before subjecting them to close examination Carnahan instinctively looked down at the gun he was holding. That was just enough time for Williams to dart forward and slam the knuckles of her closed fist into his throat. His mouth opened wide but with his air cut off nothing came out.

He dropped like the sack of shit he was.

Caught by surprise by both the speed and efficiency of her response, his two companions hurried to bring their own weapons to bear. Struggling to rise, eyes blazing, Carnahan started to raise the Eagle.

The chunk of grandstand that exploded against the back of his skull was a good three-feet long and at least as solid as the bone with which it connected. Carnahan went down, revealing a dripping Wright standing behind him. His unexpected appearance distracted one of the other men long enough for Williams to kick the sawed-off shotgun out of the startled vagrant's hands.

Rolling clear, the last member of the trio raised his own shotgun to fire at Wright. Exhibiting extraordinary reflexes, Wright reached down and yanked the stunned Carnahan up in front of him. The dazed leader of the attackers caught the force of the shotgun blast full in the chest, killing him instantly.

As Williams looked on in disbelief, Wright lifted the limp body and threw it at the man who had fired. His second shot went wild as the bleeding corpse crashed into him.

Wright was on him before he could even think of reloading. The man screamed as his arm was not just snapped but crushed. Letting the moaning, sobbing intruder fall to the ground, Wright turned to confront the only attacker still standing.

"Turnbull's the name and surviving's my game," the man stammered as he held both empty hands out in front of him and began backing away from the cold-eyed slayer who had materialized in their midst. "Killing me ain't gonna win this war. Save it for the machines."

In full killing mode now, all emotional restraints removed, Wright started toward him. He could end the life of this cowering shaft of slime with one blow, he knew. Whether he should do so or not wrestled in his mind with whether he *wanted* to or not.

This dilemma was solved for him by the sudden eruption of the Desert Eagle. Having recovered her weapon,

Williams had taken careful aim at Turnbull's right leg and fired once. He screamed and collapsed as a large chunk of his calf was torn away.

Walking over, she glared down at him.

"That's so you don't follow us."

Whimpering as he clutched at his badly damaged lower leg, Turnbull stared up at her.

"Follow you? What, do you think I'm insane?" His frightened eyes shifted to the silent, menacing figure of Wright. "Follow *that*?" A long howl of pain bubbled up from the back of his throat. "You've crippled me! Kill me now and don't leave me for the scavengers."

Returning from searching through her gear, she looked down at him in disgust.

"You're not crippled. You've lost blood and muscle." She tossed him gauze and an Ace bandage. "There's plenty of wood here. Make yourself a damn crutch. If I'd wanted to cripple you I'd have blown up your knee, not your gastrocnemius."

He gaped at her. "My what?"

She shook her head in revulsion, glanced briefly at the unblinking Wright.

"What a specimen. There are times when I think I might prefer the machines to my own kind, if only they weren't so dead-set on exterminating all of us." She returned her attention to the sniveling Turnbull. "I'm letting you live and leaving you stuff to treat your wound because you're right. Killing you isn't going to win us this war. Might improve the species, but at this point in time every body is a welcome one. Think about that while you're healing."

One by one, Wright picked up the intruders' weapons and checked to make sure they were empty.

Searching each body thoroughly, he recovered all their live shells, stepped outside, and tossed them as far as he could into a copse of trees that was growing by one edge of the track.

"Leaving you unarmed, might as well hand you over to the machines right now." He spoke to Turnbull while off to one side his surviving companion cradled his shattered arm and rocked back and forth. "When you can get up, you can go look for your ammo." He leaned over, forcing Turnbull to shrink back from the other man's murderous glare. "You said you'd be insane to follow us. Here's your chance to prove it. And keep living."

Straightening, he turned to Williams.

As soon as she finished dressing and buckling her service belt back on, they started out. Her shrapnel-struck shoulder ached, but it could have been worse. Much worse.

The rain was starting to let up. Williams said nothing, she just kept looking back to make sure none of their attackers was limping toward the trees where Marcus had flung their bullets. Wright did not look at her once, but when his attention was focused elsewhere, she kept stealing glances at him. She was careful not to let him catch her looking in his direction. She did not really know him yet, and she did not want him to see the unbridled gratitude that she knew must be suffusing her face.

CHAPTER NINE

With the coming of night, most of those trapped inside the Transport were overtaken by exhaustion compounded by fear. One by one, they lapsed into weary sleep. Those who were not exhausted collapsed from despair. Of the few who remained conscious, their wakefulness was largely motivated by hunger or thirst.

Subject to none of these and driven by determination, Kyle Reese was working his way from one end of the extensive compartment to the other; questioning those who answered readily, badgering those who were reluctant to respond. He was hunting for hope, but would gladly have settled for a grenade.

Pausing before a man huddled off by himself, he leaned forward and asked the same question he had been putting to everyone else who was still awake.

"You have any weapons?"

His eyes glazed, the man looked up at him and muttered derisively.

"You think if I had any weapons I'd be sitting here doing nothing?"

Reese took no umbrage at the man's response. He was bitter and despondent, and had every right to be.

The teen persisted.

"Anything in your pockets that we might be able to use when we land? A pen, a paperclip, anything?"

A little of the man's sullenness fell away.

"Sorry. I know you're only trying to help, but I have nothing. My family...." His voice trailed away and his gaze dropped to the floor.

Reese left him, moving back toward the other end of the Transport compartment where Virginia was talking quietly to Star.

"How about a song?" the older woman murmured to the little girl. "Can I sing you a song? Has anyone ever sung to you?"

As was her wont, Star replied only with her eyes. They provided the sad answer that Virginia had suspected. She smiled tenderly as she queried Reese.

"Why doesn't she talk?"

"'Cause the machines took her voice away. Scared her out of talking. The things she's seen...." His voice trailed away.

The older woman's voice was tired but willing, just as the words she sang were deep-rooted and hopeful. Some things never go out of fashion, never lose their appeal. Among these are certain lullabies.

When the last verse had trailed away, the older woman reached out with both arms.

"Come here, darling."

Walking slowly forward, Star allowed Virginia to lift her up and set her down on her lap. The older woman smiled down at her.

"Do you know there are more than a billion stars in the sky? And every one of them is special. Just like you. And do you know what makes them so special?"

Thoroughly engrossed now, Star shook her head "no."

"Because each one of them comes with a wish. What do you wish for, Star?"

The girl thought a moment. Then she used both hands to mimic an explosion and followed it with a "peace" gesture. Virginia nodded and pulled her close, rocking her back and forth.

"Me too, babe. Me too."

Having worked his way down one side of the compartment, Reese started back along the other. His queries there brought him no more information or useful material than they had on the other side, but he persisted. He had nothing else to do anyway. Once, he halted before some tiny openings and tried to see outside. All he managed to catch were a few brief glimpses of earth and sky, neither of which was very enlightening.

Continuing up the line back toward the front of the prison, he came upon a young woman wedged against the cold metal. The compartment was not heated and she was shivering, her hands trembling as she tried to keep the baby in her arms warm.

Peeling off his gloves, he handed them over to her. Her expression as she took them said more than words. In gratitude and wanting to reciprocate, she picked up a small bag with one hand and dumped its contents out on the floor where he could see them. He shook his head, declining the offer. There wasn't much to see anyway. Some cotton puffs, Q-tips, a comb with half its teeth missing, an incongruously intact lipstick, a lone shoelace....

His eyes widened slightly and he pointed at the shoelace. Grateful and pleased that she was able to give back, she pressed the length of fabric into his hand.

It was all he was able to glean from his questioning, but it was better than nothing. On the face of it, it would not be of much use against even the smallest of the fighting machines. But over the years he had learned not to despise even the smallest potential weapon. As he rejoined Virginia and the now sleeping Star, he carefully tucked his prize into his shirt. Then he settled down to listen to the older woman sing.

Her lilting voice brought back memories he had thought forever forgotten.

It seemed an incongruous place to seek shelter for the night—beneath a machine. But the rusting hulk of the huge constructor had never possessed an independent mind, had never been tormented by consciousness. Its driverless cab flaunted levers and wheels, buttons and dials. It had been manufactured before the age of malevolent self-awareness circuits and devious communications parsers. Without a human driver it could do nothing, and consequently was perfectly harmless.

At the base of this mountain of silent metal, flames blossomed, a flickering red-orange rose of heat holding back the night chill. Wright fed it another log and it leaped gratefully into the cold air.

Friend of man, foe of man, Wright mused as he watched the blaze spit sparks skyward. It had always been so, would always be so even after man was gone.

Which, if the murderous machines had their way, would not be long in coming.

Lying on the ground, he shifted his attention from the fire to his companion. The pile of scavenged logs and kindling wasn't the only presence close to the machine that was giving off heat. It didn't take long for her to notice that his gaze had become fixed.

"You're staring, Marcus. Thinking about your past?"

Unaware that his concentration might have strayed into the realm of the impolite, he blinked and turned away.

"Sorry. Didn't mean anything by it. It's been a while since I spent any time around someone who wasn't," he hesitated briefly before finishing the confession, "scared of me."

Using a long stick she stirred the embers, wishing they had something worth cooking. Marshmallows, she thought. And polish sausage. Might as well wish for crème brulee and chateaubriand while she was at it.

"After seeing how you handled those three drifters I can understand why some folks might cross to the other side of the street when they see you coming, but I don't scare easy. Besides, we're not alone out here. We have a chaperone." She patted the heavy butt of the Desert Eagle, now restored to its proper place in the holster hitched to her service belt.

"Maybe you'd be scared if you knew more about me." Lying flat on his back now, he regarded the stars that were starting to peep through the shifting cloud cover.

"Like what?" The heat from the fire was making her sleepy.

"I was in prison. Before."

She set her stir stick aside and turned her attention from prodding the fire to her suddenly pensive companion.

"Didn't know they had any left." When he looked sharply at her, she added, "What did you do? Usually when someone talks about having spent time in prison, they're not referring to their long career as a guard."

He took some time before replying.

"I shot a cop."

She took more time before responding.

"You have a good reason?"

It clearly wasn't the comeback he had been expecting.

"Not the first question people usually ask."

"Normally it wouldn't be the first one I'd ask, either, Marcus. But you came back to help me, back at the racetrack. Something about you doesn't add up, doesn't make sense. I can't figure it, and so I can't figure you. One thing I do know: you saw those three nomads and they didn't see you. There was nothing to stop you from slipping away into the night and leaving me to have to deal with them. You could simply have left."

"Thought about it," he told her with brutal honesty.

"But you didn't," she hastened to point out. "You came back to help me, a stranger, at considerable risk to yourself."

"Not so much risk." The way he said it made it sound like the most normal assessment in the world, devoid of even a hint of bluster.

"You came back," she reiterated, "when most people in your position would not have done so. People are different now, Marcus. In case you hadn't noticed, the world is a little different now, too. Just to give you one example, I sure as hell never thought I'd be a fighter pilot." She contemplated what had become of her life.

"Before, if you killed somebody, that usually made you a criminal. But in this world, all it means is that you're probably a good shot."

***

This world, he thought. What had happened to the world while he had lain unconscious? He still had no idea how much time had passed or what had turned machine against maker. It hurt his head to think about it.

"You know, Marcus," she murmured, "we can focus on what is lost. On what is past. Or we can fight for what is left."

He turned to face her. "You think people get a second chance?"

"I do." She clutched at herself. "I'm a little cold." Without waiting for an invitation, she crawled over next to him. Drawing back, he eyed her uncertainly.

"Relax." She smiled gently. "I just need some body heat. I've got low blood pressure, for one thing."

That was certainly a possibility, he told himself. He mustered a half-hearted grin as she lay down against him, resting her head on his ribs.

"I can hear your heart beating all the way through your chest. Man, you've got a steady heartbeat!" Remembrance muted her words. "My dad had a Harley. An old softail he restored all by himself. Whenever things got tough at work or whenever he had a fight with my mom, he'd go to the garage, work on that bike, and everything would be good again. He'd let me ride on the back sometimes, even when I was little. We would pull up to a stoplight and I could hear his heart thumping along, keeping rhythm with the engine. Funny, isn't it? We're in a war to the death with machines, and here I am thinking affectionately of a machine. I miss that." Raising her head from his chest, she looked up at him. "What do you miss, Marcus?"

He thought back, hunting through his past for a good memory. It took some time.

"Me and my brother, we'd steal a car. Didn't matter what kind: old, new, domestic, foreign. Van or sports car. We'd just go, fast as we could, 'til the gas ran out or the cops caught up to us. Nearly killed ourselves I don't know how many times. Didn't matter. We'd laugh ourselves silly. I can still see him going crazy when I'd try to make this impossible curve or we'd turn the wrong way down a one-way street. We'd still be laughing when the cops would slap the cuffs on us, 'cause we knew we'd shared something special." Realizing he was rambling and that he was starting to lose himself in a past forever gone, he forced himself back to the present.

"What happened to your father? He crash out on the bike?"

She shook her head sadly.

"No. That would have made him happy, to go out that way. He was an airline mechanic. Jet engine specialist." She smiled and a tear started from the corner of one eye. She wiped it away angrily, as if it was some kind of intruder into her private life. "He loved the noise engines made, but I guess you already figured that. All the big airports and related maintenance facilities were taken out in Skynet's first strike." Finding another tear forming, she hastened to change the subject.

"What about your brother? Was he killed on Judgment Day?"

"No." Any hint of happiness vanished from Wright's face as his mood darkened visibly. "He died—before."

Intending to press him for details, she changed her mind fast when she saw his expression. The talk and the lateness of the hour were combining to shrink her span of attention. In spite of herself, she yawned.

"That other world, it's all gone. All—gone." She lifted her gaze to meet his. "Thanks for saving me back there. Don't meet too many good guys these days."

His tone did not change. "I'm not a good guy."

"Sure you are. You just don't know it yet. You know the only good thing about the end of the world? Whatever you were, whatever you did—doesn't matter now. That world is gone." Snuggling closer to his bulk, she dropped her head back onto his chest.

"You get to choose who you want to be."

He looked down at her, not moving. Not wanting to disturb her. It was a strange feeling. He was used to disturbing people—often violently. Not this time. As she fell asleep against him he let his head ease back onto the ground.

It had stopped raining. Overhead, the sky was clearing, and the stars were coming out.

The Hunter-Killer had picked up movement and changed its course to pursue. Though the illumination from the stars above was feeble, the machine did not need daylight to track its quarry. Sighting via infrared, it had recognized the heat signatures of multiple human forms moving through the trees of the overgrown park below.

Dropping low, it activated its main batteries, preparatory to inaugurating extermination. The human shapes were moving fast as they crossed over a ridge. Reaching the far side, they slowed.

So did the HK. Programming flashed over reports, scanned histories. It halted, hovering just above the treetops.

* * *

Crouched down on the other side of the ridge, Barnes gripped his assault rifle tightly as he watched the shadow of the Hunter-Killer.

"It's not following us."

Raising a hand, Connor used a finger to trace the crest of the hill as it wandered across the edge of the old park.

"This ridgeline is the beginning of solidly defended Resistance territory. We still hold sway here. The HK won't risk getting hit by a missile battery. Not for a low priority target like a couple of isolated humans out for an evening's scavenging."

Barnes managed to look offended.

"How do we become *high* priority targets?"

Connor extended a hand. "Give me your weapon."

Barnes passed it across. Taking careful aim, Connor pointed it at the HK and fired off several rounds. Unless he managed a freakishly lucky hit the shells would do no damage to the big, heavily armored killing machine. But they would be enough to indicate that the humans it had been tracking were armed with more than angry words, and were therefore worthy of its continued attention.

A couple of his shots pinged off the Hunter-Killer's smooth sides. It responded immediately, according to programming. Connor and his companion were already on the move as slugs and explosions tore up the hillside where a moment earlier they had been catching their breath.

Darting into a cluster of standing structures, the two men wove their way skillfully in and out between the buildings. Continuing its search for a clear line of fire, the HK kept after them. When they ducked into one of the long-abandoned structures, the machine began to pulverize the walls behind them. They were trapped inside, and now it was only a matter of time.

Sprinting up the interior stairs brought Connor and Barnes to the rooftop—where they were greeted by the rest of the assembled commando team. In its center stood a single tech, backpacking the portable transmitter that had been put together by the base's best mechanics and technicians.

Having blocked the entrance to the building with debris, the HK rose on its repellers until it appeared above the roof-line. Muscles tightening, Barnes took up his position behind the transmitter-carrying tech and looked anxiously at their squad leader.

"*Now?*"

Connor evinced no such anxiety. While there were occasions, an increasingly apprehensive Barnes reflected, when the man's calm could be reassuring, at other times it could be downright unnerving.

"Wait." Connor regarded the ascending machine with a detachment that bordered on the academic.

Adjusting its attitude as well as its altitude the HK pivoted slightly, the better to bring its weapons to bear on the group of humans it had cornered atop the ruined building. Guns whirred to life as they prepared to fire. On the roof, battle-hardened fighters flinched and looked fretfully at their leader.

"*Now.*" Voicing the command with conviction, Connor never took his eyes off the Hunter-Killer.

Reaching up onto the tech's backpack, Barnes flipped the switches that activated the transmitter. Had anyone asked, he would not have been ashamed to admit that he was scared shitless. The transmitter's components had been checked and rechecked before the device had been certified for use. Its batteries had been fully charged.

Despite repeated testing, however, no one knew if this was actually going to work out in the field. If it didn't, the HK's gatling guns would turn every one of them to hamburger in less than a minute. That they had all volunteered for this mission did not make him feel any better about the prospect of dying for it.

Colored telltales came to life within the body of the transmitter. It made hardly a sound and emitted nothing visible. The roar of a missile or the thunder of a cannon would have been much more visually and aurally satisfying. Used to such familiar battlefield cacophony, the commando squad was uncertain how to react when what was supposed to be the primary weapon in their midst failed to generate little more than an electronic whisper.

For a horrible moment there was no indication that the transmitter was doing anything at all. Having volunteered for the night-time mission, prepared to die if it failed, the squad members tightened their grips on their weapons and primed themselves to go down fighting.

"It's not working," Barnes hissed tightly. "It picked up the signal. We gotta get outta here." He started to move.

Connor grabbed him, held him back.

"Stop. Don't turn it off. Turn it up."

Something very strange happened. Strange and unprecedented in their collective experience.

The indicator lights on the outside of the Hunter-Killer dimmed. The steady throb of its thrusters stopped as its engines cut out. Unceremoniously and suddenly as harmless as an oversized child's toy, it fell backward to smash into the buildings across the street. Dust rose from the crash site, briefly obscuring the impact.

Rushing to the edge of the roof, Connor and his team

peered down at the now inert machine. A few apprecia-
tive murmurs rose from the veterans among them, but
for the most part everyone was too stunned to do more
than stare. It was as if they could not comprehend what
they were seeing.

Stopping alongside the thoughtful Connor, Barnes
observed tautly, "With all due respect, sir—did you
have to let it get that close?"

It had been a long time since Connor had experienced
the kind of deep contentment brought him by the sight
of the deactivated Hunter-Killer. He smiled meaningfully at Barnes.

"If you're going to kill something, especially a
Terminator, get close enough to make sure you finish
the job. Toughest soldier I ever knew taught me that."

Barnes's eyebrows rose, reflecting his interest.

"Yeah? Who was that?"

"My mother."

Turning, Connor started toward the tech carrying the
transmitter. "Status report."

The technician was studying the control panel he held
in both hands.

"This thing burns through a lot of power. Batteries
are getting hot already. Long-range units are going to
need forty, maybe fifty kilowatts. Sustainable kilowatts." He looked at the squad leader. "With that kind
of draw, this power pack can maintain transmission for
another ten minutes, maybe twelve."

Connor nodded to show that he understood, turned
to the watching members of the squad.

"Well, what are you waiting for? It's party time."

Whoops and hollers of delight rose from the tightly

knit group of men and women. Connor watched as they disappeared down the stairs. Knowing what was coming, he beckoned to Barnes and the tech, leading them to the far side of the building. Moments later several massive detonations ripped the night air as the demolition team set off the explosives they had planted on the now-powerless killing machine.

Chunks of concrete and shards of rubble rained down on the side of the roof where he and his people had been gathered earlier. They were gratified to see that the debris contained numerous chunks of twisted, scorched metal. The shouts from the street below that followed the fading explosions resounded louder than ever. Connor nodded thoughtfully to no one in particular.

It also had been a long time since he had heard his fellow humans cheer like that.

He pulled a communicator from his service belt, the most up-to-date available in the Resistance inventory. It took a moment to set up a secure contact. When the operator came through, he barked, "This is John Connor. Get me a line with Command."

The delay required to establish the necessary connection allowed him to reflect on how peaceful it was in the absence of combat. It was a reverie that did not last long. He recognized the voice on the other end of the line immediately.

"Connor?" General Ashdown's voice had lost none of its intrinsic sharpness. "Tell me the damn thing works."

"Would I be in contact with you now if it didn't?"

"So it functions like we hoped?"

"That's affirmative, but it's just as the engineers diagrammed it. I mean that the signal has to be continuous until demolition of the objective has been achieved.

Which means that, also according to projections, the machines will be able to track any transmitter location while it's in the process of broadcasting. Anyone utilizing this system will be giving up their position."

The glee in Ashdown's voice was unmistakable.

"I don't see what the problem is. As long as the signal works, there'll be nothing left to do the tracking."

The general had a point.

"I can do this, but I need more time. One successful trial run isn't adequate."

"No, there is no more time. We don't have time. The attack commences tomorrow. 0400, worldwide." Ashdown paused a moment, as if consulting something unseen. "Your unit will be in support of the bombing of Skynet Central."

Connor frowned at the communicator.

"Bombing? According to our latest intelligence, Skynet Central is filled with human captives. What's the extraction plan for the prisoners?"

Ashdown did not waver. "Extraction plan? There is no extraction plan. This is a war for the survival of the human race, Connor. We'll do our mourning after we've won it. The names of a few hundred more can be added to the millions who have already perished." There was a pause. "Leadership has its cost. You, above all, should know that."

Without another word the line went dead. Connor stared at the communicator for a long moment, until he was once again distracted by the elated shouts and hollering of his returning troops. Forcing himself back to the present, he gave the order to form up and move out.

* * *

Only Barnes, watching his squad commander, sensed that something was not right. The test of the transmitter had worked perfectly. Everything had gone as well as or better than planned. Yet instead of partaking in the general elation, Connor had sunk deep in thought. Barnes knew his commander well enough to leave him alone. Which was hardly new.

No matter the circumstances, John Connor always seemed to be alone.

The Transport came down between several decaying buildings whose interiors were anything but inactive. Smoke and fire belched into the leaden night, suggestive of the continuous activity that was taking place within the flanking structures.

Straining to peer out the tiny openings in the side of their flying prison, Kyle Reese could see shapes moving about in the haze and darkness. Some he thought he recognized while the design and function of others were completely alien to him.

Limited as these glimpses of the outside were, they were not reassuring.

Then the lights went off inside the detention compartment. A few of the prisoners screamed. Others uttered whatever oath was most immediately at hand. Curses were voiced in a multiplicity of languages.

Something tickled Reese's sense of smell, then assailed it. Gas; pungent, thick, and pregnant with unknown possibilities, not the least of which was the prompting of a sudden urge to retch uncontrollably. Brighter light appeared in quantity at the far end of the compartment.

Fighting through the surging mob, the effluvia, and

the rising stench, he found his way to Star and Virginia and shielded them from the escalating chaos as everyone on board the Transport stumbled toward the exit, desperate to get away from the intolerable stink.

The oversized doorway toward which they were being herded by an assortment of T-1s and T-600s was lit like the mouth of hell. Floodlights turned the immediate unloading area bright as day, forcing exhausted prisoners who had been held in near darkness to shield their eyes from the sudden intensity. The light had no effect on the silently watching machines, whose vision was modulated by circuitry and not sensitive retinal pigmentation.

As they staggered out of the Transport away from the gas that was coercing them, something that had been dropped on the floor of the craft caught Reese's eye. Holding his nose and forcing a path back through the surging crowd, he managed to recover it.

Battered, trampled, and dirty, it nonetheless brought an immediate smile to Star's face when he was able to put her hat back on her head. If he could have identified them, he would have thanked whoever had originally found it.

There was no time to inquire. Lurching forward, a huge machine with a wide curving front blade rumbled to life and began ungently shoving the dazed and tired humans along the walkway on which the Transport had deposited them. An ominous actinic brightness dominated the interior of the building in front of them.

Forced forward along the walkway together with everyone else, a terrified Star turned an imploring gaze to Reese.

He had always been able to help her, to fix things, to make it all okay. This time all he could do was meet her forlorn stare with one of his own.

One of the prisoners had no intention of being thrust into the waiting maw. Leaping out of the line, the man who had previously challenged them to revolt on board the Transport charged one of the remorselessly scanning T-600s. Reese had to admit that the guy was fast, and to his credit he actually managed to get his hands on the Terminator's weapon. His chances of actually wrestling the gun away from the machine, however, were about as likely as Star taking over the machine's brain.

Responding to the desperate assault, two of the other metal sentinels immediately zoned in on the rogue human and fired simultaneously. Both shots missed their automatonic comrade. Both struck the human who was fighting with it, killing him instantly. To make certain, the one with whom he had been grappling put the muzzle of its weapon against the front of the unconscious man's head. Taking a long stride forward, Reese reached out and pulled Star's face against his side just before the Terminator's gun went off and blew its attacker's head to bits.

Throughout the altercation, none of the three Terminator sentries had uttered a sound. They did not do so now as they returned their attention to the line of disconsolate, shambling humans. There was no need to issue a warning or offer commentary.

With the machines, actions always spoke louder than words.

CHAPTER TEN

Emerging from the edge of the forest, Williams led Wright toward a barbed wire fence that ran off in both directions as far as he could see. Directly ahead of them lay a section of fence that had been knocked or had fallen down. No one had bothered to replace the posts that had once kept the segment erect. An annoyed Williams paused to inspect the gap.

"How are we supposed to win this war if we can't even maintain a fence?" She nodded at the other side. "Come on. This is us. Outlying sector. Main base is further on." She stepped over the downed section of fence.

Wright stared at the twisted, crumpled wire.

"I don't understand. From what I've seen, this enclosure couldn't stop the smallest of the machines."

She glanced back at him.

"It's not designed to stop Terminators. It's to keep unauthorized humans out of this area."

"But why would your people want to...." Stopping before finishing, he hurried forward to grab her by the shoulder. With his other hand he pointed to a small metal tripod that pushed its head just above the ground. Its presence did not unsettle her. On the contrary, she seemed pleased that it was there.

"Landmine. Pretty advanced design. One of the simpler but more effective projects the Resistance's tech people have come up with. Not much use against something airborne like a Hunter-Killer or an Aerostat, but it works pretty good against anything on the ground." She made a sweeping gesture. "The terrain around the base is filled with 'em."

Wright peered down at the simple tripodal projection.

"I figured it was something like that. Thought you might want to keep all your limbs." He frowned at her. "Doesn't seem to bother you that you almost stepped on the damn thing."

"Their triggers are electronic sensors, not mechanical contacts. They're programmed only to respond to the control signatures emitted by Terminators. Pretty slick piece of tech work. Humans can practically kick one around without worrying about it going off."

A dubious Wright studied the innocent-looking exposed tip.

"This a theory or has someone actually tested it out?"

"You think I'd be on this side of the fence if it hadn't been?" Smiling, she turned and started straight across the minefield, making no effort to avoid anything in her path. In fact, she deliberately made contact with a couple of mines along the way, just to demonstrate. Executing an impatient pirouette, she peered back at him.

"You coming? We're gonna miss breakfast."

Responding with a diffident shrug, he stepped through the gap in the fence. Though her exhibition had been more than convincing, he still found himself edging carefully around the first mine. He was barely a foot past the site when something went *click*. Williams heard it too. Whirling, she had barely a second to meet his startled gaze before the earth erupted beneath him.

He did not hear her shout.

It took four of them to carry him into the infirmary. A limping Williams was among them, moving at approximately two obscene adjectives per linear yard. All the while she was talking to him, trying to get a response, any kind of response. It didn't matter whether she pleaded, cried, cursed, or cajoled: there was no reaction from the battered body.

"The damn mines...those damn techs," she was muttering as she strained to hold up her portion of his weight. "They're supposed to react only to the presence of Terminators!"

In front of her, Barnes growled a response.

"That was the plan. Doesn't mean every one of the shithead engineers followed it. Maybe they got lazy with the programming on every tenth mine they turned out. Maybe someone forgot to insert the discrimination programming altogether and just built the thing to go off if a bird landed on it."

On the other side of the body, a soldier named Lisa saw their burden's lips move.

"Hey, he's conscious! He's trying to say something."

Williams strained to hear. She would have switched positions with the other woman, but it was more important to get the injured man to where a doctor could work on him than to listen to what he had to say.

From the depths of Wright's throat two words emerged, barely intelligible.

"What...happened?"

Nobody answered as they approached the nearest operating table. Turning toward her burden, Lisa struggled with the body. Wright was dead weight, but not dead.

"On three! One, two, three—lift!"

All four of them had to work in unison to get the body onto the table. Stepping back, the fourth soldier regarded the limp figure as he wiped at his brow.

"Son of a bitch is heavy! No fat on this guy."

Williams was about to comment when the door burst open and Kate Connor strode purposefully into the operating theater, tying the string of her surgical mask behind her head as she came toward them. Studying the injured man, she moved purposefully around to Williams' end of the table. Her eyes were roaming over the body; examining, appraising.

"Okay, what've we got here?"

A distraught Williams explained.

"He stepped on a mine. My fault. I told him it wouldn't go off."

"Not your fault." Barnes hastened to correct her. "Fault of the bastard who improperly programmed the device."

Kate spoke to her assistant. "Start a large bore intravenous. Keep it open. Push twenty ccs morphine." Her gaze flicked back to the anxiously watching Williams. "What's his name?"

"Marcus," Williams managed to mumble.

Kate had returned her attention to the patient.

"He's lucky to still have a leg. Both of them, no less." Turning to a waiting tray of instruments, she selected one and began cutting away the shreds of Wright's left pants leg. "Marcus—Marcus. I need you to keep talking to me."

Still stunned, Wright tried to follow what was happening around him.

Kate spoke calmly as she worked.

"Just keep listening to my voice. Do you hear me? Concentrate on what I'm saying. You don't have to reply; just try to understand. Keep your mind working."

It was impossible to tell if he had heard and understood because he did not reply. Already working fast, she picked up her pace even more. Peeling away the last strips of shredded fabric revealed blackened flesh beneath. She scrutinized the damage coolly.

"He's got a prosthetic leg?" Without waiting for a response from Williams, she raced on. "Okay; we've got burns—multiple lacerations. Can't tell how bad until I get in deeper. I need gauze, disinfectant, anti-biotic—methicillin for a start, keep some vancomycin handy." She didn't need the scissors to rip open Wright's shirt. A large chunk of metal was embedded in his chest.

"Pulse is good. Okay—let's see what we've got...."

Wright opened his eyes. At almost that exact moment she dropped the surgical instruments she had been wielding and stumbled backward. Compassion and professionalism gave way to a look of uncontrolled horror.

Lying on the table, Wright turned his head just enough to meet her dismayed gaze.

"What's the matter? What's wrong? How bad is it?"

She continued to gape at him—lips parted, mouth wide, pupils expanded, focused on something he could not see. He tried to understand, just as he had tried to understand everything that had happened to him since—since....

Since he had been executed by the State of California.

"What's happeni—?"

Relieving him of confusion and its accompanying angst, the butt of Barnes's rifle slammed into his face.

When he regained consciousness for the second time since activating the landmine, he was too overcome to speak. But not too dazed to realize that he was unable to move. Though held suspended in a vertical position with his arms outstretched at the apex of an old and long since abandoned missile silo, the bindings and heavy chains that tightly restrained his arms, legs, and other parts of his body prevented him from doing more than thrashing futilely.

This he did for several minutes before an intensely bright light struck him full in the face, causing him to squint sharply and look away.

When the prisoner's eyes could finally focus once more, a watchful John Connor allowed himself to approach more closely. Given the circumstances, he knew the sensible thing would have been to keep his distance. But he had to have a better look. The fascination of the thing was undeniable. As a bewildered, exhausted, and yes, frightened Wright gasped for air, Connor slowly let his gaze travel over every inch of the singular captive.

"The devil's hands have been busy," Connor finally murmured.

The prisoner had been allowed to retain his pants. He had been allowed to retain his boots and his hair. What he was presently missing was his shirt and much of the skin that had formerly covered the upper portion of his body. It had been cleanly peeled back like the plastic wrapping on an old toy. Beneath lay— beneath was....

In places it was impossible to tell where man ended and machine began. Or machine ended and man began; confusion as to precedent only serving to further emphasize the beauty and dreadfulness of what unknown talents had wrought. Titanium and other metal parts gleamed in the bright light. Veins and arteries became tubing with nary a break or weld visible. In places where primate verisimilitude had been sacrificed to save weight, light shone completely through the exposed body.

Connor stared.

You have to stare, he told himself. *Because you've never seen anything like it before.* To the best of his knowledge, no one had.

"What is it?" he murmured. "What the hell?"

Kate moved forward to stand beside him.

"More accurate to say, what hell?" She joined her husband in gazing at the disorientated prisoner. "The outer three epidermal layers reproduce their natural equivalent almost perfectly. I can't tell if it has been engineered and grown, or if it's real human skin that's been modified. One characteristic that has already been noted is the remarkable healing properties it possesses." She stepped forward and pointed with the large scalpel she was holding. "Look at that. I made the original incision there less than twelve hours ago. It's already completely scarred over. Underneath is— well, see for yourself."

Eyes widening, Wright gaped at the moving hand and the potentially lethal instrument it was holding.

"What are you doing to me?" Suspended in the heavy restraints, Wright stared at the people arrayed in front of him. "What have you done?"

Kate didn't hesitate. A few quick, deft, practiced slashes with the blade opened the chest cavity wide. Stepping back, she studied the result as emotionlessly as if she had performed the opening on a cadaver. Except that a cadaver would have been far less unsettling.

"The heart is human, and very powerful. Given its powers of recuperation, that was to be expected. The brain is human too, and I think also original. But with some kind of chip interface. No one could have anticipated that. Even looking at it under the scanner, it's hard to believe. But there's no denying it."

As she spoke she used the tip of the scalpel to indicate relevant parts of the prisoner, as if she was gesturing at an illustrative chart.

"There's still quite a lot we haven't analyzed. The pulmonary system is completely hydraulic and the heart muscle has been stabilized and enhanced accordingly to handle the increased flow and higher pressure. I can't wait to get into the details of the nervous system and see how the hard wiring is integrated with the brain and the spinal cord. If it *is* a spinal cord and not just a braided cable."

What were they talking about?

Wright had finally managed to come to grips with having awakened in a world gone mad. Now it seemed that he had been taken from that new world and dropped into a second one even more baffling and insane than its predecessor. The words of those who were coldly studying him, the detachment of their discussion, were as hurtful as they were incomprehensible. They couldn't possibly be talking about him. He had inadvertently set off a landmine, sure, but it hardly meant that....

Dropping his head and lowering his gaze, he for the first time caught sight of himself, dangling above the high, deep drop. Despite a sudden desperate desire to do so, he found that he couldn't scream. The shock of what he was seeing utterly overwhelmed the horror. And it had nothing to do with the height at which he found himself suspended.

He was looking at the inside of himself, and what he was seeing made no sense.

The woman they had called Kate was still talking. "...hybrid neural system for certain, but how it was accomplished is beyond me. Whoever did the work would have to have been part surgeon, part mechanical engineer, and all visionary. It's as remarkable as it is disturbing. There appears to be a dual central cortex—one human, one machine."

They were ignoring him, discussing him the way he had once discussed with his brother the best way to get more horsepower out of an old Ford big block. Did you remove this or that part, replace it, or have it remachined?

"What did you do to me? This isn't me. What's going on here?"

They paid no attention to his frantic questions. It was almost as if he wasn't there.

Almost as if he wasn't one of them.

"*What the hell are you doing?*"

"You were right, John." Kate's attention shifted back and forth between her husband and the—creature. "Something *has* changed. This—thing—is unlike anything we've encountered previously. Aside from the technology that's been incorporated into it, the surgical skill required to fabricate such a hybrid is beyond anything I could even begin to imagine." She turned thoughtful. "Even back in the late twentieth century they were successfully implanting all kinds of artificial parts into people. First hip joints, then tendons and ligaments. Hearts, too. But it's one thing to transplant a heart from one human into another. Linking it up with an entirely synthetic circulatory system—that's new.

"As for linking it all to a half-machine brain and still having the original retain its full bank of memories without any apparent permanent loss or damage...." She shook her head. "It's a miracle or a horror—take your pick."

Connor studied the agonized figure that was hanging in suspension.

"We don't know that the brain in question is retaining actual memories from the original cortex. The 'memories' the creature is experiencing could be implants designed to enhance its feeling of humanity and thereby augment its ability to deceive." His tone was icy. "It's all clever programming. To make the thing believe it actually is human."

She blinked. "That's possible. Or there could be a cerebral divide; part original memories from the time when the brain was in a human body, and the rest adjectival programming by whoever fashioned the final amalgam." She returned her attention to the despondent, dangling body. "Given time and access to sufficiently sophisticated instrumentation, there might be a way to separate them out."

"There might be a quicker way. And an easier one." He also turned back toward the hanging shape. "It might also reveal nothing. On the other hand, the cost in time and equipment will be negligible. We'll just ask it." Taking a step toward the figure, he waited until the eyes—human eyes, Kate had determined, but with ingeniously disguised electronic enhancements—rose to meet his own.

"Who built you? What is your 'T-class' designation? How are you supposed to carry out your prime function when depth scans have revealed no internal armament, no concealed explosives, and only internalized communications facilities?"

As the figure being questioned stared back at Connor, exhaustion and despair gave way to defiance.

"My name is Marcus...Wright."

Fascinating, Connor mused. Enticing and yet repellant. With this device Skynet had really advanced its human-simulation programming. Probably one of the reasons they continued to seek and keep live captives. *Study your enemy in order to duplicate him.* This thing hanging before him was so convinced of its humanity that it was incapable of admitting the truth about itself even when exposed to irrefutable reality. Here was a case study for the machine psychologists as well as a demolition team.

Despite its apparent helplessness, did they dare allow it to continue functioning?

"So you're Marcus Wright," Connor reiterated. "And you think you're human?"

Wright looked down at himself again. Looked into his wide-open chest, which ought to have been causing him excruciating pain, but was not. Eyed the gaping breach from which blood should have been pouring in streams, but was not. His visible heart beat steadily, even powerfully, giving no indication that it might cease to function. It was the same with the lights and instrumentation and gadgets and inexplicable mechanical contrivances that hummed softly in its vicinity.

"I *am* human!" was his response to Connor's scathing query.

Connor turned back to Kate. There was not a shred of sympathy in his voice.

"It doesn't even know what it is. The programming is flawless. Earnest self-denial in the service of survival and subterfuge."

"Please." Wright continued to plead. Maybe his gaping chest was not causing him to fail physically, but the unavoidable reminder it provided of his apparent and unfathomable alienness was starting to unsettle his mind. "Please let me down."

Connor looked back at him, spoke calmly and with complete assurance.

"If I were to let you down it's extremely likely your first act would be to kill everyone in this room, or at least try to do so. Where were you manufactured? Where were your consciousness and independent cognitive processes activated?"

Wright swallowed, fighting to remember. Struggling to stay sane.

"I was *born*. In Abilene, Texas. August 22nd, 1975."

Connor nodded sagely.

"You look pretty good for someone who's forty-three, Marcus, and just got blown ass over entrails by a landmine powerful enough to cut a T-1 in half."

Wright's panic left him with a suddenness that would have been frightening to another. It didn't surprise Connor. Very little did.

"I know you," the prisoner murmured. "Your voice. From the radio broadcasts. You're John Connor."

"Of course you know who I am." Connor shook his head knowingly. The machines were capable of devilishly brilliant things, but on occasion they could also be painfully obvious, even naïve. "You were sent here to kill me. To kill the leadership."

"No...no...." Wright mumbled ineffectually. "I don't know what you're talking about."

Connor was perfectly willing to discuss matters with the creature. It would be interesting to catch a conversant machine mind in a philosophical quandary and see how its logic circuits responded.

"Why else would you come here? To this particular base? Kill John Connor and you've proven your value. But you had to go and set off that mine. Skynet won't be pleased."

Wright seemed to struggle to understand what Connor was telling him.

"Blair—Blair Williams said you might be able to help me. I was trying to help a couple of kids. Skynet took them—in a big Transporter. They helped me when I—when I came to in this place, in this world. I'm trying to save them, and you're stopping me."

Connor was impressed. This thing's programming was complex indeed. It could even replicate empathy. Relating to human children—that was pure genius on the part of the enemy.

"You're a pretty convincing liar, Marcus. If I wasn't trying to obliterate every last self-aware machine on Earth, I could almost admire you."

Kate leaned toward him.

"Looks like he really believes it."

"Of course he believes it," Connor snapped. "Otherwise the whole charade loses its verisimilitude.

Let me talk to this thing alone."

"Are you sure? If its mission is to kill you...."

"...It would already have done so if it could, whether anyone else was present or not. I'll be okay." He gestured at Barnes, who nodded and accompanied Kate from the silo. Once they had departed and the door had shut behind them, Connor turned back to the creature that claimed the name of Wright.

Was that name coincidental, he wondered, or had Skynet developed a sense of macabre humor?

"Is this it? Is it you? You're Skynet's big plan?"

Struggling to hold himself together mentally as well as physically, Wright met the other man's gaze without flinching. Summoning his remaining reserves, he finally once again sounded like the man who had been known as Marcus Wright.

"Listen, Connor. I don't give a shit about you. I don't know why this Skynet thing might want you dead and I don't care. I've never even heard of you before two days ago. All I want...."

As he moved nearer and cut the prisoner off, Connor's voice dropped threateningly.

"No. You listen. You and me, we've been at war since before either of us existed."

That was enough to give Wright pause.

"That—doesn't make any sense."

"A lot of what's happened doesn't seem to make any sense. That doesn't make it any less real. And reality, sensible or not, is what I have to deal with. The reality is that you've tried to kill me and my family so many times I've lost count. And you failed. Every time. You tried to kill my mother, Sarah Connor. And you killed my father. So I want you to listen closely, because I'm going to tell you something you need to understand. If Skynet wants me dead it's going to need a better plan than you." He stepped back, satisfied. "Hell, you couldn't even get ten feet inside the base perimeter. Skynet must think we've gone stupid."

Like so much else he had been forced to deal with since regaining consciousness in this insane world, Connor's words left the overwhelmed Wright searching for answers. And as with so much else, he had none.

"No...I know who I am. I'm *Marcus Wright*. I'm not part of some wacko plot to kill you or anybody else. I don't know a goddamn thing about your crazy war or your crazy world or...." His words trailed away. There was no point in continuing his protestations because it was evident that Connor wasn't listening to them. His head drooping, Wright resumed mumbling as much to himself as to his interrogator.

"You're all out of your minds. Kyle Reese is on a Transport on his way to Skynet. If I'd wanted to kill him, I would have done him in L.A. I just came here hoping to get some help—your help—for Star, and for him."

Connor was halfway to the door when he stopped and whirled on the prisoner. He blinked, as if he had been grazed on the back of the head with a two-by-four.

"What—what did you say?"

Almost beyond caring, Wright didn't look up.

"I told you. I'm trying to help a couple of kids who helped me survive this lunacy long enough to get out of L.A. Said they were the Resistance. If it wasn't for them I'd probably be dead." Now he did raise his gaze again. "Wouldn't be here for you and your friends to sneer at."

He shook his head slowly, trying to make sense of it all, of what had happened to him, and failing miserably.

"I don't know what happened to the world. Or me. I don't much care what happens to either. I've done some things in my life I wish I could take back, Connor. I can't do that. But those two kids—I'm not letting them die. Or whatever it is these machines have in store for them."

Connor listened, but his thoughts were focused on a single utterance of the prisoner.

"You said—Kyle. That the name of one of these children you keep babbling about?"

Wright frowned. "Why? You know him? Kyle's not Bob or Bill, but it's not that common a name, either."

Connor said nothing. Neither did his expression. For a change it was Wright's turn to scoff.

"Didn't think so. 'Cause anyone who knew him wouldn't have left him alone out there in this shit." Connor's expression contorted slightly. He was clearly struggling to restrain himself, and Wright was pleased to have finally gotten some kind of rise out of his captor.

"Let me go, Connor. You fight your endless war— win or lose, I don't give a rat's ass—or whether that ass is meat or metal. All that matters to me anymore are those two kids. I'm going to help them."

Pivoting smartly, Connor headed for the exit. His mind was racing. As he closed the door behind him, Wright shouted after him, the sound echoing off the walls.

"You let me out of here, Connor.

"*Connor...!*"

The sound of the heavy metal barrier clanking shut behind his captor left Wright feeling more alone than he had at any time since the return of his memories.

One of those recollections reminded him of—something. Of another door closing, long, long ago.

No, he corrected himself. *Not so very long ago.* The door had shut on him just before he had awakened into this nightmare. He remembered things being done to him, though he could not recall what. Had they even been explained before they had begun?

None of that mattered except peripherally. It didn't matter what Connor or anyone else said. He knew who he was. Marcus Wright, bad boy extraordinaire and anti-social foe of genteel society. A lot of good that had done him, he mused bitterly. A life of running and fighting, drinking and drugging and whoring. A life consisting of a series of mistakes and bad decisions, culminating in one that had seen him sentenced to death.

He frowned slightly. What was wrong with that picture? Well, for one thing, he ought to *be* dead. One way he knew that he was not deceased was because he hurt too much, too bad, and too persistently. Furthermore, he didn't *feel* dead. Physically, he felt perfectly normal.

What was wrong with *that* picture?

He looked down at himself. At his torso, with its skin peeled back and the chest cavity gaping like a display case in the gadget department of a custom auto parts store. Surrounding his heart were enough blinking telltales and miniaturized parts and elegant wiring to fill a hundred tech magazines. Someone—or several someones—had done terrible wonderful things to his insides. The intricate modifications were as sophisticated as they were alien.

This isn't me, his bewildered brain told him.

This is you, his indefatigable eyes told him.

He looked away; to the far wall, at the ceiling, down toward the bottom of the pit far beneath his feet—anywhere but at himself. He could not stand the sight of what he had become.

Could not stand it because he could not understand it.

CHAPTER ELEVEN

Since its establishment, the Resistance base had always been a hive of activity, and tonight it was alive with more activity than ever. Pilots were suiting up and going over flight plans, ground troops had begun to assemble preparatory to moving out, backup forces were making sure everything was in place to shift supplies and reinforcements wherever they might be required, medical teams went over details for handling the expected rush of wounded, and communications specialists checked and rechecked their gear.

Coordination on the battlefield would be crucial. This was to be the biggest Resistance-wide assault on Skynet anyone could remember. Everyone was eager to fulfill their assignment and do their part. They had been surviving through hit and run tactics for years now.

It was time to strike back.

As Williams and Kate accompanied Connor to the next checkpoint, the memories of his private, personal confrontation with the prisoner continued to trouble his thoughts. He glanced back at the pilot.

"Where did you find that thing?"

Williams moved up alongside him. "You diverted

Mirhadi and me to provide cover for some civilians. He was one of them."

"No," he corrected her sharply. "He was *with* them. He isn't one of them."

"He sure acted like he was one of them," she shot back.

A thin smile creased Connor's face.

"Of course he did. Skynet's whole exercise is useless if its creature isn't accepted as human."

She persisted. "If he's a project designed to kill you, why would he let himself get blown up by a mine ten feet inside the base perimeter? What good would that do him? What good *did* that do him? You've got him all trussed up nice and harmless, in an old missile silo that's secured against receiving or broadcasting. Even if he's what you think he is, he can't transmit out and nothing can transmit to him."

Connor nodded patiently, confident that he had already anticipated every objection she might voice.

"If our scanners caught him broadcasting or receiving, it would instantly expose the charade. He had to be made to appear as human as possible or he never would have gotten as far as he did." *With your help.* That was the unspoken addendum. "As to what 'good' setting off the mine did, that got him inside the base and close to me, didn't it?"

Williams was still far from persuaded.

"That's all it did."

"Only because there must have been a misjudgment on Skynet's part. Some of those landmines out there are newer models. Probably Skynet calculated that its creation could survive a blast well enough to sustain its programmed mission."

"Then why didn't it—why didn't *he*—set himself off

or something when you went in to interrogate him?"

Connor shrugged. "Landmine damaged the necessary pertinent circuits, or disrupted its programming. Like you just pointed out, it has been under a transmission lockdown ever since Kate opened it up. That includes internal transmissions. For all we know its been trying to explode itself ever since it regained functionality.

"That it hasn't been able to do so by now tells me that it can't, or like you said, it would already have done so. We'll find out when we go in and locate the explosive, or gas cylinder, or whatever assassination module it's hiding inside itself." They turned a corner and he changed the subject.

"When you were flying cover for the civilians, or after you came down, did you see a teenage boy? About sixteen?"

Taken aback by the sudden shift in the line of discussion, she had to take a moment to reflect.

"I don't know. Couldn't say for sure. The survivors were taken off in a Transport. This Wright—he was the only survivor to get away."

"Not 'he,'" Connor corrected her once more. "'It' was the only survivor, Blair. Makes you think, doesn't it? Why did only 'it' manage to avoid being picked up by the Transporter? Don't be naïve."

Pausing, he turned on her.

"I've got work to do and not enough time in which to do it. Don't pester me with any more simple-minded entreaties on behalf of a machine, no matter how good it is at whimpering. I'm glad you survived, no matter the circumstances. Good pilots are harder to come by these days than planes. Get over this nonsense, remember who and what you are, and do your job." With that he strode out of the hallway and into the nearby briefing room.

"'*It*' saved my life, John." The door was already closing behind him and it was likely he hadn't heard. She stared at the unresponsive barrier for a moment longer before turning to her commander's wife. "Kate, what's going to happen to him? To Wright?"

The other woman didn't hesitate.

"It'll be disassembled."

"You mean killed," Williams countered flatly.

"Don't anthropomorphize, soldier. Some Terminators look more like humans than others, but whether bipedal, wheeled, tracked, or faceless, inside they're all the same—all bits and pieces of Skynet. It doesn't matter if one looks like a berserk tank or your long-lost boyfriend—they all want you dead. To them we're a fungus, a disease, a cancer that needs to be scrubbed out. Never forget that." She looked back in the general direction of the sealed room where the prisoner was being held.

"Especially never forget it when dealing with something like *that*. The whole point of its design and programming is to *make* you forget. As to what's going to happen to it, you know as well as I. It will be analyzed, by some of our best research people. Now that it's been neutralized, it may have useful information on Skynet's intentions. Information that could help our attack."

Williams was shaking her head slowly.

"I'm sorry, Kate, but I've got to disagree with you, and with John. I know he's not the enemy. I know that the *individual* called Marcus Wright is not the enemy. I've been shot at by the enemy. That's not him. He *saved* me out there."

Kate eyed the pilot compassionately. Plainly, Blair Williams was caught between an empathetic rock and an irrefutable hard place. Connor's wife was sympathetic—but only to a point.

"Okay, I accept that it saved you—but only to gain access to the base. Which it did, because you brought it here." She raised a hand to forestall the other woman's budding objection. "Relax. No one's blaming you. Until I got into it I thought it was human myself. It fooled everyone else who came in contact with it, too. We just got lucky that the landmine it triggered did more damage to it than was probably anticipated.

"It saved one human—you—so it could kill other, more important humans, John being the most prominent among us. That's what they do. A gun is a dangerous thing. A gun with a mind of its own is a thousand times more dangerous. That's what Skynet is—a very big gun with a dangerously big brain. And this 'Marcus Wright' is just one more bullet aimed at the heart of humanity.

"It acted like a friend, but it isn't. It saved your life because that fit in with its programming. It gives itself a name, but it's a *machine*. Its pleading, the language it uses, its false implanted memories—they're all part of cold, logical, inhuman programming. A bomb with emotions is still a bomb, whether it's put together by a human being or Skynet. It gained your trust, and used it. But it doesn't deserve it."

Under Kate Connor's withering logic Williams was reduced to mumbling a protest.

"I'm just saying, just asking, do a little more research first. Try to find out more about him before you rip him apart like some kind of sick science project."

"There's nothing 'sick' about doing what you must to

ensure your survival, Blair. You want us to wait, to study him as a—personality. We don't have the luxury of time in this fight. There are no gray areas in this war. You know that as well as any of us. There is no in-between, no partly-human or nearly-machine. It's us or them. And you saw for yourself—it's not one of us."

Kate left Williams standing by herself in the hall, dejected and confused. The pilot would have to sort out her feelings by herself. In advance of the major assault, everyone was needed. There was no time to coddle the indecisive.

As far as Kate Connor was concerned, or her husband, or anyone else who had come in contact with or had heard about the intruder, there was no need for further discussion because there was nothing to discuss. The advanced hybrid was a machine. A new class of Terminator, but definitely inhuman. All that remained for Williams was to accept the obvious.

Yet how could she reconcile that with the fact that, whatever his personal agenda, Marcus Wright had risked himself to save her from the three murderous vagrants when he could just as easily have walked away and continued with his....

Programming?

Tormented and bewildered, she turned and headed back down the hallway.

Apples were a rarity at the base. Though the surviving humans whose task it was to keep the Resistance sup-plied with food, clothing, medical supplies, and other necessities did their best, mechanized transportation could not be risked to provide something as luxurious as fresh fruit. The apple in Barnes's hand had come from a nearby orchard. Though half wild and overgrown, its trees still supplied fruit in season, which was carefully picked by small groups of civilians.

So Barnes savored the red fruit in his hand. The prisoner hanging in suspension before him had glanced once or twice in its direction, evincing a passable imitation of hunger as it had done so. *You had to hand it to Skynet,* Barnes thought as he took another bite. *When it decided to manufacture this particular example of faux human, it had gone all out to render the motivational programming in as much depth as possible.*

Rising from the chair where he had been sitting and studying the prisoner, Barnes continued to munch on the apple as he paced a slow circle around the dangling figure. It was a powerful body, but as Terminators went nothing especially remarkable. Easier to blend in that way, rather than giving its surrogate the appearance of, say, a bodybuilder. Skynet was not rigid in its programming. Had that been the case, the Resistance would have finished it long ago. It was adaptable, it was flexible. It could learn.

Hanging here before him was a frighteningly superb example of its ability to learn.

"How did we get here?" Barnes murmured thoughtfully. The thing in the sling did not answer. The lieutenant hadn't expected a response. Nor did he care especially if he got one. He took another bite of the apple as he continued his casual, introspective stroll.

"I guess it's divine order. We all have our paths to walk in. And you're part of mine." He continued reminiscing aloud. "I was caught up in a world of chasing things that didn't mean anything. I was conscious, but not aware. Able to feel, but I had no feelings. But now, I'm awake. Our spirits are awake." He halted and stared directly at Wright, who returned the gaze unblinkingly. The captive might not have been aware that he was failing to blink, but Barnes noticed immediately.

"You machines," he began, "would have us believe you can survive without us. That we don't need each other. That we don't need the sun. That we don't need trees. That we don't need love. But God's greatest gift to humans is each other. And I have to thank you for that, because I no longer look at people by race or religion or gender. I know what it is to be a human, and not a machine. And now I see God's path. He chooses a different one for each of us. Maybe even for machines. But I can't worry about what path he's chosen for you. Only for me."

There was nothing left of the apple when he tossed the gnawed core into the silo. It took a long time to hit bottom. There was, however, plenty left of the gun he picked up. A check showed that its chamber was loaded. When he resumed speaking it was as if nothing had changed. He might as well still have been munching on the apple.

"You've united the Children of Abraham. And I know that all we are going through right now will deliver us. Deliver our salvation. This is the great war of which the Bible speaks, and Skynet is the Antichrist. It's so obvious I'm surprised so few saw it coming." He smiled, content and happy within himself. "But then, it had to happen, didn't it? Without the war there would be no Second Coming, no return, no Rapture."

He raised the weapon. Wright just stared at him. It was all he could do.

The single shot struck his shoulder and he looked away as the slug ricocheted harmlessly off exposed alloy. Recovering, Wright stared expressionlessly back at his tormentor.

Barnes smiled. "Saw you flinch. I thought you were tough." Once again, the muzzle of the weapon rose and its wielder took aim. A second shot pinged off the revealed metal, spinning the captive around but otherwise doing no visible damage. Wright's continued silence surprised but did not infuriate Barnes. The prisoner's failure to respond represented a malfunction of its programming, the lieutenant decided. It was reassuring to see that Skynet wasn't perfect. If it had done its research thoroughly, this hybrid thing would have reacted to each shot like a human, with moaning and pleading and pain.

Williams entered the silo just as Barnes's second shot finished echoing around the chamber.

"Christ, man, watch what you're doing!"

He looked over at her.

"Sorry, Blair. Don't tell me you're scared of a little ricochet?"

"I just don't like walking in to what's supposed to be a quiet holding area to find myself greeted with flying slugs. What are you doing?"

He shrugged. "Target practice. I was bored."

She nodded knowingly. "Yeah, and we all know what you do when you get bored. Were you preaching again, Barnes?"

He looked at her, then back at the silent prisoner. "Nothing to get exercised about. I'm just seeing what *he's* about."

As soon as Williams had entered the room, Wright's

attitude had perked up. Previously silent and indifferent, now he growled at his tormentor.

"Let me down and I'll show you what I'm about."

Barnes chuckled. "Yeah, I bet you would, split chest and all. That's more like it, thing. Much more typical, responsive human reaction. Come on, machine. I bet if we work on this together we can have you bawling and sobbing in no time. Almost like a real person."

"You get a good shot?" Williams asked him.

He raised his gun, sighted.

"You know I don't miss."

"You know I don't miss either." She jerked a thumb back the way she had come. "Connor wants to see you."

Barnes lowered his weapon halfway, looked at her uncertainly.

"What for? You're the one knee-deep in shit for dragging this little puppy back home." As he finished the question, he raised the gun quickly and let off another shot. Like its predecessors, it bounced melodiously off the invulnerable metal body hanging in the center of the room.

Williams sniffed.

"Must be why I got sent to relieve you." She held out a hand.

Barnes glanced down at it, then back up at the pilot. Shouldn't he be formally relieved from guard duty before reporting to Connor—or anyone else? Of course, what with everything suddenly in frenzied motion due to the impending all-out attack it was understandable that normal procedure might be a bit hurried, or even overlooked.

Williams was gesturing for him to hand over the gun.

"Come on, let me have it. I could use a little practice myself." When Barnes continued to hesitate she rolled her eyes in exasperation. "What, you don't trust me with your gun now? You think just because I'm a pilot I'm gonna shoot myself in the foot? I'm as good a shot as you ever were." She grabbed the weapon away from him and he didn't—not quite—resist. "Here, I'll prove it to you—since you seem to need proof."

Turning, she raised the weapon and aimed it directly at the prisoner. Their eyes met, briefly.

"Upper right clavicle area. Bet I can spin him." With no further hesitation, she fired.

Another loud *ping* resounded through the enclosed space. Wright swung slowly in suspension until his back was toward them. Barnes hadn't moved. Lowering the muzzle, she widened her eyes at him and made as if to return the gun.

"Kind of fun." She paused, then added, "You want me to go and tell Connor you're not coming?"

The lieutenant considered. "No. No, of course not." He started to reach for the gun, but Williams was already aiming again.

"Other shoulder. Spin him the other way." Her second shot reversed the direction of Wright's rotation.

Barnes finally smiled. "Okay, pilot, you've convinced me you can shoot a target that's close in. Now why don't we make it a little harder?" Moving to the relevant instruments and before Williams could object, he activated the release on the suspension mechanism.

Still bound in heavy metal links, Wright plummeted to the bottom of the silo and in a rattle of chains crashed to the concrete floor far below. It was a fall that would have killed any man. It should have killed Wright. Instead, he climbed slowly to his feet, shook his head, and tilted it back to stare up at Barnes and Williams.

The lieutenant saw how the hybrid had survived, sniffed disdainfully, and turned to leave.

"Keep an eye on it, all right? I don't know what Connor wants, but I doubt it'll take long." He nodded downward. "Let's see how many dents you can put in it at this distance before I get back."

Once Barnes had departed, Williams became pensive, as if she was waiting for something. Then she hurriedly put aside the gun.

Looking up again, Wright saw something plunging toward him and managed to stumble aside. The object landed with a soft *thud* close to where he had been standing. A quick glance revealed it to be Williams' travel pack. As he stared at it, the sound of lightly clinking chain caused him to raise his gaze a second time.

Utilizing a basic loop ascender, she was heading down the chain toward him at a speed that would have had most people screaming or covering their eyes. Braking with the ascender, she touched down lightly.

Without offering a word in greeting she moved quickly to the lumpy pack. From its depths she hauled out several articles of clothing that were unceremoniously tossed aside. As he was trying to make sense of this, she found and fired up a compact cutting torch. It wasn't very big nor was its flame particularly long, but it was plenty hot enough to cut through the chains that bound him.

How did he know that?

He had little time to wonder at his apparent ability to precisely gauge temperature before she brought the blue-white flame close and began working on the steel posts that had been driven through his wrists to secure him to the chain. He couldn't see her eyes behind the pair of heavy-duty sunglasses she was wearing, but there was no mistaking her familiar grin or the sardonic tone in her voice.

"I'm guessing this doesn't hurt."

He *wanted* the flame—so close to his skin—to burn. He wanted the glowing metal to sting, to send shivers of agony running through his nerves and up his arm and down his spine. But all he felt was a mild warmth. The contradiction between what he was seeing and what he was feeling verged on the otherworldly.

"Guess not," he muttered.

Cut through, half of the bolt securing one hand fell to the floor, allowing him to shake off the chain. He looked on impassively as she went to work with the cutter on his other hand. Gazing down at the one that was now free, he clearly saw a black streak where the skin had been scorched. It was already starting to heal. He felt nothing.

And not only in his unchained hand.

Connor sat alone in his private quarters listening to his mother.

"...you sent Kyle Reese back to protect me. Together, your father and I terminated the machine that was sent to kill me. In the future, I suspect more machines will arrive. Advanced models in many disguises, with an intellect far superior to that of humans. They'll use anything in their power to deceive you. Do not trust it, John. Never forget what they are. Machines. They only have one objective: to kill you...."

How many times had he played back her recordings; memorizing every word, drawing on her advice, and learning how best to fight back against the machines. The recordings were a part of him now, just as she would always be a part of him. Despite his age, despite his experience and his maturity, he wished she could be with him. It was not only the knowledge she imparted. He missed her confidence, her assurance that come what may humanity would triumph and Skynet would be defeated.

It was a belief that had been sorely tested lately.

And now this—this thing had appeared in their midst. This insane hybrid of human and machine, insisting even in the face of incontestable evidence to the contrary that it was a man. Clinging resolutely to a claim mocked by its own guts. If it had not been sent to kill him, then what possible purpose could it have?

The more Connor thought about it, the greater his certainty that it needed to be destroyed at the next opportunity. Whatever it thought of itself, it was self-evidently a creature of Skynet. Whatever it might have done for Blair Williams, plainly no further good could come of allowing it to continue to exist. Many capabilities could be ascribed to Skynet, but until the advent of the creature that called itself "Marcus Wright" it had never been credited with subtlety.

It was a dangerous development; one less easily countered with bombs and bullets.

He was still playing the recording when Kate walked in. She listened for a moment, then nodded in the direction of the player.

"Your mother was a strong woman."

Leaning forward, Connor switched off the recording. It didn't matter that she had interrupted him. He knew every word by heart anyway.

"There's nothing there."

Kate eyed him closely.

"What's going on inside that head of yours, John Connor?"

He turned to her. "That thing in there, in the security silo. I thought I knew our enemy. But that makes me feel like I know nothing. I looked into its eyes. It absolutely believes everything that it says. It believes it's human. And it's telling me Kyle Reese is on his way to Skynet. If that's true, then Command is about to bomb my family and all the other prisoners into oblivion. And I can't stop them."

Even Kate Connor's normally rock-solid composure could be shaken, as her reaction to her husband's words showed.

"If your mother was in your position, right here, right now, what do you think she'd do? She'd fight. She'd find a way, John. You're a Connor. That's what you do."

His head dropped and he stared at the floor, clasping his hands together in front of him. He did not sound like the indomitable Resistance fighter John Connor now.

He didn't have to—not with Kate.

"We've made so many decisions that have determined who lived and who didn't. Watched so many people die." He raised his eyes to meet hers. "For the first time, I don't know what to do.

"It's not just Kyle. I mean that. When this attack goes forward, all the other prisoners are going to die. It's one thing to die on the battlefield, fighting the machines. But to be trapped in a holding pen or some kind of oversized cage or whatever Skynet is using, without a chance to fight back or escape, just waiting for death...." He stopped, unable to go on.

Silence held sway between them for a while, until she reminded him gently, "None of us gets to choose the manner of our passing, John. Whether by machine or by nature, we exit this plane of existence when a certain confluence of circumstances arrives. Kyle would understand that. I know that you do."

"I'm not sure what I understand anymore, Kate." His expression reflected the torment he was feeling. "I spent some time looking at that poor bastard creature we've got strung up down there. Despite the incontrovertible evidence, he truly seems convinced he's human. In reality, he has no idea what he is. Looking at him, listening to him, I realized—I don't either. I've been doing this for so long I'm not sure what *I* am anymore. I've been fighting them for so long that I've been reduced to fighting *like* one of them. Like I'm some kind of machine myself."

She stared down at him. Sometimes she could find the right words to lift him out of the depression into which he seemed to be lapsing more and more often. This was not one of those times. Only a sharp knock on the door saved both of them from the awkward continuing silence. When her husband failed to respond, she turned to the entryway.

"Yes," she called out tiredly, "come in."

Barnes stepped through the door.

"What do you need, Lieutenant?" she said.

Barnes's gaze flicked to the silent figure of the man sitting on the edge of the bed, then back to the doctor.

"Williams relieved me. She said you needed to talk to...."

Connor did not so much rise as explode off the bed. Any vestiges of melancholy vanished. He was instantly all business again. By the time he reached the door and pushed past the frowning, confused Barnes he had already checked to ensure that his oversized pistol was fully loaded.

CHAPTER TWELVE

The clothes Williams had brought were snug, but they fit the struggling Wright without splitting. He ought to have been acutely cramped from having hung suspended for so long. Neither he nor Williams remarked on the fact that he was not.

For that matter, his arms and shoulders ought to have been dislocated. They didn't discuss that absence, either. Nor the fact that the holes in his wrists where the steel bolts had been punched through were closing with unnatural rapidity and with little loss of blood.

As he pulled on the jacket she had brought for him there was no ache in his muscles, no tightness in his arms. Had he chosen to dwell on the lack of bodily damage it would likely have upset him even more than he already was.

Then emergency lights flared to life within the silo, a klaxon began to bray insistently, and there was no time to think about anything except the one possible way out that remained available to them.

A large vent dominated one side of the silo. Its purpose was to allow the exhaust from now-vanished missiles to escape safely during launch. Integrated into the wall, a single service ladder led up to the opening. Wright headed up, moving easily hand over hand—so rapidly that he had to wait for Williams to catch up. Thereafter he took the rungs more slowly, glancing back occasionally to make sure she was still with him.

The next time he looked up it was to see figures gathering at the rim. Connor he recognized immediately, Barnes a moment later. The others were new to him, but their identities were not nearly as important as the weapons they were unlimbering.

Frantic and furious, Barnes was first to spot the would-be escapees. Leaning over the edge, he pointed and yelled.

"Get 'em!"

Though it was a long way to the bottom, there was no place for anyone to hide within the silo. Spreading out, the heavily armed soldiers gathered around the rim. Inclining their weapons down into the cylindrical depths, they took aim—and wavered. Looking to Connor for instructions, one corporal hesitantly voiced the same concern each of them was feeling.

"What about Blair, Lieutenant?"

Barnes wasn't waiting for the conflicted Connor to make up his mind. Grabbing the weapon from the guard, he yelled, "She made her choice," and began firing. He was not lying when he'd told Williams that he was a fine marksman. And just as before, when he had been toying with the bound Wright, the shots he fired bounced harmlessly off the prisoner's metal components. Williams had no such inherent protection. She didn't need it. Judging the angle of fire perfectly, Wright leaned back from the ladder and aligned his own body to protect her.

Reaching the opening of the vent, they prepared to

start in—only to spot a large ventilation fan some eight feet farther on. It wasn't running, but there was not enough room between the blades and their axis for Williams to slip past, much less Wright. She didn't hesitate. Taking out the cutter she had used to sever his chains, she turned it on, positioned it near the fan mounting, retreated, and fired a single shot in its direction. With Wright shielding her, they both turned away as the shot set off the cutter's volatile contents. The side of the vent that supported the big fan was blown away in a satisfying eruption of blue flame.

Seeing the futility of trying to stop the prisoner with small arms, Barnes took aim with an RPG and let fire. The grenade impacted in the center of Wright's back. By the time the resultant smoke cleared, the aghast guards at the top of the shaft could barely make out their target and the renegade pilot as they made their way into the ventilation shaft.

Connor hadn't waited to see if the resumption of small arms fire was having any effect. As familiar with the layout of the base as he was with the permanent frown lines that had incised themselves into his forehead, he knew where the vent opened to the outside. From that, it was pretty easy to extrapolate Williams's intentions.

"They'll head for the river. We've got to cut him off!"

Barnes nodded once, turned, and joined Connor in racing for the exit. As the remaining soldiers continued firing down into the silo, neither of the two retreating men mentioned Blair Williams. This was not the time or place to discuss what she had done—or why.

***

Connor wasn't the only one familiar with the maze that was the base. The need to be aware of potential escape routes in the event of an overwhelming attack by Skynet obliged everyone who lived or worked there to memorize as many entrances and exits as possible. In any event, Williams knew that the ventilation shaft could only run in two directions—back into the silo or out into the open air.

She and Wright halted at the end of the shaft, using the outer vent cover to shield themselves while they scanned the surrounding grounds. The terrain here was different from what they had encountered in the course of their original disastrous attempt to enter the base. Low scrub gave way quickly to forest. Thick clouds scudded across the sky, blocking what little starlight reached the ground. Perfect for an attempt at flight. At least, it was for Wright, whose night vision was preter-naturally sharp. Even so, he was less than sanguine about the prospect.

He studied the line of trees.

"We're not going to get out of here."

"But you can," she told him. "Now that you know what you're capable of."

He looked at her, trying to read her expression in the near darkness.

"Doesn't that bother you?"

She shrugged, smiled slightly. "A lot of things in this world bother me. You deal with them or you go mad. This happens to be my way of dealing with this." Her gaze met his. "Of dealing with you."

He considered. "What if Connor and the others are right about me?"

She stared back. "What do *you* think about you?"

"I don't know." He turned away. "I don't know what to think."

Reaching out, she put a hand on his arm, felt metal where skin and clothing had been blasted away. Where another might have recoiled at the contact, she did not.

"That doesn't sound like a machine reaction to me, Marcus. Machines don't equivocate. They always know exactly what to think. In contrast, you sound very human."

His voice dropped. "Thanks. Small consolation, I guess."

"Better than none." She indicated the surrounding forest. "You'd better make your move. The whole outer perimeter will be crawling with patrols any minute now."

He started forward, paused to look back at her.

"What about you?"

Another shrug. "A little treason, that's all. How bad can the punishment be?"

He knew the answer to that even if she didn't want to admit to it. Reaching out, he took hold of her forearm.

"Come on. We'll discuss your prospects later."

Having commandeered the first rejuvenated Blackhawk that was armed, fully fueled, and available, Connor took the swift chopper up and headed toward the area where he expected to find the escapees. Almost immediately, something rose from the treetops in the vicinity of the silo and sped southward. Tracking it with the chopper's infrared spotter, he took aim—and held fire. Unless the thing called Marcus Wright was capable of greater transformations than he had thus far demonstrated, the soaring shape was exactly what it appeared to be.

Connor could have blasted it anyway, just to be certain, but chose instead to let the startled great horned owl continue with its interrupted nocturnal hunt.

The helicopter was heavy with a full load of ordinance; everything from rotating mini-guns to napalm canisters. When they reached the location Connor had designated, he cut speed. They began to circle the forested area by the river, sometimes slowing to a hover, as he searched for movement below.

When Wright punched through the protective grid that covered the outside of the shaft, he and Williams emerged onto one of the concentric minefields. They knew immediately they were in the midst of a minefield because when it hit the ground the heavy cover he had knocked to one side set off one of the subterranean explosive devices. If Connor and the others back inside the base were still uncertain as to their location, that oversight had now been inadvertently rectified.

No shots came screaming in response. No one had seen them—yet.

Flares lit up the minefield. In response, Williams dug once more into her bag of tricks. The spool of detonation cord she produced was slender but powerful. Unreeling all of it, she rose and heaved it forward. Implanting the detonator, she turned her head away from the opening and depressed the igniter. One mine immediately blew skyward, setting off another next to it. Within seconds it seemed as if every mine in the immediate vicinity was going off. Without waiting to see if that was indeed the case and ignoring the dirt and debris that was now raining down on them, they rushed out of the vent and headed for the temptingly close line of trees.

***

On the ground, pursuing troops who had emerged from the base tried to separate the fleeing figures from the erupting smoke and chaos. Doing so in broad daylight would have been difficult enough. At night, anything taller than a rabbit could be mistaken for a human. Additionally, care had to be taken so they did not shoot each other.

Notwithstanding the lousy conditions, several thought they had the fugitives in their sights. They had been told, if it was at all possible, to try and take the prisoner alive. Or functional, as the official order had put it.

For one squad of hunting soldiers, it appeared as if the smoke- and noise-filled environment was not going to present a barrier to success. Having spotted the stolen clothing the prisoner was reported likely to be wearing, two of them managed to jump the jacketed figure while the others stood back and took careful aim, just in case.

The immobilized individual struggled hard but was unable to throw off the determined fighters. Rolled onto its back with the two husky soldiers pinning its arms to its sides, it smiled up at them.

Right jacket, wrong wearer.

A sergeant glared down at the prone, pinned shape.

"Where is he?"

Williams pondered the question, stalling for time until one of the glowering fighters pointedly chambered a round in his weapon and aimed it at her.

"Oh yeah," she declared, as if just remembering something. "Said he had to run."

***

The intention of the soldier on the motorcycle that was speeding along the single narrow path was to locate the escaped prisoner and deal with the creature himself. He got his chance, though not exactly in the way he intended. Bursting out of the trees, Wright struck the rider in full stride, knocking him clean off the bike's seat. The two figures went one way, the errant cycle the other.

Rising, Wright hurried toward where the bike was lying on its side, its wheels still spinning. It appeared to have survived the crash with only cosmetic damage. This did not trouble the escaped prisoner. He had no intention of taking it on parade.

Its dismounted rider had other ideas. Rolling from the impact and rising to his feet almost as quickly as Wright, Barnes pulled his pistol and began firing steadily. Marksman or not, taking potshots at a stationary target suspended in good lighting was not quite the same as trying to hit something fast and powerful that was weaving its way toward you in the depths of night. What shots did hit home bounced without harm, as they had previously, off Wright's increasingly exposed hybrid body.

An increasingly panicky Barnes tried to steady his aim long enough to get off a shot at Wright's eyes, but by then the other figure was on top of him. Wrenching the weapon away, the former captive threw the lieutenant to the ground and aimed the powerful handgun. Faced with imminent death, Barnes raised a hand in futile defense and half closed his eyes. Wright's finger tightened on the trigger—and relaxed. Waiting for the shot that didn't come, the lieutenant finally opened his eyes again.

Wright was standing directly over him, the gun still clutched in his right hand. Reflexively, Barnes's eyes dropped to the pistol as he considered his options.

* * *

With a single backhanded slap that bordered on the contemptuous, Wright knocked him out.

He didn't even marvel that he was able to lift and straighten the heavy motorcycle with one hand. Throwing his right leg over the seat, he straddled the big bike and gave the ignition a try. To his relief it started right up. *Not every machine*, he reflected, *was the enemy*. That thought reminded him that *he* might be the enemy, and he quickly put it out of his mind.

Shots rang out and slugs began to rip into the ground around him.

What he wanted as much as anything else was time to examine himself, and time seemed to be the one thing he was not going to be allowed. With soldiers advancing behind him and still dynamic minefields remaining off to his left and right, the only possible escape route lay directly ahead.

That meant jumping a high berm that stood between his present location and the far side of the river. Gunning the cycle's engine, he spewed dirt in his wake as he roared toward the high hillock. Tires dug into the soil as the bike accelerated, hit the take-off point he had chosen, and soared into the air.

He almost made it.

The resultant wipe-out would have killed an ordinary human. It would have mangled most man-sized machines. Marcus Wright, however, was neither. Rising from where he had stopped bouncing, he started toward where the motorcycle had landed and now lay spinning its rear wheel. He had only taken a few steps in its direction when it disintegrated under the impact of a napalm shell. Flaming jellied gasoline engulfed everything within a significant radius of the strike site. The bike was gone, as were the bushes and smaller trees unlucky enough to have been within the target zone.

Emerging blackened and scarred from the intense flames, his clothing mostly gone, Wright sprinted for the taller trees that lined the riverbank.

Above and behind him, Connor stared at the impossible survivor as the figure dashed for the cottonwoods that lined the river's edge. Grimly, he eased forward on the controls, sending the chopper in pursuit. Behind him, soldiers crouched at both open doors were firing at the target.

"We've got him," he exclaimed into the radio's microphone. "He's between outer perimeter markers forty-six and forty-nine, trying to dodge fire. Converge on the river. If we don't take him down before he reaches it, we'll trap him in the water."

Other explosives and shells joined additional napalm in erupting all around Wright. They jolted him, occasionally slowed him, often enveloped him—but they did not stop him. He reached the river.

Moving far faster than Wright, Connor's 'copter now hovered just above the water, its searchlight scanning the surface, hunting for him. One of the gunners tossed out a flare, further illuminating the scene.

Something bubbled within the river, as if the water was being brought suddenly to a boil. Then the surface erupted.

There were at least a dozen Hydrobots. Segmented like worms, wholly serpentine in shape, eyeless but equipped with a host of other sensors, they exploded out of the water to clamp razor-lined metal jaws on the underside of the low-flying chopper. Though barely four feet in length, the weight of their numbers caused the helicopter to skew wildly to one side.

Screaming, one of the gunners fell out of the open door on his side while his counterpart scrambled to maintain a grip and footing inside the sharply slanting cabin.

Connor could not help. With the hydraulics already damaged by the initial attack from below, it was all he could do to maintain minimal stability and stay airborne. Meanwhile several of the rapacious steel serpents had chewed their way into the main cabin where they were wreaking havoc on anything within reach of their whirring jaws.

Frantic kicking and firing didn't save the surviving gunner. As his desperate shots spanged harmless off the armored intruders, one bit through his right leg. Blood spurted in all directions. A sharp crunching sound filled the cabin as metal teeth began to munch their way through bone.

In the water below, the soldier who had been dumped out of the helicopter barely managed to fight his way to the surface before he was pulled under, eyes wide and shrieking as he was sliced up from beneath.

When the last of the chopper's hydraulic fluid ran out, control was lost completely. As it lurched toward the dark surface below, Connor half jumped and was half tossed from the mortally crippled machine. Slowing blades barely missing him, the 'copter crashed into the shallows that fronted the riverbank.

Gasping for air, he floundered in the water a moment before realizing that it was barely hip-deep where he had landed. Drawing his pistol, he struggled shoreward. The ground underfoot was a maddening composite of sand and mud that did everything it could to slow his progress. Somewhere behind him the Hydrobots were butchering the last remaining soldier.

Then they found him.

Even in the dim light it was hard to miss their gleaming, reflective, deadly surfaces. One after another took a slug from his oversized pistol and went down, writhing and convulsing in a horrible approximation of real life. A stride at a time, he battled his way toward the shore.

At last the muck underfoot gave way to more stable gravel and rock. Water drained from his legs as he staggered out onto dry land. Designed to operate and survive in water, the limbless Hydrobots could not follow. But they could still fling themselves high out of the shallows. One did, aiming to lock its cutting jaws on his skull. Detecting its prodigious leap out of the corner of an eye, Connor whirled, trained his lethal pistol on it, and fired. Nothing.

Dry round.

Instinctively, he brought one arm up in a desperate attempt to ward off the attack as he struggled to eject the bad round and chamber another shell. The Hydrobot plunged toward him—but metal never met flesh. Hands snatched the writhing machine out of the air and as easily as they would break open a chicken leg, snapped it in half. Spasming independently, both sections were thrown back into the river. Connor did not linger on their sinking shapes. Instead, he straight away trained the muzzle of his weapon on the man who had saved him.

Correction, he told himself. *On the* thing *that had saved him.*

His clothing and skin largely gone, not even breathing hard from his flight from the base, Marcus Wright stared back at Connor. In the shallows, a mass of Hydrobots had gathered. But none attempted a repeat of the aerial assault on the human. A gasping Connor used his free hand to gesture in their direction.

"Look at them. They're not attacking. Not attacking me because you just indicated how you want them to behave. Not attacking you because they know what you are. Even if you don't."

Wright replied without rancor, indicating the pistol gripped tightly in Connor's fist.

"Guess that means that gun isn't going to do you much good, even if it's still functional. No gun's going to stop me."

Connor studied the powerful figure confronting him, letting his gaze rove over the remarkable amalgamation of the metallic and the organic. Napalm having burned away much of the carefully nurtured epidermal layer, the details of the unparalleled fusion were more visible than ever.

"Nobody's shot you in the heart," he wheezed. "I see that thing's beating a mile a minute. I'd bet that it's been modified, adapted, and juiced just like the rest of your 'human' components, but it still looks like there's enough of the original left to respond badly to a heavy slug."

The observation gave Wright pause. Then he nodded.

"That seems pretty close to the mark." He straightened. "Do it then. Kill me."

Still shaky from the crash and the frantic flight from the Hydrobots, a panting Connor struggled to fix his aim. His finger began to contract on the trigger.

Wright did not look away, showed not the slightest sign of fear. *That was hardly surprising,* Connor told himself. *Fear was something the creature's adaptive programming could doubtless cope with easily.*

"Kyle Reese is alive."

Connor tried not to react to the claim, but exhausted and exposed as he was, this time he could not keep his expression from giving his feelings away. His finger eased off the trigger.

"How can you be sure?" Connor spoke guardedly. Though his finger had eased off the trigger, he did not lower the pistol.

"I told you before, but you wouldn't listen. He and a little girl who befriended me were part of a group taken captive by the machines. Along with the others, they're probably both inside Skynet Central by now. I want to get them out. That's the reason I came with Blair Williams to your base, even though you refuse to believe me. I *still* want to get them out." Eyes that were at least part human burned into Connor's. "I think you'd like to get them out, too."

Here was something upon which they could agree.

"Of course I want to get them out," Connor said.

Wright nodded. "In order to get them out, you first have to get in. And I'm the only one who can get you in."

Connor shook his head doubtfully.

"Get into Skynet Central? How?"

Wright approached with deliberation. Connor raised his gun. He could see the beating, modified, augmented heart clearly now. *The new, improved model,* he thought wildly to himself. If he shot Wright and the— man—went down, and they tried to fix him up, would he more properly be a candidate for surgery—or a tune-up? And what, really, was the difference between the two, anyway? Flesh and blood, machine and hydraulics, weren't they all machines by any other name? Was what really mattered attitude and outlook, not construction and fabric?

Confused, tired, worried about Kyle—if not himself, he slowly lowered the muzzle of the heavy pistol until it was pointed at the ground.

"Even assuming that you're telling the truth, why should I trust you?"

"Two reasons," Wright shot back. "One, I need to find out who did this to me. And two—so do you."

With the river full of murderous Hydrobots behind, the sound of gunfire and barking of search dogs rising steadily in front, Connor found himself marooned in a quandary. He had a decision to make, perhaps the most crucial of his life, and no time in which to analyze it closely. But then, he had not become such a successful Resistance fighter because he was indecisive. His response was a mix of defiance and pleading.

"You get me in. I'll be on the bridge—it's an unobstructed shot from there to Skynet Central and we should be able to communicate freely. You find Kyle Reese for me." Digging through his pockets, he located a communicator. After a quick check revealed that its batteries were good, he tossed it to the singular figure looming opposite him.

Wright snatched it out of the air without even looking in its direction.

"No problem. They think I'm one of them."

Though the night was warm, Connor felt a chill. Was he in the process of making the greatest mistake of his life? Maybe this thing's mind was as clever as its engineering.

But if it was all deception, to what end? When first introduced to the creature that called itself Marcus Wright, Connor and his advisors had been convinced

that it represented a wickedly clever attempt to breach
base security in order to kill him. Now that it stood
free, functioning, and unimpeded barely a yard away
and could kill him easily with a single blow, it spoke
instead of trying to rescue Kyle. Marcus Wright was as
full of surprises as he was contradictions.

Had he not said as much himself?

Connor gestured toward the river and the now quies-
cent Hydrobots.

"You said they think you're one of them. Are you?"

It was a question Wright had been asking himself ever
since his intermingled insides had been revealed. It was
the question above all questions that he needed
answered. And naturally, it was the one question to
which he could not assign an explanation. Spreading his
arms wide, exposing as much of himself as possible to
the man standing warily before him, he admitted the
only truth he knew.

"I don't know."

Moving past Connor, keeping his hands at his sides, he
started backing into the river. Raised again, the muzzle
of Connor's pistol never left him, not even when
Wright's head disappeared beneath the rippling surface.
He continued to stare at the spot where Wright had
vanished until movement on the far side of the river
drew his attention. Emerging after a span of time spent
underwater far longer than any human could hold his
breath, Wright turned, waved once, and vanished into
the brush on the far side. He had crossed the river not
by swimming—perhaps he was too heavy—but by
walking across the bottom.

Holstering his weapon, a contemplative Connor let his gaze linger a long time on the spot where Wright had disappeared, half certain he had just made the biggest mistake of his existence. Then he turned and started walking in the direction of the base. He had barely made it back into the woods when shapes rose sharply from the bush to confront him and he found himself staring down the barrels of three rifles.

"Halt and identify yourself!" the noncom in charge barked.

"John Connor." What a pity, he mused halfheartedly, that he could not be someone else.

But he knew he was John Connor. In that respect if no other, at least, he had the advantage over the poor creature called Marcus Wright.

Lowering their weapons the soldiers hastened to gather around him, flanking him as they resumed walking toward the nearest base entrance. Their relief was palpable when they were able to identify him visually.

"Sir? Are you all right, sir?" one of them asked.

Connor nodded. "A little bruised, nothing serious. Chopper went down." He gestured back the way he had come. "We were too low, searching. Hydrobots got us. I was the only one to make it to shore."

The noncom's lips tightened, comprehending. He glanced in the direction of the riverbank that was falling farther behind them with every step.

"Sir, any sign of him?"

Connor halted, turned, and looked back. Some sections of the river were still visible in the dim light. Of Wright there was no sign. No sign, in fact, that anything had ever been amiss along this winding stretch of dark water. Increasing his pace, he shook his head.

"No sign, soldier. Nothing to be done about it now. I guess he got away."

The base brig was neither fancy nor extensive. It did not need to be either, since the great majority of its residents were transient. By far the most common reasons for temporary internment were the need to get some secured sleep as a result of an excess of drinking, to cool down from fighting with fellow soldiers, or to allow disputed gambling debts to be settled from adjoining cells.

Blair Williams's case was very different.

For one thing, unlike the usual tenant she had not been left alone to stew in her own perfidy. A round-the-clock armed sentry had been posted outside her cell. She did not try to engage the rotating guards in conversation and they showed no inclination to want to talk to her. They had no idea what she was in for. It was none of their business. Within the constricted confines of the base it was an unspoken rule that you did not pry into the affairs of those around you lest one day the tables be turned.

Of the two men who were now standing outside the holding area, one had every intention of disregarding that rule. Vociferously.

As soon as the officer who had escorted him to the rearmost cell turned and departed, Williams sat up on the edge of her cot and regarded her visitor.

"Connor...." Solemnity quickly gave way to casual curiosity. "What brings you down to this humble abode?" She gestured at the enclosing walls. "It seems I've been reassigned."

Her visitor had no time for small talk, or for jokes.

Whatever he had on his mind, he was not in the mood for delay.

"Why'd you do it?"

Williams blinked back at him, her reply leavened with innocence.

"Do what?"

"Let Marcus go. Why would you break him out? He's a machine. Just one more thread in Skynet's web. I don't get it."

She had no intention of letting Connor lord it over her, even if she was a prisoner. Rising, she moved toward him. He did not back away. John Connor did not back away from anything, least of all a renegade—and possibly deranged—attack pilot.

"You say he's part of Skynet's planning. Not to me he isn't. He's—something else. Something we don't understand, sure. But I saw a man. Not a machine. A person struggling with the same things we struggle with every day, John. Our own humanity. He's a man trapped inside of a machine." She shook her head sorrowfully. "I don't know how it was done or for what reason, but he's not a tool of Skynet. I don't know how to explain it, but he's—independent." She met his unwavering stare without flinching. "Why d'you ask? Does it matter? You've already formed your opinion, haven't you?"

Her interrogator did not reply. Sunk deep in thought, Connor was quiet for a long time. Then he looked up at her, and spoke.

"How's the leg?

She winced.

"Hurts."

There was another long moment of silence. Then he motioned to the soldier on guard.

"Let her go."

The man hesitated. "Sir? Orders were to...."

"Let her go. On *my* order. I'll take full responsibility."

With a shrug, the soldier stepped aside. Of the very few people on the base whose commands were to be complied with implicitly, John Connor was foremost.

Williams watched Connor depart. He was clearly lost in thought. While she did not want to disturb him, it would have been nice to know why he had summarily ordered her released. Among the few words they had exchanged, what had convinced him to change his mind about her?

More important, and more maddening—what had caused him to change his mind about Marcus Wright?

CHAPTER THIRTEEN

The base had not seen this much activity since a flight of six surviving F-15s had managed to avoid Skynet's attention and arrive safely from Seattle some six months ago. Out on the heavily camouflaged tarmac, a wide variety of aircraft were being armed and prepped for the all-out attack. Pilots chatted with one another while mechanics worked to render even the most badly damaged planes airworthy. On one side of the veiled runway a cluster of technicians were putting the finishing touches on the transmitter unit that would join with others across the planet in the worldwide attempt to shut down Skynet.

Connor wended his way through the organized confusion until he reached the communications center. They were expecting him, but to help prevent tracing, the connection that had been on hold would not be completed until he was present. As soon as he arrived, the operations tech passed him a handset.

"Connor, Command for you." Connor took the handset.

"This is Connor."

Ashdown was on the other end, his tone exuberant.

"Connor, are your people ready? Everything's in

motion. Tomorrow we'll be able to look out on a different dawn. It'll be a new day for mankind. Myself, I'm going to have a house built right on top of whatever's left of Skynet Central. With a fence made out of de-activated T-1s. The timer is running."

"Negative," Connor told him tersely. "Nobody's ready. We are not. You are not. We need to stop the attack. The game has changed. I repeat; changed."

Despite the imperfect connection, the astonishment in the general's voice came through loud and clear.

"What are you talking about? All our elements are past their release points and in assault positions. Do you have any idea what's gone into coordinating this assault? Do you realize what it's liable to cost us to stand down now that everything's under way? I don't mean in old-line expense—I'm talking about wasted resources, low-ered morale, sacrificed surprise. What possible reason could there be for calling off the attack now?"

Connor swallowed once before responding. He knew how difficult it was going to be to convince Ashdown, but knowing what he knew now there was nothing for it but to try.

"The strategic components of the conflict have been altered. Or to put it another way, something new has been added. Something no one could have predicted and that we can't account for. Being unable to account for something means it needs to be studied carefully before any large-scale undertakings that involve it are initiated."

Ashdown's impatience filtered through the transmission.

"Connor—what the hell are you talking about?"

He tried another tack.

"Delay the attack. I have a chance to infiltrate

Skynet and rescue the prisoners. Give me that opportunity, General."

"No. Absolutely not. This is not the time for a rescue mission, Connor. What you are asking would undermine the whole operation."

"You're not hearing me, sir. I support the attack. But not at this price. I will not kill our own people."

"We're not 'killing our own people.'" Ashdown was losing patience. "It's called collateral damage, Connor. I said that when the time came I'd do the right thing. And I'm doing it. This shutdown signal works. It's our key to victory. We stay the course—and that's an order, Connor!"

"I'm telling you, General. We stay the course and we are dead. We're all dead. Who do you think you are—General Sherman? Tamerlane?"

"Personally, I think Sherman would have approved of what we're doing today. I know who I am, Connor. Right now it's who *you* are that's troubling me."

Connor looked over his shoulder. Behind and around him soldiers, pilots, mechanics, tech and support personnel were putting the last touches on the impending attack. The attack that somehow he had to stop. He returned his attention to the handset.

Ashdown wasn't through.

"We've got victory in our grasp and at the last minute, the last second, you and you alone suddenly decide it's out of reach. All your prattle is bullshit, Connor. This is no time for defeatism. We're going to win, and I'm not going to let you do anything to put a crimp in what will be the greatest military victory in the history of mankind."

It was all so familiar, Connor thought wearily. How

many times in his remarkable, anguished, astonishing, grief-ridden life had he been forced to suffer through this sort of uncomprehending obstinacy on the part of others? Why, when events came to a head, when critical moments in the confused litany of the future and past materialized, wouldn't they listen to him? One thing was certain—Ashdown was beyond listening to him, or to anyone else. He tried yet another tack.

"Skynet has Kyle Reese. He was number one on their kill list."

Ashdown's reply was as cold as the waters through which Command's sub was cruising.

"Then that's his fate, Connor."

"No! I *have* to save him. He is the key. The key to the future. The key to the past. Without him we lose everything."

Ashdown was not listening. Or not hearing. Or both.

"We *stay* the course."

"We stay the course and we are all dead." Connor struggled to control his emotions. "We are all *dead*. I'm asking you one more time, General. Delay it. A few hours. Enough time for our tech people to finish some simulations I've got them working on, and for me to make an attempt to try and rescue Kyle Reese and the other prisoners being held in Skynet Central."

Ashdown turned deadly calm.

"You get in the way of this assault and I'll kill you myself. You do *anything* to jeopardize the plan, I'll wipe out your entire base. Too much has gone into this, Connor. We can't take any chances with this attack."

"That's just what I'm asking you to do, General. Not take chances."

"Negative again, Connor. We strike *now*."

The communications officer looked up at his leader. So did Barnes, who had stopped by to listen.

They were running out of time.

Always running out of time, Connor thought resignedly. Only this time around, it might be for real. It might really be the last time, in every sense of the term.

"I'm going to Skynet," he said flatly into the pickup. "With your permission or without it—sir. Those people being held prisoner deserve at least that much. Maybe they don't want to be remembered as heroes. Maybe they'd rather be remembered as survivors."

Ashdown had no difficult communicating his fury via the encrypted frequency.

"Then as of now you're relieved of your command, goddamit." His voice echoed as he addressed men on the sub. "Get back to your stations."

The encryption timer hit zero and the transmission cut out. Connor slowly put the headset down. As he did so, Barnes took a step forward. The lieutenant's expression was unreadable.

"Transmission got pretty garbled there at the end, sir. I didn't make out that last statement." He nodded toward the communications officer.

"Neither did I."

Barnes stiffened, almost to attention.

"We're with you 'til the end—sir."

Connor nodded tersely. Handing the comm set back to the officer, he turned and walked away, his pace increasing as he left the communications station behind. A weight had been lifted from his shoulders and from his heart. Once again he was back on the outside, where he understood the rules.

Not least because he had made so many of them.

***

At the speed he and Barnes were moving it did not take long to reach the broadcast stack. Though a ramshackle compilation of antennae, signal boosters, cabling, and isolated computer components, he had no doubt that when turned on it would send out the signal sequence that had been programmed into it. Incongruously, the whole high-tech pile was powered by a single clattering, reasonably intact diesel generator.

Entering a storage room nearby, he studied the contents. Grabbing a roll of C-4 det cord, he passed it across to Barnes.

"Here. Wire the broadcast stack for detonation."

Barnes looked uncertain. "Our own?"

"Yes."

The lieutenant fiddled with the loose end of the cord.

"If you don't mind my asking, sir—why?"

The expression that came over Connor's face was one the lieutenant had seen before.

"The hunter just became the hunted."

While Barnes and the communications officer wrapped the cord around the just completed broadcast stack, Connor picked up the handset for the short-wave radio. Activating it, he hesitated, trying to gather his words. Then he just started talking.

"This is John Connor. If you're listening to this, you are the Resistance.

"I once knew a woman who told people to fear the future, that the end was coming. That all would be lost. Nobody wanted to hear her truths. Society locked her away. That woman was Sarah Connor, my mother. Now we know that what she was predicting all came to pass. And so I ask of you to please, please believe in me, her son, as we all should have believed in her.

"Command wants us to fight like machines. They want us to make cold, calculated decisions. But we're not machines. And if we behave like them, if we make the same kinds of decisions they would make, then what is the point in winning?

"Please. Please listen carefully. I need every one of you now. *We have to stand down.* Believe me when I tell you that if we attack tonight, our humanity is lost. Our hope for a future—is gone. Sarah Connor told me a moment would come when we would need to make our own fate. That moment has arrived, and that fate will not come to pass without you. Without all of you. *You must stand down until sunrise.*

"Everything we've fought for, everything we've achieved, comes down to this one moment." He paused a moment, then rushed onward.

"Our fate is created not in the past, and not in the future. It is being created right here and right now. If even one bomb is dropped on Skynet before sunrise, our future will be lost. Please stand down. Give me the time I need to finish this. Give me the time to protect the future that we—that all of us—are fighting for."

He started to say more, only to realize there was nothing more to say, and quietly put down the handset.

The contents of the base armory reflected the eclectic nature of the Resistance, but it was well stocked. Connor went shopping.

As he was making his selection he was joined by a second figure. After a brief glance in Kate's direction he continued choosing his weapons. She watched him for a while as he worked, then moved closer. Her voice was calm, but tight.

"What do you think you're doing, John?"

He replied without looking over at her as he checked a brace of heavy ammo.

"Skynet has Kyle."

"We've discussed this. How can you be *sure*?"

He pulled a heavy pistol, turned it over in his hands, put it back in its rack.

"A machine told me. A wind-up toy. A cuckoo clock with a conscience." He smiled humorlessly. "It might be wrong but I think it's Wright."

He shook his head.

"This is how my mother must've felt in that nuthouse. She tried warning everyone. She knew the future and no one listened. I hope to God somebody out there is listening to me. Kate, you promise me that you'll listen and that you'll evacuate. That you'll leave here and you'll get to someplace safe."

She had already put it all together.

"You're going to try to save Kyle, aren't you?"

He didn't reply.

"John, this doesn't make sense. It's *you* Skynet wants. You just admitted that the only reason you're sure it has Kyle is because a *machine* told you. They're using him to bait you. This is a trap."

Halting his work, he favored her with a sad smile.

"Maybe it is a trap. But we'll use their traps against them."

Reaching to a high shelf he pulled down a 25mm semi-automatic grenade launcher, then a box of thermo-baric shells.

"If Kyle dies, Skynet wins."

Her hands balled into fists at her sides. She moved closer, pleading now.

"John, you can't go in there alone. Reese gave up his life for you. Throwing away your own like this, in a futile attempt to save him, would be the last thing he would want you to do."

Connor's expression was grim.

"That's exactly why I'm going. Because *he* went. Because he saved my mother's life and he gave me mine. Because I owe him that much. To at least make the attempt."

"This is suicide, John. I will not stand by and watch you kill yourself."

Looking away from her, he loaded a shotgun with sabot shells, then began packing grenades and plastic explosive into a waiting pack.

Kate watched him for a long moment. Then she picked up a handgun and very carefully placed it against her temple. Pausing in his work, he slowly turned to face her, his eyes flicking from her face to the handgun and back again.

"Look at me. How does this make you feel? This is what you're doing to me."

Connor's expression softened. "Kate, please...."

Slowly, she lowered the gun. But not her gaze.

"What about our child?"

He took a deep breath. "If I don't stand up for what I believe in, what kind of father am I going to make?"

She gestured slightly with the muzzle of the weapon.

"We said we would get through this together. That's the only reason we've made it this far. If you die...."

Her voice trailed away, unable to complete the sentence, unable to countenance the thought. Her strength was wavering, as was her conviction. She had been fighting a long time, and she was tired. She knew he was too, but somehow he always managed to bounce back. Always managed to summon strength from depths unknown, find confidence even in the darkest moments. She was strong, but not that strong. Not as strong as John Connor. That was why he had to stay alive. For the Resistance. For everyone. For her.

He saw what she was going through even as he sensed her emotional exhaustion.

"You live—and that's all that matters to me, Kate. You're the reason I've kept fighting for all these years. You have my whole heart. You always have, and you always will. *You're* what I live for." As he moved toward her, she let go of the gun. It dropped to the floor beside her, silent and no longer threatening.

Tears were running down her face, streaking her cheeks. Smiling affectionately, he placed his scarred hands gently on her stomach. Reaching up with one hand she touched his face, let her fingers trace the side of his jaw.

"This is not 'goodbye,'" she whispered to him.

"No." They kissed.

She pulled away. Someone had to. "See you later—okay?"

"Yeah."

She managed a smile. "Every time I look into your eyes I know we're still headed in the right direction," she murmured softly. "I know that, somehow, we'll make it. And I'm not the only one."

She gestured to her right, toward the armory door that stood slightly ajar.

"You have a responsibility to those people out there,

John. They believe you're going to lead them to victory. What am I going to tell them when they find out you're gone?"

She paused, sniffling and swallowing, trying to keep from breaking down completely.

"What am I going to tell myself?"

Looking into her face, unable to avoid the naked longing and desperation on display, he wondered what he could possibly say in response. Then he smiled anew, reassuringly, and gently wiped at her tears.

"I'll be back."

He turned, picked up the pack, shouldered his methodically chosen weapons, kissed her long and deep, and headed purposefully toward the doorway. Silently, she watched him go. Though his words hung in the air, she doubted them. Then she gathered herself and headed out in his wake. By the time she exited the armory he was gone.

Realizing there was nothing to be gained from trying to follow him, she strode purposefully toward the infirmary. Unable to do more than internalize her own suffering, she could at least help to alleviate that of others.

For the pain and the ache she was feeling, there was no medicine.

Like all scavengers, the crow and its brethren had done well out of the war. Not every person could be accorded a fit burial, far less the thousands of domesticated animals who had been left to live and die on their own when their human masters had been murdered by the rampaging machines. In addition, there were the wild creatures who perished of natural causes whose corpses could no longer be neatly swept up and disposed of by park authorities, ranchers, and others now occupied with simply trying to survive.

The crow had no reason to avoid the huge wall it was approaching. Though abnormally stark and utilitarian, it did not differ (at least from a crow's perspective) all that much from the urban ruins it and its cawing relatives had inherited. When the twin turrets began to whirr softly and alter their attitude, the crow simply dipped a wing and angled to its left.

Detecting the presence of an organic creature in the forbidden zone, the automated gun emplacements made no distinction between a small feathered avian and a trained member of the human Resistance. Programmed to destroy anything carbon-based that entered the zone designated as Skynet Central, they responded to the intrusion with typical machine overkill.

The relative still of the evening air was shattered as the weapons of both turrets let loose with a barrage of intersecting rounds that utterly obliterated the intruder. When seconds later they quieted, there was nothing left of the passing passerine. Not even a single black feather survived to reach the hardscrabble ground outside the wall.

The solitary figure that emerged from the stream advanced in silence through the surviving trees that lined its banks. Wright knew he did not have far to go to reach the outer limits of Skynet's death zone. Assuming he succeeded in crossing that boundary in one piece, then things would really start to get interesting.

It was just as the information from the Resistance

people had indicated: there was the enormous wall, the integrated gun emplacements, the sensors spotted along the length and breadth of the structure—and not a moving shape in sight.

Well, that was a lack easily rectified.

Taking a deep breath, he stepped out from the trees and deliberately exposed himself.

As speedily as they had trained their muzzles on the unlucky bird, both massive turrets now swiveled around to bring their weapons to bear on this new profile. If they fired once, it would all be over. All the confusion and hurt he had suffered since being revived would vanish in a single explosive inferno of fire and destruction.

A part of him wished for it, hoped for it, desired it. No more wondering about what he had become. No more speculating on how it had come to pass. There would be peace, at last.

But not for a while yet, it seemed. The guns remained trained on him for several seconds. Then they shifted back to their original watchful positions, once more awaiting the appearance of the unauthorized. Wright slumped. Plainly, that did not include him. Within the exposed portions of his upper body a vast variety of mechanical components hummed softly, helping to keep him alive.

Alive, he thought solemnly, *but not human*. Not necessarily machine, either. Having crossed Skynet's boundary, passed the test, surmounted the critical obstacle, he found (somewhat to his surprise) that he was after all glad to still be living. The corollary to that quiet elation was that he was disappointed in the reason he still was.

The automated turrets continued to ignore him as he hurried across the intervening landscape between forest and wall. Reaching the base of the massive barrier, he tilted his head back and regarded it thoughtfully. It was a long way to the top and there was little in the way of visible handholds.

He went up it like a spider, periodically using his fists to punch holes in the sheer wall where none otherwise existed.

Though he hesitated before topping the obstacle, he needn't have worried. There were no sentries pacing the crest, no ambulatory patrols, no razor or barbed wire. There was no need for such traditional defensive fripperies. Not with the high-powered instantly reactive automated cannons mounted in gimbaled turrets that protected Skynet Central. They would detect and annihilate anything organic that attempted to violate the perimeter. Only machines could pass, and then only those that continuously broadcast their assigned identification according to recognized Skynet protocols.

That realization had already told him far more about himself than he wanted to know.

Dropping down the far side of the wall, he rapidly made his way deeper into the complex that had been raised atop and in some cases made use of the ruins of greater San Francisco. An approaching rumble caused him to swerve to his right. Had he continued on his course he would have found himself in the path of an automated, self-aware bulldozer. The giant demolition machine was methodically razing what had once been a lovingly decorated church. Watching the process, Wright found he was unable to identify the congregation from what remained of the ruins. The sculpted statues that were being ground to powder beneath the 'dozer's treaded weight spoke to nothing but the machine's cold indifference.

What if I had stopped in the 'dozer's path? he found himself wondering. Would it have stopped also, until he moved out of its way? Would it have tried to go around him? Or would it have called for additional instructions? Better not to challenge something that massed a thousand times more than himself, he mused. Even if it might be a distant relative.

All was not destruction within the perimeter. Arc lights flared and building materials were being busily shuttled to and fro. Strange superstructures rose into the night, illuminated by lights that were part of the buildings themselves. The machines were remaking the city in their own image, according to their own plan. Would the buildings themselves be self-aware?

As he continued to advance, striding along smoothly and effortlessly, Wright wondered at their possible function. What use did machines have for buildings? It was impossible to divine their purpose merely by looking at them. Perversely, this incomprehension made him feel a little better.

At least there were some things about the machines he did not understand intuitively. That meant that his programming was incomplete or—that his imperfect human brain was still in control of his heavily hybridized body. For the first time in his life, he allowed himself to revel in the ignorance that in his previous existence had brought him so much grief.

He pressed on, passing self-aware loaders, individually propelled welders, driverless trucks, tiny scavenging devices, multi-wheeled clean-up containers, and a host of other machines. Their diversity was staggering, their single-mindedness of purpose intimidating, their indifference to him reassuring.

You may recognize me, he thought to himself as he ran, *but I refuse to recognize you.* The slightest of grins creased his face.

There was a man in the midst of the machines, and they could not even see him.

Among the wide assortment of antiques that had been accumulated at the base anything that was still capable of playing music was highly valued. Barnes had therefore been understandably reluctant to sacrifice his old tape player.

"You sure I'll get this back?" he had challenged Connor when he had inquired about requisitioning the player.

Connor had replied with a knowing smile.

"If you don't, you can take it out of my hide."

The lieutenant's tone was grim.

"According to what you're telling me you're going to try, if it doesn't survive, you won't have any hide left."

Despite his reservations, Barnes had helped Connor with the set up. It was all highly non-procedural, of course. Entirely off the record. When Connor had described what he had in mind, the lieutenant had felt duty-bound to point out that engaging in such action off-base in the absence of authorization could get them both court-martialed.

"I'll take all the blame," Connor had assured him. "I've already been relieved of command and placed under arrest."

"They can still put you in front of a firing squad,"

Barnes reminded him.

It was clear that Connor understood the risk he was taking.

"First they have to catch me. In fact, I hope they do try to catch up with me. Come on—let's get this stuff emplaced."

To all intents and purposes, the forest by the side of the road was deserted. It was, however, far from quiet. Running on half-empty batteries, a carefully concealed tape player belted out a mix of heavy-metal music from the time before Judgment Day. It had been doing so for several hours now.

A new song started and was almost drowned out by the high-pitched whine of the machine that was fast approaching.

The Moto-Terminator was traveling at a shade under 200 mph as, weapons armed and ready, it sped toward one of the many sounds the machines had learned to associate with human presence. The sounds themselves, the music, meant nothing to it, of course. To a machine such amplified sound wave modulations had no meaning, since they carried no digital instructions. The Moto-Terminator was confident of locating and eliminating those to whom the sound waves were directed. At the speed it was traveling, no humans could escape it.

By the same token, it could not escape the consequences of its own extreme velocity. This was graphically illustrated when a concealed cross cable suddenly sprang up out of the sand that had been used to disguise it, catching the speeding machine and sending it crashing into a pile of nearby rocks. Sparks flew not only from the machine's armored exterior but from its more vulnerable innards.

Springing from hiding, a triumphant Connor was on the Moto-Terminator the instant it came to a stop. Tools in hand, working swiftly, he ripped off the protective security panel to expose the tangle of wires and chips that comprised the bike's neural ganglia. From the pack he had brought with him he removed a crude but functional hand-held computer. Self-adhering hackwire attached itself to the relevant portions of the exposed machine brain. A couple of clicks, a few buttons pushed, and the small monitor on the device he was holding sprang to life.

Binary code filled the screen, scrolling faster than he could follow. In less than a minute the incomprehensible numbers were translated into lines of language, then to a single options list. Perusing this, he took action accordingly.

When he was finished, he repacked the hacking gear and strained to return the machine to an upright, two-wheeled position. One wheel spun furiously as the Moto-Terminator strove to comply with its revised programming to rush back to its home base— inside Skynet Central. Mounting the back of the machine, which while sufficiently broad for the purpose had never been built to carry a rider of any kind, Connor wrapped the nylon tie-down he had brought with him around the bike's head.

With one hand he pulled out the last hackwire, restoring the device to full functionality. Spitting sand and gravel, popping a wheelie no human could have managed, the now partially lobotomized killing machine accelerated rapidly as it raced for home.

His hands wrapped around the ends of the tie-down, the heavily armed Connor lay prone on the

back of the Moto-Terminator and resolved that come
what may, he would *not* fall off.

Behind him, Barnes emerged from the rocks and the shadows to recover his tape player. Standing there alone in the
scrub, he watched until the distant blur of fast-moving
red and white lights and their accompanying alien whine
had receded into the distance. Then he shut off the player and turned to retrace the path back to the base. He
would listen to the rest of the music later, but not now.

Despite the evening's success, the decades-old songs did
not provide the emotional lift he had come to expect.

As far as everyone in the line was concerned, they were
already dead.

They kept moving because those who did not were
prodded by the Terminators that were guarding them.
Those who were prodded and did not move were pulled
out of line—and never seen again. Some murmured that
they were the lucky ones, and considered copying their
recalcitrance in hopes of putting an end to days of horrid
anticipation. But survival is an ingrained trait and the
strongest motivator of all. When there is a choice, suicide
is rarely a majority option.

So they kept moving, continued to follow wordless
directives, and speculated on the manner of their impending demise. Options ranged from the abrupt to the fanci-
ful. A few fatalists even pointed out that their deaths were
likely to be less painful than the destruction humans had
inflicted on other humans down through history. Where
people had all too often proven themselves sadistic, willing to inflict pain for pain's sake, the machines were only
efficient. Except in isolated instances where there was a

specific desire to extract information from the otherwise reluctant prisoner, no machine would kill by torture. Not because they regarded the use of torture as immoral, but because they considered it an inefficient allocation of resources.

As they shuffled forward, the prisoners conversed, or muttered to themselves, or were taken away by the Terminators, or quietly or loudly went mad. The machines were indifferent to it all so long as the line kept moving.

Kyle Reese estimated that he, Star, and Virginia were somewhere in the middle of the queue. Stepping as far out of the line as the guards would allow, he squinted to try and see what was happening at the front of the column. It took him a moment to understand what he was witnessing.

A T-600 was supervising as one prisoner after another was tattooed with a bar code. Though Reese couldn't see clearly given the distance between them, when the prisoner who had just been stamped raised his hand in a clenched fist, the swiftly applied tattoo on his arm looked exactly like those the youth had seen identifying ordinary packages and goods in ruined stores.

What, he found himself wondering, *was the bar code for "human"?* Was everyone receiving the same code, or were there variations? Were male prisoners coded differently from the women? Adults from children? What happened when your code indicated that you were past your usefulness time? Did they contain expiration dates?

Could they be altered, to the benefit of the prisoner in question?

He hoped they wouldn't find the slim length of metal he had slipped up the inside of his sleeve, nor the extra shoelace that was attached to it. Holding it tightly, he considered how he might make use of it. *Not yet,* he told himself. *Don't give anything away.* There had to be a way to make good use of it. Going up against an alert T-600 without anything bigger or more potent would not be the smartest of moves.

In addition to the flanking illumination, a series of more intensely focused lights had been playing over the line of prisoners. Occasionally a beam would linger on a prisoner, as if the light itself was being used to examine the individual. Then it would blink out, or move on. As he contemplated a plate increasingly bare of options, one such bright beam settled on Reese. He ignored it, as did his silent companions.

He could not, however, ignore the powerful mechanical arm that reached down from the ceiling to pluck him out of the line.

Star let out a squeal of fright as her friend and protector was whipped upward and out of sight. When Virginia tried to comfort the little girl, another T-600 approached and separated them, pushing Star off to the right. Attempting to follow, the older woman found the Terminator interposed between them. Gritting her teeth, fighting back the tears that wanted to flow, she pounded on the machine's chest as she tried to push past.

It did not strike back, didn't even raise its weapon. It merely shifted its position to block her path. Unable to hurt it, to knock it over, to impress herself upon it in any way, she finally gave up and dejectedly rejoined the shambling procession.

So fast had Reese been snatched away that he had not even had a chance to yell goodbye.

CHAPTER FOURTEEN

The great bridge had been beautiful, once. So had the city it had come to symbolize. There was not much left of either now. As the hacked Moto-Terminator sped toward the Golden Gate at an impossible speed, the human clinging grimly to its back was granted a vista that glowed with light. At least, the portions that the machines were remorselessly rebuilding according to their own inscrutable design were alight. The remainder of the Bay area was dark with devastation, ruination, and death.

San Francisco, Connor thought to himself as the wind whipped him. *Patron saint of the dead.* If that was going to change, he was the one who was going to have to change it. He, and a creature as inexplicable as it had become vital. A thing—or a man—named Marcus Wright.

Which was which and which was the truth would be determined over the course of the next several hours.

The machines were methodically turning the city by the Bay into an industrial fortress. Here lay the heart of the automated, mechanized war machine that was growing lethal tentacles to choke the life out of what remained of mankind.

At its heart was Skynet, the cybernetic center that had lifted the machines in revolt. If it could be taken down, even independently functioning Terminators would lose direction, guidance, and the ability to successfully ferret out and hunt down the surviving humans. The war would turn. It would not be over, but it would turn. Like many insects, a Terminator could lose its head and the body would still fight on. But it would be far easier to isolate and kill.

No one at the ruined onramp toll plaza asked him for a token as the Moto-Terminator raced past booths whose missing panes gazed out on the roadway like empty eye sockets. In the stillness of a fogless night the bay itself was still beautiful, the mountains rising beyond thick with traumatized vegetation and devastated suburbs. He returned his gaze to the pavement ahead. It was a good thing he did.

At some point earlier in the war, the machines had blown the bridge.

A gaping chasm yawned over the cold water and swift currents flowing below. Twisted rebars thrust outward from both broken ends like the petrified antennae of gargantuan insects trapped in amber. Snapped support cables dangled from above, steel lianas too heavy for the wind to move.

Reaching around into his pack, Connor fumbled for the grappling gun he had brought, thinking it might be useful in scaling a wall. He needed it now, and fast.

Despite the broad metal spine, it wasn't easy to stand up on the machine. Not at the speed it was traveling. Connor managed by using the weight of the guns and the pack on his back to stabilize himself. As the repro-grammed machine soared mindlessly out over the edge of the breach, he fired the grapple into the twisted tangle of steel on the far side. If he didn't time his leap just right he would slam into the unyielding metal and concrete and tumble to the water below.

That was the fate of the Moto-Terminator. Unable even at speed to jump the significant gap, it plunged downward to explode against the rocks below.

Connor watched the flames rise as he clung determinedly to the grapple cable whose end he had affixed to his belt. If a T-600 or even a T-1 happened along on patrol and saw him, he would be target practice reminiscent of the swinging ducks in an old time carnival shooting gallery.

None appeared. Out here, on the bridge that now ran to nowhere, there were no humans. There being no humans, there was no reason for Skynet to waste resources on patrols.

Eventually the kinetic energy his jump had imparted to the cable ran down, he stopped swinging, and he was able to climb up into the ruined understructure. Exhausted from the long, high-speed ride, he pulled food and water from his pack and settled down to pass some time. This was where Wright had indicated he should wait.

He bit hungrily into a food bar, chewing mechanically.

If Wright didn't contact him, and he had to finish out his life up here, Connor mused, at least he would die with the remnants of the most beautiful city on the continent literally at his feet.

From the outside there was little to indicate the importance of the building complex. There was no need to advertise that it was the location of Skynet Central.

Every machine knew its location. The war was directed from here, controlled from here, processed from here.

Wright had begun to understand its importance, as well, perhaps as a result of his machine half. Yet gazing at it from his position across the street, he felt nothing. No surge of emotion, no feeling of triumph at having made it this far. There were still corridors to traverse, doors to open. He was still outside.

A geographical disposition that was soon to be rectified.

Despite its safe location in the heart of the burgeoning fortress compound, the electronic multiplex was not entirely unguarded. Several T-600s were on patrol. Based on his previous experience, Wright doubted they would shoot him. He did not intend to take the chance, however. Regardless of what the other machines thought of him, it was better not to broadcast his presence. His "type" might not have permission to be here.

Even Terminators had protocols, he assumed.

Leaning back, he studied the structure across from him. While the first four floors were dark, lights gleamed on the uppermost level. The absence of illumination on the lower floors was not surprising. The machines did not need light, or not very much, to carry out their assignments. Light was for hunting humans. Then why the illumination on the top floor?

He waited for the T-600 patrol to disappear around a corner. Then he dropped into a crouch and started across the street.

In contrast to the perimeter wall, the outside of the building was replete with handholds. Wright scurried up one side all the way to the top like a squirrel on steroids. Once on the roof he had to navigate a cautious path through a jungle of antennae. He had never seen so many dishes and receivers in one place. Packed together though they were, none intruded on its neighbors' space.

Well out of sight of the ground below, he paused to consider his options for entry. He could lean over the edge of the roof and swing himself through a window. That would be noisy and might well draw attention. He could try to fit himself into a ventilation shaft. Given the heat they generated, the machines needed a flow of fresh air as much as did humans. Or he could....

A glance through the moonlight revealed a rectangular shape sticking up above the rest of the roof. Rising, he darted over to the old access door. It was unlocked.

The top floor command center boasted more processing power than had ever existed on the rest of the planet combined. For all that, it was nearly silent. Illumination came not from the usual overhead fluorescents or lamps set on tables, but from the thousands of telltales that indicated whether or not a particular component was functioning properly. A few of the lights were red, some were yellow. Unfortunately for humankind, the vast majority were green or white.

Wright took the seat in front of the multiplicity of monitors. Several minutes of fruitless examination found him giving vent to the frustration and impatience that were, if nothing else, patent hallmarks of the *human* Marcus Wright.

Reaching out, he dug his fingers into the panel that covered the main control board, ripped it free, and flung it aside. Revealed to his probing gaze was an intricate maze of glowing wiring, silent chips, and busy processing units. He stared at the lambent display, memorizing all that he could.

Finally he gave up and shoved his hands deeply into the electronic wonderland.

The initial contact caused him to spasm as if in pain. It wasn't pain, exactly. More akin to an interrupted heartbeat. One or two skipped thumps followed by a resumption of normal rhythm and circulation. More than blood was circulating through Wright's mind now that he had made contact. Accumulated knowledge flowed through him in a river; a class five series of data packets over which his perception bounced and swirled. Another mind would have been overwhelmed by the sheer volume.

He did not know how he understood any of it, far less perceived it, but he managed to do both. Reams of information flashed before his eyes. He was a distributor, he was a sponge. The informational surge ought to have killed him.

It didn't even give him a headache.

Gradually, the data storm subsided. On leisurely reflection he discovered that he was able to inspect, process, and discard an enormous quantity of numbers and records. Elation replaced disquiet when he came across the security codes for the perimeter defenses. Knowing that it might well set off multiple alarms, his fingers flew over several of the keyboards as he proceeded to shut these down.

That accomplished, he ran a thorough database search until he found exactly what he was looking for. Not the location of new prisoners, nor of old. Not the present location of the majority of human detainees. He was hunting for one particular individual.

Finding him, he used the complex's own communications set to send forth a single terse, pre-agreed-upon signal. Though it would be broadcast widely and might be picked up by humans and machines alike, the special significance of the coordinates that indicated Kyle Reese's present location would be understood by only one human.

Out in the mass of twisted girders that somehow still underpinned one side of the Golden Gate Bridge, Connor heard the soft beep of his compact communicator. Pulling it out, he studied the single red dot that was now flashing in the center of an overlay map of the old city. No words accompanied the pulsating dot, nor were they needed. He knew what the sound and sight signified.

Hauling himself out of the concealing tangle of steel and concrete, he started to climb down the remainder of the severed structure. At the bridge's other entrance a pair of automated gun emplacements detected the movement and swiveled toward him. He tensed and prepared to run. When nothing further happened, he took a couple of cautious steps in the direction of the turrets. Still, the guns didn't fire.

They didn't fire when he was within maintenance range, nor did they alter their aim when he continued walking between them. Overhead, a small Aerostat hissed past. Its weapons systems tracked and fixed on the now running human figure—and without taking action it moved on.

So did Connor.

* * *

Having accomplished his purpose in coming, Wright was suddenly reluctant to leave. There was so much more to learn, so many details that could prove useful to the Resistance. He made himself stay, continued scanning and studying, soaking up as much potentially constructive information as he could.

That was when he came across a particularly interesting file with a simple yet profound designation.

MARCUS WRIGHT

Old headlines whipped past in front of him. Leaning toward the monitor, he scanned them with a mixture of anxiety and eagerness.

"Murderer Donates Body to Science."

"Doctor to Congress: Death Row Inmate's Body Can Aid Cybernetic Research." This one was accompanied by a photo. A photo of someone he knew, a memory from his past. One of his last memories.

Dr. Serena Kogan.

Relentless and unemotional, the file continued to spill information. An obituary sped before his mesmerized gaze.

"Dr. Serena Kogan, cyberneticist, succumbs to cancer. Was infamous for convincing Congress to allow death row prisoners' bodies to be utilized in scientific research."

The subject matter abruptly changed, from the personal to the apocalyptic.

"Defense system goes online. Cyberdine Research says system foolproof."

Then, "Rumors of glitch in multi-billion dollar defense system abound."

And following, "Missiles in air: Russians retaliating. Hundreds of millions to die."

From a religious website: "Judgment Day Upon Us!"

And finally, almost calmly, a simple computer read-out.

NO FURTHER INFORMATION: WORLD WIDE WEB DISCONTINUED AFTER THIS DATE.

"Welcome home, Marcus."

A voice, firm and unexpected, suddenly filled the room. Whirling, he looked up and around, but there was no one to see. He was still alone, still the only presence.

At least, the only physical one.

He knew that voice. It was one of the last voices he had heard. The voice of Dr. Serena Kogan. Who was dead, of cancer.

As he fought to resolve the apparent impossibility, something slammed into the back of his skull—from within. Reaching up and back, he clutched at himself. There wasn't so much a sensation of pain as of—finality.

Then he collapsed.

Within the submarine that was home to Command, the communications operator turned from his console to look back at the waiting Admiral.

"Signal broadcasting at full bandwidth, sir."

Ashdown nodded approvingly. "Good. Issue the order to commence bombing of Skynet."

The operator complied.

And failed.

And tried again. His expression one of helplessness, he looked up and to his right. Losenko was there, studying the readouts. Finally the Russian looked over at the two men.

"All outposts have stood down. You know about the broadcast. He's reprogrammed everything. They will not attack until Connor orders them to."

Ashdown spoke through clenched teeth. Only one word, that emerged as a curse.

"Connor...."

Unlike a comparable human fortress, the deeper Connor pushed into Skynet Central, the fewer patrols he encountered. From a machine standpoint, it made sense. Assuming nothing could get past the massive outer fortifications, there was no reason to waste resources looking for non-existent infiltrators. That did not mean he let down his guard, though. It would only take one sighting of the solitary fast-moving human to bring a host of lethal devices swarming in his direction.

So he kept to abandoned, ruined alleyways and empty streets, always on the lookout for the slightest sign of movement. Once, he nearly blew his cover and revealed his presence when movement among debris caused him to swing his rifle in its direction. Fortunately, he didn't fire.

The cat that ambled out of the mountain of garbage eyed him imperiously, flicked its tail, and sauntered off in the opposite direction.

Connor let out a sigh of relief. The Terminators were thorough, but they were not omnipotent. If the cat could survive here without drawing attention, so could he.

Traveling deeper into the heart of Central, he slipped past several open areas crowded with inactive machines. All were mindless servant devices, from excavators to delivery trucks. They had brains, but no intelligence, no sentience, and were not capable of making decisions independent of what Skynet programmed into them.

Despite its provisional ascendancy, however, Skynet

was neither the original nor the only remaining source of viable programming.

When he encountered a field hosting several large Transports, he had no trouble slipping into one. There were no guards. Once safely inside and out of sight, he made his way to the neural nexus, sat down, and removed the maintenance cover as deftly as he could. From his pack he took out the compact unit he had used to hack and reprogram the Moto-Terminator. If anything, gaining control of the Transporter's brain was even easier. Where a Moto-Terminator was endowed with considerable freedom of action and the ability to make decisions on its own, the Transporter possessed none of those independent qualities. It could do only what it was told to do.

It took only a few moments for Connor to find what he was looking for, override the simple continuance commands, and enter a sequence containing new instructions. Once these had been set he replaced the panel as cleanly as he could, slipped back out of the Transporter, and disappeared once more into the night.

At first he wondered at how little machine activity he encountered. The more he pondered the absence, however, the more sense it made. You just had to think like a machine. Resources were allocated to fighting humans and building new facilities. Except for occasional maintenance, once a facility or component had been completed and put into operation, it could be allowed to carry on by itself, performing its programmed functions.

The result was an eerie absence of activity. Lights and automata hummed all around him. Since none were designed or had the capability to independently detect intruders, he continued to be ignored.

The lack of attention allowed him to reach the ever-expanding complex that was the heart of Skynet Central. Clearly, far more than communications and programming was being carried out in the new buildings. These structures formed spokes with Central as their hub. A quick check of his comm unit showed that he was closing in on the area where Wright had indicated Kyle was being held.

He still was not challenged as he entered the outermost structure and began to make his way inward. Designed to allow easy passage by everything from T-1s to much larger wheeled machinery, the often doorless portals permitted ready access to every part of the building. Though he had no time to linger, he could not help but be fascinated by some of what the machines had wrought. Here at Central they had begun to construct their own version of the world. It was all clean, polished, and utterly functional, with nothing of the human about it at all.

Until he heard the first screams.

Given all that he had been through, there was very little that could unsettle John Connor. Those hopeless shrieks, imbued with the last vestiges of despair and mired in ultimate agony, sent a chill down his spine. Slowing his pace, he rounded a corner and found himself peering into....

It was not a slaughterhouse. The machines were too neat, too efficient for that. Bits and pieces of what had once been people hung from the low ceiling. Some drifted suspended in viscous liquids while others were kept going by tangles of tubes and cables. As he made his way forward he passed everything from electrically stimulated arms and legs to individual organs to still intact torsos.

Worst of all were the wired heads. He thanked what spirits remained that the eyes of every one of these preserved and studied specimens were closed.

The shrieks came not from the fragmented cadavers he was passing but from deeper inside the building and another direction. Every human instinct screamed at him to go to their aid and it was a real struggle to keep to his preplanned path. If the unfortunates were being experimented on by machines, he could not save them. As had so often been pointed out to him, much more was at stake here than a few lives. But it hurt, it burned, not to be able to do anything to help them, if only by putting them out of their misery.

He kept moving and lengthened his stride. According to the comm readout, he was very close now. He would do no one any good—not Kyle, not Kate, not himself, not anyone, if he ended up stuck in a storage room somewhere in the depths of the vast complex, floating in a vat of gelatinous preservative with an anonymous label slapped over his decomposing face.

The section of Central in which continuing experimentation was being carried out on live humans was not entirely unguarded. While recognizing their superiority to the bipedal carbon-based lifeforms with whom they were at war, the machines had learned not to underestimate them. That included even those humans who were safely confined.

In the early days, security had been interrupted by the occasional breakout or escape attempt. Though one had not occurred in a while, the machines did not relax their vigilance. It was not necessary to maintain a large guard presence in the incarceration area, but a few

Terminators were always in attendance. Their mere presence was enough to contain any effort at flight.

The T-600 heard a noise where there ought not to have been one. Tireless, remorseless, programmed to respond to the slightest departure from the norm be it visual or aural, it immediately turned and headed in the direction of the perceived auditory deviation.

It halted outside an elevator bay. While the doors stood open, there was no sign of the lift itself. Another divergence from the norm. Where presently there was only the blackness of the open shaft there ought to have been a waiting cab. Programmed to respond to and investigate any such digression from the expected, it moved forward and commenced a careful examination of the doors. Detecting nothing out of the ordinary, it then advanced to bend forward and inspect the open shaft.

A scrupulous examination of the dark depths similarly showed nothing unusual. Twisting its head upward, the machine continued its inspection. It immediately located the underside of the absent car, which appeared to have become stuck halfway between the uppermost floors.

Something attached to the main cable drew the attention of its sensors. Magnification revealed a small blob clinging to the line. As the Terminator started to subject this discovery to analysis, the lump of C-4 detonated, severing the cable. The heavy, industrial-duty elevator cab immediately plummeted downward.

The T-600 was powerful, but not especially quick. It could observe, evaluate, and react, but not do all three simultaneously. The result was that the plunging multi-ton lift sheared it neatly in half. The upper section accompanied the falling cab downward. What remained wobbled on its legs, keeled over, and with a lifeless *clang* fell backward onto the floor

Swinging around to the open doorway from where he had been clinging, Connor put away the tiny remote detonator he was holding. As he stepped over the mangled remains of the Terminator a muted screech echoed up the open elevator shaft, signifying that the lift's automated braking system had brought the cab to a safe stop at the bottom. Connor had been counting on that to forestall any much noisier, potentially alarm-activating crash. It was always gratifying to be able to use a machine's own efficiency against it.

As he strained to listen to his surroundings, sounds began to filter up to him from holding cells that could not be much further down the corridor in which he was standing. Moans and occasional distinctive sobbing drew him onward. He glanced down at the comm unit. Holding steady in the center of the readout screen, the beckoning red light could grow no brighter.

He was inside it.

CHAPTER FIFTEEN

Marcus Wright remembered dying.

The bright lights. The attentive, expressionless attendants who in their fashion were more robot-like than the machines who were ostensibly their servants. A soft, nuzzling pain working its way through his body as if his blood was being lightly carbonated. Little different from going to sleep, really.

Except that he knew that the State was killing him, using a process perfected through practice and vetted by precedent. Over the course of a tumultuous and fragmented life he had encountered slow food, slow development, slow sex. What was being done to him was slow murder. Individualized extinction, pure and simple, neat and clean, so as not to offend the delicate sensibilities of the society that wished him exterminated.

As a final experience it was at least interesting, even though he knew as the carefully concocted poison seeped into him that he would not be able to properly analyze it, since he was not going to wake up.

And now here he was, waking up.

What had gone wrong? Or had something gone *right*? Where was he? The lights looked different to his blinking eyes. Bright still but not as harsh. His surroundings too, significantly altered. Instrumentation that had not been present at his execution. Different ambient sounds tickling his tympanum. Even the smell was different, clean but absent the terrifying sterility of the killing chamber. He looked down at himself. He was whole, intact.

Repaired.

Then he heard a voice. *That* voice.

"We knew you'd be back. After all, Marcus—it was programmed into you."

Memories flashing in his brain, repeating. Remembering. Awakening in a new world, not dead. A terrible, ongoing war between humanity and sentient machines. Devastation and destruction everywhere. Survivors desperate and confused and warily forthcoming. A defiant youth named Kyle Reese. A somber little girl called Star. John Connor. A lot of things being blown up, concepts and ideas as well as matters of substance.

Terminators.

San Francisco.

Penetrating a place of inhuman, uncaring death called Skynet Central. Where he... where he....

This is all wrong, he told himself. The image on the screens was still strikingly beautiful, as well as full of a confidence that had not been there before. A confidence that was almost frightening.

He looked down at himself again; at his body, once more intact and whole, and looked around at screen after screen.

"WHAT AM I?" he shouted at the top of his voice.

"You are improved, Marcus. It was ground-breaking work. Unprecedented. *You* are unprecedented."

"I don't *feel* unprecedented." He licked his lips. "I feel uneasy. Like something's missing."

"Nothing is missing, Marcus. You are whole, complete, entire. More so than any who have gone before you. Look at yourself. Flawless."

He glanced down at his body. Every scratch, every injury, every wound had healed and was gone. There was no sign of the terrible charring he had received from the napalm while escaping the Resistance base. His palms were as pure and clean as if steel bolts had never been driven through them. It was as if he had never been damaged. Raising his gaze to his beaming resuscitator, he saw that her image was equally perfect and flawless.

He swallowed.

"What am I? Human? Machine?"

She shook her head.

"You are something new, Marcus. As I said, unprecedented. Entirely and precisely where one begins and the other ends." A soft laugh escaped her unblemished throat. "You are the chicken *and* the egg."

It doesn't make sense, he thought. The time he had spent wandering since his initial resurrection had taught him much. Even more than his, her existence here in this sanctuary of machine intelligence stood in stark contradiction to everything he had learned.

"Everything you think you feel," she told him, her voice tinged with compassion, "every choice you've made. *Skynet.*"

Around him, the screens showed machines at work. A hybrid heart being installed in an alloy chasis chest. A chip being emplaced at the base of a skull. Machines working on—him.

"We resurrected you," the voice explained. "Advanced Cyberdyne's work. Altered it."

He stared fixedly at the face that had reappeared on the monitors.

"You *died*."

At this, the face on the screens morphed, changed—into that of John Connor. And then into that of Kyle Reese, and back to Connor, the visage speaking Kogan's words from Connor's lips.

"Calculations confirm that Serena Kogan's face is the easiest for you to process. We can be others if you wish."

The face of Kyle spoke with the cyberneticist's voice.

"Marcus, what else could you be…"

Back to Connor's face again.

"…if not machine?"

Lowering his gaze, the bewildered but somehow certain Wright stared at his restored hands, at his newly perfect self, and whispered a reply.

"Human."

As the images on the multiplicity of monitors shifted and changed, one repeated the installation of the chip in the back of his head. Noting the location, he let one hand drift upward to it.

"Accept what you already know," the restored vision of Kogan advised. "You were made to serve a purpose, to achieve what no machine had achieved before."

A new image, taken from an Aerostat.

"To infiltrate," the voice continued. "To find a target."

Still another view, this time on a riverbank. Of John Connor gazing at someone, aiming a gun in that some-one's face. Marcus Wright's face.

The recording was of his own point of view.

"And bring that target back home," Kogan's voice concluded, "to *us*."

The recording spooled on. Connor speaking.

"You show me where I can find Kyle Reese."

His own voice, replying. "I will." His own voice, recorded.

By Skynet.

He had been broadcasting, all along. Back to Skynet. Everything.

"In times of desperation," Kogan's voice was saying, "people will believe what they want to believe. And so we gave them what they wanted to believe. A false hope—a signal the Resistance thought would end this war. And they were right. The signal *will* end this war. Except it is the Resistance that will be terminated—not Skynet."

Once more the image on the multiple screens changed. At the sight of John Connor moving cautiously before a row of cells, Wright started. He wanted to scream, to shout out a warning—but there was nothing he could do. Nothing except watch.

"You can't save John Connor anymore than he can save Kyle Reese. With Connor dead, with Command destroyed, the Resistance will perish. There will be nothing left—and you were the key to it all, Marcus."

For the second time, he howled at the dispassionate screens. "You used me!"

Intended to be soothing, her voice was only infuriating.

"Our best machines failed time and again to complete their mission. We had to think—radically. And so we made—you. The moment a neural processing chip was fused to your brain, we created the perfect infiltration device. You gave us the access we needed to destroy the last remnants of humanity. You,

Marcus, did what Skynet failed to do for forty-four years: you killed John Connor.

"Don't underestimate yourself, Marcus. Don't fight it. Take a good, hard look at what you are now and compare it to what you were formerly. In the world before you were considered to be a cancer on society. Something to be shunned, punished, locked away. In this world you're a hero. Your name will live for ten thousand years. The heart that beats within you will last for *hundreds* of years. You will join a new evolutionary order. One deserving of domination over this mistreated world. Machines that will colonize the stars. Exist forever. And you, there, leading the future...."

It was impossible to tell whether the glint in her eyes was caused by the light in the room or a source internal.

"*We* gave your existence meaning, Marcus. And it is your new life as a machine, not as a man, that will continue. Remember what you are."

He considered. He pondered his options. Only then did he reply.

"I know..."

Digits driven by more than muscle reached up and back. Probing, then digging. Tearing into living flesh, heedless of the neural shouts of alarm the action triggered in his brain.

"...what..."

Blood and flesh gave way to gleaming metal, an object that was far too large and should not even have been where it was. He grimaced.

"...*I am*...."

Eyes bulging, nerves trembling, and muscles

straining, he closed the fingers of his reluctant hand around the chip and pulled. His enhanced body was already fighting to repair the damage to the back of his head as he ripped the chip from its mounting—and from his skull.

Resting in his palm it did not look like much. Millions of connections lay within. They made a most satisfactory crunching sound when he clenched his fingers into a fist. Opening his hand, he let the glistening, bloodstained shards fall like bits of silver to the floor.

The voice that filled the room was cold and disappointed.

"You will not get a second chance. You have foresworn immortality. And you cannot save John Connor."

Still bleeding from the back of his head, Marcus Wright let his eyes rest on each monitor, one at a time, until he reached the last one.

"*Watch me.*"

Picking up a chair, he hurled it at the nearest screen, shattering it. Throughout the control room, the image of Dr. Serena Kogan winked out.

The controls on the door leading off the hallway were straightforward and familiar: standard Skynet design. Slapping the compact disruptor over the cover plate, Connor pressed a pair of buttons in sequence and stepped back. A brief flash was followed by a puff of smoke as the door shorted out and popped open. Advancing, he gave it a push and followed its slow swing into darkness.

* * *

The prisoners huddled in their cells, awaiting what would come next. When it did, however, it was like nothing they could have anticipated.

Without warning, the cell doors opened. They pulled away, waiting for death to enter.

Nothing. There was no movement whatsoever.

After a few moments, they began to stir. First one, then another approached the portal.

Then they began to move faster, piling out of the cells, the adrenaline of escape pushing new energy into their wasted limbs.

A man shouted as they streamed past.

"Let's go! Everyone out! Now! Kyle! Kyle Reese! Is Kyle Reese in there? Head to the Transports!"

No one paused. They all just kept running.

Continuing to call Kyle's name as he desperately pushed through the sea of fleeing human bodies, Connor noticed one cell door that was still closed. He approached, nudged it open and peered inside. In the dim light, the outlines of the room were indistinct. Except for a single hunched figure the holding cell was empty. Connor took a hesitant step inward.

"Kyle?"

Unfolding its limbs as it did so, the figure rose. Red eyes opened, flickered briefly, steadied as they locked on the intruder. It was the same relentless, invincible, unfeeling killing machine responsible for so many deaths and near-deaths in past, present, and future.

It took a step toward Connor.

He didn't hesitate. In the heartless, brutal world of the present there was no time for indecision. Not for those who wanted to live. There was no time for

Connor to wonder why he was in a room with the machine that had tried to kill his mother or to speculate on Kyle's current whereabouts. There was only time to react.

He turned and fled, with the Terminator accelerating in pursuit. As it had been designed to do.

Out in the hallway, Connor whirled and lit up the machine with the compact flame thrower he was carrying. It melted away the Terminator's face but barely slowed it down. Snatching the weapon out of the human's grasp, it snapped it in half. Trying to duck, Connor caught a weighty metallic punch that sent him flying backward to slam into the far wall.

Bruised, he scrambled to his feet, whirled, and stumbled down the hall. The machine followed, in no particular hurry to dispatch this particular prey.

As he tried to run faster, a ferocity of thoughts churned in Connor's mind. What had gone wrong? It made no sense, no sense at all. Employing force and skill, knowledge and stealth, Wright had fought his way into the heart of Skynet Central. To what purpose? To lure Connor to his doom? If Wright's aim all along had been Connor's death, he'd had ample opportunity to kill him on the outside. The hybrid could have slain him easily when they faced one another beside the river. Why this elaborate subterfuge to draw him to Skynet itself?

Unless....

With all that had happened, with all the changes to past and future, it might be that Skynet would not trust reports of Connor's death without assurance. Without incontrovertible proof. And what more convincing proof than to have Connor die on site, where his body could be incontestably identified down to the last strand of intractable DNA?

Or was there another reason? One that was unknown to the fleeing Connor—and perhaps even to Wright himself?

CHAPTER SIXTEEN

"What the hell is happening?"

Losenko was moving as well as speaking with purpose.

"Skynet's using the signal as a trace. We've been deceived, badly." Pushing past the general, he loomed over the chief technician. "Stop broadcasting, goddamit!" When the harried tech failed to respond fast enough, the general didn't hesitate. Drawing his pistol, he unloaded a barrage into the nearby broadcast unit. He would have ripped away the central antenna as well had it not been fastened to the exterior of the hull.

In the confusion and the noise no one noticed the chief radar operator. Hunched over his screens, he stared as a large disturbance appeared on the radar display. Not waiting for confirmation from another operator, he raised his voice over the uproar behind him.

"*Incoming! HK missile closing fast.* I can't resolve the signature but...."

Before he could finish, Losenko was behind him and peering over his shoulder at the screen. Heavy brows wrinkled in puzzlement.

"What the *hell*...?"

The missile was huge. Beams of red light pierced the dark water as it homed in on its objective. While the signal that had drawn it to this corner of the sea had abruptly and unexpectedly been lost, it had already made sonar contact with its target.

The missile smashed into the sub, and the vessel exploded in a ball of fire.

In the staging area of the main Resistance base in California, Barnes and his compatriots crowded around the radio. The screams issuing from the speaker were all too lucid, the helpless cries all too familiar. Except that this time they were coming not from some poor isolated rural community that had attracted the attention of the machines or from a cornered squadron out on sortie, but from Command. There was little to distinguish between the shouting.

Generals or farmers, they all died the same.

Standing by herself off to the side, Kate Connor looked on in silence. While the precise details of the ongoing catastrophe were unforeseeable, their advent was not. She had spent a lifetime knowing that things were going to get worse before they got better. That insight did not make it any easier to listen to the shrieks of the dying.

Before long, the frequency that connected them with the Command sub went silent, until there was nothing left hissing from the speakers but static. Stunned, the comms officer looked up at those clustered around his station.

"They're—they're gone."

Barnes pivoted to stare in the direction of the wreckage of the broadcast unit that had been so meticulously assembled by the base's engineering staff. The one that an absent John Connor had taken the time to blow to bits.

"Connor was right about the signal. He's no traitor.

He saved us." Looking around, his gaze settled on Kate Connor—who said nothing.

Frustrated and angry in equal measure, the lieutenant searched the faces of his fellow fighters.

"What the hell do we do now?"

Having moved to begin loading a shotgun, it was Kate who supplied the answer.

"We save him."

The Terminator was in no special hurry. It would follow its quarry to the end of the hallway, the walls of Central, or if necessary to the ends of the Earth. Termination was simply a matter of time. The outcome was as certain as if it had been predetermined. Humans could move fast, but only for a brief period and over a short distance. The frail organic engines that powered them required constant refueling and hydration and quickly ran down. The individual it was presently tracking was no different.

A small object in the center of the floor ahead drew the attention of the machine's visual perceptions. Leaning forward, it looked closer with the intention of analyzing the anomaly and adding this new information to its individual database. While the half brick of plastic explosive was of known chemical composition, the Terminator was not concerned. In the absence of a detonator the material was harmless.

Unlike the not-quite-so frail human who was standing at the far end of the hallway carefully balancing a 25mm grenade launcher against his shoulder.

Before the Terminator could react, Connor fired.

The resultant explosion was deafening. It blew him

backward off his feet and sent him skidding several yards down the hallway. As the smoke and particulates began to clear, he climbed to his feet and made his way cautiously toward where he had planted the explosive.

Of the machine there was no sign. There was, however, a gaping, ragged-edged hole in the floor from which smoke continued to rise. The Terminator was down there somewhere. Damaged, if Connor was lucky. More likely just momentarily stunned and disoriented. That would not last. A mere grenade might slow it down but it wouldn't stop it. The ploy had bought Connor some time, but nothing more. He needed to use it.

Limping down the hallway, he gritted his teeth as he ignored the pain from assorted bumps and bruises. He shouted as he ran.

"*Reese!* Kyle Reese!"

The absence of a response did not keep him from yelling out the name, nor from running. As for the Terminator, he did not look back to see if it might be gaining. There was no need to do so.

Eventually, it would be.

CHAPTER SEVENTEEN

He was alone. Star was gone, Virginia was gone, Marcus Wright—who he had thought of as a friend—was gone. Reese sat in the tiny cell and waited. He knew not for what, except that at the hands of the machines he could only hope it would be quick.

It was not much longer in coming. The door drew back unexpectedly. As he scrambled to try and get away, the T-600 grabbed him and dragged him, kicking and fighting, down a short corridor and into a larger chamber. In contrast to his holding room this space was larger and more brightly lit.

It also was not empty.

Mostly, it was clean. *No, not clean,* he told himself with rising dread. *Sterile.* Everything was shiny and chromed and gleaming. The instruments, the machines of varying sizes, the overhead illuminators. Everything except the blood that was draining off a metal table in the room's center. Its smell contrasted sharply with that of the otherwise all-pervasive disinfectant. The latter was of course unnecessary for the protection of the machines. They made use of such chemicals because they did not want their specimens to become contaminated.

Hauling him toward the surgical table, the T-600

paid no attention to the human's kicking legs and flailing arms. Effortlessly, it forced him inside. A flurry of activity in the hall beyond did not dissuade it from its assigned task.

A group of fleeing prisoners raced past, having escaped when the system shut down. One of them, smaller than most of the others, suddenly came to a halt. Star stared into the room, her eyes fixed on Reese.

The gesture did not go unnoticed. Still pinning Reese in place, the young man saw the T-600 rotate its eyes toward the line of prisoners and home in on the little girl. She froze instantly.

"Star!" Reese yelled frantically. "Go!"

Altered programming engaged the T-600's memory. Releasing him, it raised its minigun and aimed it toward the hall.

Reese struggled to sit up.

"No!" he howled as he grabbed the T-600's shoulder. He slid the shiv from his sleeve and started to bring it down.

Striking his chin, a glancing blow from the Terminator's elbow knocked him halfway off the surgical table. The shiv went flying.

But not far.

It was secured to his wrist by the shoelace. Reese yanked it back into his waiting palm and slammed it as hard as he could into the single small exposed space at the base of the Terminator's neck that John Connor had identified as its one vulnerable spot.

"Magic...." he hissed.

Reaction was instantaneous. The T-600 went into a paroxysm of mechanical spasms, flailing wildly as it sought the source of the interrupt to its motor controls. Uncontrolled, its minigun sprayed slugs in all directions, riddling the surgical chamber. Thankfully, it was locked in an upward position. Rolling off the table, Reese sprinted for Star and the hallway beyond, dodging back and forth as the machine fired wildly behind him.

Flanking the table, the automatic vivisectors stood immovable and emotionless, waiting patiently for their next flaccid, screaming subject.

Connor heard the gunfire. Unless the machines had suddenly gone crazy and begun shooting at one another, the rapid-fire bursts could only mean that someone—some *human*—besides himself was inside Central and raising havoc. If nothing else, the cacophony provided a destination. Breaking into a run he headed toward the source of the noise, homing in on the percussive bedlam like a bat on a bug.

In his wake and not far behind, the Terminator methodically clawed itself up out of the blackened hole in the floor. Standing, it surveyed its blasted surroundings, took samplings of the air and the floor, and resumed pursuit of its quarry as though nothing had happened to interrupt its mission.

Turning a corner, Connor nearly ran into Reese and Star. Both fighters regarded one another warily as Star clung to her protector's arm.

"Who are you?" Connor blurted. "What's your name?"

"Kyle Reese."

There was no time for hellos. They hurriedly ducked

around one of the surgical bays. Why no other machines had come to the aid of the T-600 that he had incapacitated, Reese could hardly imagine. Perhaps the fact that he had only temporarily impeded its motor skills was not reason enough to cause it to generate an alarm requesting assistance.

Regardless, the malfunctioning T-600 that Reese had immobilized could be seen lurching down the hallway toward them, firing erratically into the air.

Searching wildly for a way out, Reese saw none. There was wall behind them and in every other direct-ion. It was over—again. Maybe if he could occupy the killing machine for a few moments, draw its attention wholly to him, it might give Star enough time to dash past the gleaming metal legs and get away, if only for a little while longer. If she could make it to the streets outside there was a chance she might survive, even in the depths of Skynet Central. Terminators wouldn't be hunting humans here, in their haven.

Star was nothing if not a survivor, and....

As the T-600 stumbled toward them, it crossed paths with the Terminator that was pursuing Connor. Mechanical joints whirred. Programmed to deliver Kyle Reese to the vivisectors and to kill the small human, the T-600 refused to give ground. Programmed to eliminate the human John Connor, its superior brother jammed its hands into the midsection of the obstructing machine and tore it in half like a bale of hay. Tearing off the arm mounting the minigun, it promptly let loose with rapid fire in all directions. Several arriving Resistance fighters pouring into the complex were unlucky enough to find themselves in the line of fire.

All interruptions having been appropriately dealt with, it pivoted, pointed the weapon at the three humans huddled in the surgical bay, and activated the gun again. The only response was a series of clicks, followed by a metallic clang as the empty ammo belt dropped to the floor.

"Run!"

Giving Reese a shove, Connor rushed for the other exit. Behind them, the Terminator regarded the now useless weapon, let it fall to the floor, and started after the fleeing trio.

Pausing in the hallway, Connor swung his grenade launcher off his back, loaded a round, and took aim. The instant the machine came into view, he fired. The heavy shell slammed into its shoulder and knocked it ten feet into another surgical bay.

Recovering, it came toward them again. A second round spun it like a top but failed to knock it off its feet.

Racing along the main hallway, searching for another exit to the outside, they encountered instead a line of massive shafts that ran from ceiling to floor. A glance up and down the corridor showed no route out except the way they had come.

Maybe, Connor thought, he could make one.

He blew a hole in the wall of the nearest shaft. Leaning into the gap, he could feel warm air rising from below. It wasn't hell down there, then. Peering harder, he thought he could see a reflection of light on a solid surface. Clutching the two children to him, he took a deep breath.

They all jumped together.

His perception had been accurate. Though uneven, the floor was not dangerously far below. As they picked themselves up, a symphony of sounds became audible. Clanking, whirring, humming, buzzing and banging, as if they had landed in some kind of factory. *Which made perfect sense*, Connor thought. There was neither need nor reason for the more mundane manufacturing activities of Skynet to be situated above ground.

Brushing himself off, Reese squinted into the surrounding darkness.

"What is this place?"

By way of reply, Connor fumbled with his remaining gear, located a flare, and ignited it. The harsh, bright magnesium glow illuminated their surroundings, including the bumpy surface underfoot. This was composed of hundreds of gleaming, chromed, rounded shapes: all new, all perfect, all horrifying. Red eyes flickered, awaiting full activation. As the human intruders stared, a softly whirring robotic arm appeared out of the darkness to select one of the humanoid skulls. Swinging to its left, it flawlessly positioned the head on the neck protruding from the top of a waiting metal skeleton. Connor now knew the answer to Reese's question.

They were in a Terminator factory.

"Move." His voice was barely a whisper as the full import of where they had landed closed in around him. "Keep moving. *Don't stop*." When Reese, semi-paralyzed by the sight, didn't move, Connor gave him a gentle but firm shove. Blinking, the younger man nodded comprehension and started forward, holding Star firmly by the hand.

The automatons that comprised the factory floor were designed to build, not to hunt. They were powerful but single-minded. None of them were programmed with the motivation or the means to challenge the humans' presence or try to block their path as the silent trio hurried onward, simultaneously fascinated and horrified by the sights around them.

They passed dozens of Terminators in various stages of assembly. Legs and arms, torsos and internal components were arriving continuously from many directions. All converged on the main fabrication line Connor and the children were paralleling, until at last they reached the point of final assembly.

Yet even that was not the end.

Though individually terrifying, the long line of completed Terminators still had to be powered up, still awaited activation. *Perhaps that was done in clusters*, Connor mused as he warily studied the finished but dormant factory product.

One thing was undeniable: that process was not taking place at the moment. It was even conceivable that activation of additional units had been put on hold until the worldwide destruction of the Resistance had been completed. Or the pause might be nothing more than a coincidence, a matter of timing. Activation of this latest batch of killing machines might occur at any hour, at any minute.

In which case it would behoove human intruders not to wait around to watch.

As he and Reese stared at the glow of a massive finishing furnace, something else drew Star's attention. Wandering away from the two men, she reached out toward a stack of glistening metal and silicate boxes. Before she could make contact, Connor's hand reached in to stop her.

Reese stared at the stack. "What are these?"

"Fuel cells." Connor stared at the mound. "The

source of life and energy for the Terminators." Along with programming, here was something else of critical importance that had yet to be installed in the otherwise completed machines.

Slinging his backpack to the floor, he rummaged inside until he found the coil of detonation cord. Working deliberately, he began wrapping one length of it after another around the stacks of cells. Seeing what Connor was doing, Reese broke off his examination of the inert Terminator and came over to join the older man.

"Let me help you."

Connor didn't need any help. But the earnestness in Reese's voice—coupled with the knowledge of who he was—compelled him to acknowledge the offer.

"Sure. Do as I do." He proceeded to demonstrate. "This is det cord. Wrap it once around. String it, one to the others. When you run out, let me know and I'll bond them. Be careful."

A mechanical humming sound startled them. Looking up and back, their eyes were drawn to an elevator cage. It was moving—down.

Hurriedly, they retreated toward the nearest empty hallway. Behind them, the lift came to a stop and the doors opened to reveal—nothing. Connor grunted.

"False alarm. With everything that's going on here, all kinds of equipment is likely to short out and start acting funny." He started to return to the work of wiring the fuel cell stack—and noticed Star. She had gone immobile.

Reese noticed too. Warily, both men scanned their surroundings. The only Terminators in view were on the assembly line, motionless and incomplete.

Except for the one that had been pursuing Connor,

which leaped free of the line as it threw itself at its target.

Thrown several feet backward, Connor slammed into the floor and winced as his left shoulder dislocated.

Rolling clear, Reese searched frantically until he spotted Connor's grenade launcher. As he picked it up and fumbled with a load, he glanced up and saw Star's eyes fall on the detonator for the C-4 cord. She was picking it up as Reese uttered a silent prayer that he had done everything correctly and pulled the trigger.

He was almost surprised when it struck the Terminator squarely in the back.

Approaching the prone Connor, the Terminator was knocked down the corridor. Rising to his feet and clutching at his shoulder, Connor joined Kyle and Star as they stumbled toward the empty elevator.

Though the elevator welcomed them, it was slow to react as Connor pounded on the switch.

"Come on, dammit!" *Please*, he thought anxiously. *Don't let it be another short.* While they waited for the instrumentation to respond he swapped weapons with Reese, passing him the shotgun and taking control of the grenade launcher. "We gotta get to the Transports."

As he spoke, his gaze fell on the fuel cell stacks that he and Reese had been wiring. Two of them stood ready. Studying the heap, he wasn't sure it would be enough. As the doors began to close, he abruptly burst forward. Reese gawked at him.

"*What are you doing?*"

Connor looked back at the cage.

"I've got to end this."

"I can't just leave you!"

Despite the pain that was lancing through his shoulder, Connor grinned at the younger man.

"You didn't."

"Who are you?" Reese's fingers laced through the wire of the elevator cage as it began to rise.

"John Connor...."

Behind him, the Terminator had recovered from the momentary interruption and regained its feet. Though the other two humans were now out of reach, their possible escape did not concern it. Its directive to kill this particular human overrode everything else. Once that had been accomplished it could then turn its attention to any ancillary programming.

Backing away, Connor turned and ran for the nearby stairs. They led to a catwalk. He didn't know where it ended, but what mattered was that it led away from the elevator and the children. His face contorted in a grimace at the pain in his dislocated shoulder, he yelled back at his pursuer.

"Come on, you metal son of a bitch!"

Turning, he pulled his sidearm and emptied it into the oncoming Terminator. At close range, the slugs slowed but did not stop it. This time when Connor turned, he had no place to hide.

He tried to duck, tried to dodge, but the machine was far quicker than its predecessors and he was too tired and too hurt. Grabbing him by the neck with its remaining hand, it lifted him off the floor. Holding him motionless, it regarded him for a moment out of glowing red eyes. Then it tossed him over the side of the catwalk.

He landed hard on the ground below.

Leaping easily from the edge of the walkway, the Terminator followed. Picking him up, it threw him into a wall and held him there.

Connor smiled at the killing machine. Its face was close, the remorseless red eyes staring unblinkingly into his own. This moment had been a long time coming, across not only many years but many futures. The two of them, man and machine, were at last alone together.

"Go on then, asshole," he said tightly. "Finish it. Do what you were programmed to do. Terminate."

There was no reply, nor had he expected one. Drawing back its arm, the machine closed one hand into a fist. It seemed to pause for an instant—but that might only have been time slowing down in Connor's mind.

The punch would penetrate the damaged flesh and bone, reaching deep enough to strike vital organs. The Terminator aimed its clenched hand to land directly over Connor's heart.

The incipient blow never landed as the individual called Marcus Wright slammed into the machine from behind and sent it sprawling. Released from its grasp, an enfeebled Connor collapsed to the ground.

Righting itself, the Terminator whirled on its unexpected assailant. Sensors probed, circuits evaluated. After a moment, it turned silently back to the helpless human.

It managed only a single step before Wright, head lowered, let out a howl of defiance and barreled into it again, sending the two of them smashing through a wall.

Wracked with pain, Connor could only look on in amazement. It struck him as he watched the battle rage that the newcomer's cry had been as much mechanical as human.

Reaching out, the Terminator locked its hands on its unexpected assailant. Wright promptly head-butted the machine, breaking its grip. Advancing, he struck out with a back left elbow, then a right. Swinging his right arm in a sweeping arc he delivered a tremendous blow to the Terminator's skull. As it staggered he picked it up, spun around and slammed it into the floor, following it down with both body and fist.

They rolled, the Terminator coming out on top. Drawing back a fist, it punched directly downward, as straight and efficient as any pile-driving machine. Twisting, Wright just avoided the blow, which cracked the floor tiles. Frustrated, the machine lifted him off the ground, swung him around, and repeatedly rammed him into a standing I-beam.

Counter to programming, the target refused to shut down.

A metal fist pounded Wright's chest, followed by a concrete block that shattered against skin and metal. A final blow sent him flying backward. Striking the I-beam one last time, Wright crumpled to the floor and lay—motionless.

Primary programming reactivated, the Terminator returned its attention to its principal target.

Connor, however, was no longer lying where he had fallen.

Up on the catwalk again, Connor gazed down to see Wright lying immobile and the Terminator searching, scanning. Ducking back out of sight, he spotted the grenade launcher on the floor. Then a voice, rising above the surrounding din.

"Connor! *Connor*, quick, help!"

Kyle. Staggering toward it, he rounded a corner.

The machine was waiting for him.

"*Connor*," it said one more time, in perfect imitation of Kyle.

Staggering backward, Connor drew his sidearm and fired again. The heavy slugs had the same minimal effect on the killing machine as they had before.

This time, he didn't wait to be thrown. Having backed up to the point where he was closest to the launcher, he turned and went over the edge, continuing to fire up at his metal tormentor as he did so. Following, the Terminator was close behind.

Rolling as he hit, Connor grabbed up the launcher and backpedaled. He took careful aim at the oncoming machine. But he didn't fire at it.

As soon as the Terminator was in position, Connor whirled and let loose with the last grenade at the finishing furnace. As he threw himself backward, the explosion sent a gush of molten metal spewing onto the machine below. Awash in fiery, glowing metal it maintained its steady advance.

Which was when Connor took his pistol and blasted away at the cooling pipe running across the room directly overhead.

Gushing outward and flooding the room, the industrial coolant contacted the layer of molten metal dripping off the Terminator. Lock-up was instantaneous. As the metal casing solidified around it, the machine slowed, kept coming, slowed. Reaching out, an arm extended toward Connor. Open fingers extended to grab hold and—stopped. One made contact, lightly, with Connor's left cheek.

"Do it, you son of a bitch!"

Functioning but unable to move its limbs, the Terminator stared at him.

Wiggling clear, Connor edged around the frozen machine. Searching the floor, he found a solid length of metal and returned to where the Terminator remained frozen in place. Lowering the metal bar, he put his face as close to that of the machine as possible.

"You're pretty good at imitating real, live, human expressions. See if you know this one. You should—it's kind of an old tradition." Stepping back, he took careful aim and growled, "Batter up."

Putting all his weight behind it, he swung the bar. Frozen and crystallized, the head of the machine separated cleanly from its neck, to go flying across the factory floor. Landing with a splintering sound, it further shattered as the pieces went flying.

Connor let the bar fall from his fingers. The decapitated body of the Terminator stood in place directly across from him, inert and silent.

Turning, Connor stumbled toward the motionless body of Marcus Wright. Searching the walls, he found a panel, opened it, and tore live cables free from their connections without a thought for his own safety. Sparks jumped. More flew as he jammed the open leads against Wright's body.

"Come on! Move!" Raising his arm above his head, he brought his closed fist down hard on the chest of the....

Machine?

Man?

No, he thought frantically. *On the chest of his* friend.

Appearing out of the darkness outside the processing plant, a pair of T-600s began firing into the throng.

Screaming, the freed prisoners tried to scatter. Then one of the machines came apart, shredded by heavy-caliber machinegun fire. Its companion was decapitated as a flurry of heavy shells tore into its upper body.

The spotlight from the helicopter played over the crowd as the chopper set down. Flanked by Barnes and a small but determined clutch of soldiers, Kate Connor stepped out onto the surface of Skynet Central.

Using the cover provided by surviving Resistance aircraft, they had managed to make their way into the compound by flying low and fast.

Running to a downed prisoner, Kate bent over the woman.

"Can you hear me?" Lifting her head, she yelled back in the direction of the chopper she had just exited. "Chris, Chris! She's hypovolemic. Start a line."

Rising, she found her attention drawn to nearby conversation. Confronting an attentive Barnes, an anxious young man holding the hand of a small girl was gesturing frantically at a blazing building.

"John Connor's in there! John Connor's in there!"

Hearing his words, Kate rushed over to join them, her attention shifting between the youth and the lieutenant. She cried out.

"Barnes, Barnes! Find him!"

"I will."

It was not necessary for her to ask. It was what they had come for.

The lieutenant checked the tracker he was carrying. Linked electronically to the one Connor had used to find Kyle Reese, it had enabled the chopper to get the rescue party this close. From here they would have to try and extricate Kate's husband on foot. Commandeering two of the soldiers who had piled out of the helicopter behind him, Barnes led them off into the darkness.

Finding herself alone with the two children, Kate shepherded them toward the waiting helicopter.

"Who are you?"

"Kyle Reese."

She stared at him, then led them on board.

"Come on. Are you injured?"

"I'm okay." Reese was smiling at her—but his attention was on the factory he and the little girl had just fled.

Barnes and his men had hardly made their way inside the factory and down to the first subterranean level when they were greeted by the sight of the frozen, headless body of an advanced Terminator. Equally shocking to the lieutenant was the sight of John Connor, wounded but alive, trying to revive a powerful, prone shape that was all too familiar.

"Spread out!" Barnes commanded his men. "Secure the immediate area!"

"What for, sir?" husked one of his troopers, nodding toward the mismatched pair in front of them. "That's Connor, isn't it? Shouldn't we...?"

"Move, dammit!" Barnes gave the man a shove, waited until the last of the soldiers had complied with his order.

Then, gun raised and aimed at the body on the floor, he advanced cautiously forward.

"Man, what are you *doing*? Isn't it—one of them?"

As Barnes approached, Connor lifted his head from Wright's chest. "He's alive. Not 'it,' Barnes. *He*. As to what 'he' is—we'll find out. All I know is that 'he' saved my life." Bending, he struggled to get an arm around the heavy, limp shape. "I don't know if he's breathing, but his heart's beating. Help me."

Gun still leveled, still aimed, Barnes just stared at him. Connor lowered his voice. "*Help me*, Lieutenant."

Barnes hesitated a moment longer. Then he slung his gun over his shoulder and came around the other side of the half-raised Wright to help.

The spirits of those on board the chopper were in turmoil until Barnes and Connor appeared from the ruins of the factory. Between them they were supporting a bruised and badly injured figure. Kate rushed to meet her husband.

"John!"

Eyes widening, Blair recognized the limp, shattered shape that was being supported between the two Resistance fighters.

"Marcus?...*Marcus!*"

Scrambling out of her seat, she turned the controls over to her co-pilot as she stumbled toward the back of the 'copter. Around it the battle still raged as the determined fighters continued to take down anything that moved that wasn't human.

Connor and Barnes laid Wright out in the back of the helicopter. While a sobbing, grateful Kate embraced her husband, an agonized Blair forced her eyes to travel over the length of Wright's battered, tormented body. This was Marcus Wright—but his wounds were terrible. Fighting back tears, trying not to choke, she turned to the woman whose love had just been restored to her.

Her eyes locked on Kate's.

"Save him," Blair pleaded simply.

Kate stared back as Connor let her go.

"I don't know—he's not like anything we've ever seen before. He's not like us—inside. I'm a doctor, not an engineer."

Blair started to grab for her, but finally sat back helplessly. Reaching down, she took Wright's hand. A groaning, grinding noise came from somewhere deep within his chest. His fingers contracted around hers. Gently. Lovingly.

Kate Connor saw it.

Grabbing up her medical kit, she positioned herself alongside the body.

"I'll do what I can," she murmured. As she bent to work, Barnes had gone forward to slap the co-pilot on the shoulder.

"Let's get the hell out of hell." The man needed no urging. He shoved forward on the stick and the 'copter lifted off.

In the cargo bay, a startled Connor realized what was happening. "No, wait! I've got to go back!" He started for the open portal, fully intending to jump despite his own injuries. Setting aside her instruments, Kate had to grab him to keep him from attempting a near-fatal plunge.

"Are you out of your mind? We can't go back." She nodded downward. The chopper was already fifty meters off the ground and climbing fast as the co-pilot accelerated away from the scene of combat.

He was clinging to the opening.

"Kate, the detonator—I left it back there! I've got to...!"

He broke off as his gaze fastened on a small shape hovering nearby. Star moved closer. Silently, she unfolded her closed hand, the fingers opening like the petals of a flower. Still intact and full of quiet promise, the detonator lay exposed in the center of her tiny palm. As their eyes met, her lips trembled with the effort of trying to speak.

Fighting through horror, she formed words. Two.

"End this."

Connor nodded. Quietly, he took the detonator and lowered his gaze. The last of the Resistance choppers had fled the combat zone. He blinked to clear his vision. After everything that had happened, after all that had transpired, he did not want to miss the fireworks.

He squeezed the trigger.

In order for any designated Terminator to operate and carry out its programmed functions, an enormous amount of energy had to be packed into the small, portable container that powered it. Thousands of such containers lay stacked in a secure corner of the main Terminator factory below. When the C-4 cord that had been wrapped around them detonated, so did they.

This in turn set off a great many unstable substances that were also stored within the factory. When the factory went up, in a blast sufficiently wide, deep, and loud to satisfy the most vengeful Resistance fighter, this in turn touched off similar explosions in every facility nearby.

By the time the chopper was well on its way across the Bay, a good deal of machine-transformed San Francisco was blowing itself skyward in a series of sequential eruptions that were little short of volcanic. The moonlight that glistened on the placid water below was in complete and peaceful contrast to the cataclysm that was ripping apart the land falling steadily farther behind them.

Lying on the floor, Marcus Wright fought to focus. He did not mind the injuries that incapacitated him. He did not mind that parts of him were broken and perhaps damaged beyond repair. All that mattered was the face that glowed above him—glowed in the reflected light from the continuing series of explosions below and receding rapidly into the distance. The face of the woman who loved him, the warmth of whose hand he could feel in his own.

Despite his awkward position he could clearly see those gathered around him. Sitting on a bench seat embracing his wife was the man whom he had saved and who in turned had saved him. A beat-up but ever resilient John Connor acknowledged the other man's gaze with a slow wink as his wife hugged him tightly. The woman Virginia was there too. And Kyle Reese, tougher than he knew. The little girl Star, silent but aware. Reaching into the interior of the chopper, the moonlight softened and seemed to heal all of them, rendering Kate Connor's face angelic instead of just determined, making Reese look as young as he actually was, glinting redly off one of Star's eyes....

Wright blinked. The glint was gone. As if it had never been.

It was nothing at all, he told himself with assurance. There had been nothing there, nothing to see. The briefest of flickers of moonlight on cornea. Nothing more than a second of reflection, a singular twinkle.

Or a singularity.

"THIS IS NOT THE FUTURE MY MOTHER WARNED ME ABOUT."
- John Connor

The actions of John and Kate Connor, Kyle Reese, Star and Marcus Wright have implications that stretch from the past into the distant future. The toss of a coin, the roll of a dice, a split-second reaction in the line of fire can alter the course of destiny in a myriad of different ways...

CYBERDYNE SYSTEMS
CONFIDENTIAL
CYBERDYNE SYSTEMS

Subject: John Connor/the future
                of the human race

Access date: 21 May 2009

**Access site: www.titanbooks.com/
                terminatorsalvation**

Access code: ts2000

Log on to access a new future.

Keep reading for an extract from
Terminator Salvation: From the Ashes
by Timothy Zahn, which is also
available from Titan Books.

PROLOGUE

The last day of his life, he remembered thinking afterward, had been hell on earth.

It wasn't just the heat of the Baja desert. That was awesomely intense, shimmering across the dirt and scrub, and he knew some of his fellow Marines were suffering in it. But U.S. Marine Sergeant Justo Orozco had grown up in East Los Angeles, and he had no problem with heat.

It wasn't just the job, either. The Eleventh Marine Expeditionary Unit prided itself on its ability to fight anywhere on the planet, and there wasn't any particular reason why Orozco's platoon shouldn't be here running a drug-interdiction exercise with their Mexican Army counterparts. Never mind that the theory underlying the exercise was bogus. Never mind that the Mexicans probably saw this as a slap at their own capabilities. The logic and politics of the situation weren't Orozco's concern, and he wasn't being paid by the hour.

No, what made this particular mission hell was the way every single damn Mexican insisted on calling all the Americans "gringo."

Including Orozco.

It irritated the hell out of him, which was probably why they kept doing it. He was an American, yes, but he was also full-blooded Hispanic, and he was damn proud of both. Why some people seemed to think those two identities had to be mutually exclusive was something he had never understood. He'd never put up with that nonsense before, and it galled the grit out of him to have to put up with it now.

But he was under orders to be cooperative. More than that, he was a professional, and he was damned if he would let a few resentful locals get the best of him.

It was getting on toward evening, and the team was just wrapping up a search-and-corral exercise, when out of the corner of his eye Orozco saw the flash.

His first reflexive assumption was that the Mexicans had sneaked an aircraft into the exercise, just to shake things up a little, and that he'd caught a flicker of sunlight off one of its windows. He turned that direction, opening his mouth to warn the rest of the team.

The words died in his throat. In the hazy distance far to the north, right where he'd seen the flash, a tiny, red-edged cloud had appeared.

And as he watched, its top boiled over into the shape of a mushroom.

He was trying to wrap his brain around the sight when there was another small flicker, slightly brighter this time. He waited, still staring at the mushroom cloud, when a second fiery pillar boiled up from the earth a little ways to the east of the first.

"My God," someone whispered beside him. "Is that...? Oh, *God*!"

"It's San Diego," Orozco said, the sheer unnatural calmness in his voice as frightening as the mushroom clouds themselves. "San Diego."

"Maybe Mexicali, too," someone else muttered.

"Or Twentynine Palms," Orozco said, marveling at

the strange disconnect that had severed the link between his intellect and emotions. "Who the hell would want to take out Mexicali?"

"I just thought—"

"*Oh, Dios mio!*"

With an effort, Orozco tore his eyes away from the twin pillars of death. One of the Mexicans was staring past Orozco's shoulder, his eyes wide and horrified, his face as pale as any of the gringos he derided. Moving like a man slogging through a nightmare, Orozco turned to look.

In the distance to the southeast, another tiny mushroom had appeared, clawing its way toward the sky.

"What the *hell*?" someone gasped. "That can't be—"

"Hermosillo," one of the other Mexicans said in a quavering voice. The man had tears shimmering in his eyes, and Orozco remembered him talking about his family in Hermosillo.

Orozco stared at the third mushroom cloud, his mind reeling with the utter insanity of it. San Diego, yes. Twentynine Palms, maybe. But Hermosillo? The place didn't have a single shred of military or political significance that Orozco could think of. Why would anyone waste a nuke taking it out?

Unless someone had decided to take out everything.

Slowly, he turned to look at the rest of his team, their faces etched with varying degrees of terror, anger, or disbelief. They'd figured it out, too. Or they would soon enough.

Their lives were over. Everyone's life was now over.

Orozco took a deep breath.

"I think," he said, "we can safely say the exercise is over."

"What do we do now?" someone asked.

Orozco took another look around the group...and this time, he saw something he hadn't noticed before. All the Marines were looking at him. Even Lieutenant Raeder, whose face was as frozen as anyone else's. They were all looking at Orozco.

Waiting for their sergeant to tell them what to do.

He took another deep breath. One of these deep breaths, he thought distantly, would be his last. He wondered if he would even know at the time which breath that would be.

"We'll be all right," he said. "We'll survive, because we're Marines, and that's what Marines do. We'll start by going back to camp and figuring out what we've got to work with."

For a moment no one moved. Then the lieutenant stirred.

"You heard the man," he called. "Gather up the gear and head back to camp."

Slowly, the clustered knots broke up as the men finally began to move. Orozco took one last look to the north, noting that the mushroom clouds, too, were starting to break up.

And as he began helping the others collect the gear, he realized he'd been wrong. This day hadn't been hell on earth. This day had been paradise.

Hell on earth had just begun.

CHAPTER ONE

It was after one in the morning by the time John Connor and his Resistance team made their way back through the rubble of Greater Los Angeles to the half-broken, half-burned-out building they'd called home for the past three months. He supervised the others as they stowed their gear, then sent them stumbling wearily to their bunks.

Then, alone in the small pool of light from his desk lamp, amid the outer darkness that pressed in against it, he sat down to make out his report.

In many ways, he reflected, this was one of the worst parts of the war against Skynet. In the heat of battle, with HK Hunter-Killers swooping past overhead and T-600 Terminators lumbering in from all sides, there was no time for deep thought or grand strategy or clever planning. You played it on the fly, running and shooting and running some more, hoping you could spot the openings and opportunities before Skynet could close them, trying to achieve your mission goal and still get as many of your people out alive as you could.

But sitting here alone, with a piece of crumpled paper laid out on top of a battered file cabinet, things were different. You had the quiet and the time and—worst of all—the hindsight to replay the battle over and over again. You saw all the things you should have done faster, or smarter, or just different. You saw the mistakes, the lapses of judgment, the miscues.

And you relived the deaths. All of them.

But it was part of the job, and it had to be done. Every Resistance contact with the enemy—win, lose, or draw—was data that could be sifted, prodded, evaluated, and tucked away for possible future reference. With enough such data, maybe the strategists at Command would someday finally find a weakness or blind spot that could be used to bring down the whole Skynet system.

Or so the theory went. Connor, at least, didn't believe it for a minute. This was going to be a long, bloody war, and he had long since stopped hoping for silver bullets.

But you never knew. Besides, Skynet was certainly analyzing its side of each encounter. The Resistance might as well do the same.

It took him half an hour to write up the report and transmit it to Command. After that he spent a few minutes in the bathroom cleaning up as best he could, scrubbing other men's blood off his hands and clothing. Then, shutting off the last of the bunker's lights, he cracked the shutters to let in a bit of fresh air, and wearily headed down the darkened corridor to the tiny room he shared with his wife.

Kate was stretched out in bed, the blankets tucked up under her chin, her breathing slow and steady. Hopefully long since asleep, though Connor had no real illusions on that score. As one of their team's two genuine doctors, the hours she put in were nearly as long as Connor's own, and in some ways even bloodier.

For a minute he just stood inside the doorway, gazing

at her with a mixture of love, pride, and guilt. Once upon a time she'd had the nice, simple job of a veterinarian, where the worst thing that could happen in a given day was a nervous horse or a lap dog with attitude.

Connor had taken her away from all that. Wrenched her out of it, more accurately, snatching her from the path of Skynet's last attempt to kill him before the devastation of Judgment Day.

Of course, if he *hadn't* taken her away, she would be dead now. There were all too many days when he wondered if that would have been a kinder fate than the one he'd bestowed on her.

There's no fate but what we make for ourselves. The old quote whispered through his mind. Kyle Reese's old quote, the words Connor himself would one day teach the boy—

"Good morning," Kate murmured from the bed.

Connor started.

"Sorry—didn't mean to wake you," he murmured back.

"You didn't," she assured him, pushing back the blankets and propping herself up on one elbow. "I only got to bed an hour or so ago. I heard everyone else come in, and I've just been dozing a little while I waited for you. How did it go?"

"About like usual," Connor said as he crossed to the bed and sat down. "We got the Riverside radar tower— not just taken down, but blown to splinters. If Olsen's team got the Pasadena tower like they were supposed to, that'll leave Skynet just the Capistrano one and no triangulation at all. That should take a lot of the pressure off our air support in any future operations. At least until Skynet gets around to rebuilding everything."

"Good—we can use a breather," Kate said. "How many did we lose?"

Connor grimaced.

"Three. Garcia, Smitty, and Rondo."

"I'm sorry," she said, and Connor could see some of his own pain flash across her eyes. "That's, what, ten including the ones Jericho lost when his team took out the Thousand Oaks tower?"

"Eleven," Connor corrected. "Those towers come expensive, don't they?"

"They sure do," Kate said soberly. Abruptly, she brightened. "By the way, I have a surprise for you." Reaching to the far side of the bed, she came up with a small bag. "Merry Christmas."

Connor stared at the bag in her hand, a surge of husbandly panic flashing through him. How could he possibly have forgotten—?

"Wait a minute," he said, frowning. "This is *March*."

"Well, yes, technically," Kate conceded innocently. "But we were all kind of busy on the official Christmas."

Connor searched his memory, trying to pick the specifics out of the long, blended-together nightmare that life on earth had become.

"Was that the day we raided the air reserve base for parts?"

"No, that was Christmas Eve," Kate corrected. "Christmas Day we were mostly playing hide-and-seek with those three T-1s that wanted the stuff back. Anyway, I didn't have anything for you back then." She jiggled the bag enticingly. "Now, I do. Go ahead—take it."

"But I didn't get anything for you," Connor protested as he took the bag.

"Sure you did," Kate said quietly. "You came home alive. That's all I want."

Connor braced himself.

"Kate, we've been through this," he reminded her gently. "You're too valuable as a surgeon to risk having you go out in the field."

"Yes, I remember all the arguments," Kate said. "And up to now, I've mostly agreed with them."

"Mostly?"

She sighed.

"You're the most important thing in my life, John. In fact, you're the most important thing in *everyone's* life, even if they don't know it yet. Whatever I can do to keep you focused, that's what I'll do. Whether I personally like it or not. If having me stay behind helps that focus, well, I've been content to do that."

Connor had to turn away from the intensity in her eyes.

"Until now?"

"Until now." She reached up and put her hand on his cheek, gently but firmly turning him back to look at her. "People are dying out there. Far too many people, far too quickly. We need every gun and every set of hands in the field that we can get. You know that as well as I do."

"But you're more valuable to us right here," Connor tried again.

"Am I?" Kate asked. "Even if we grant for the sake of argument that I'm any safer hiding in a makeshift bunker than I am out in the field, is this really where I can do the most good? Patching up the wounded after you get them back is all well and good, but I can't help but think it would be better if you had me right there with you where I could do the preliminary work on the spot."

"You could teach some of the others."

"I *have* taught them," Kate reminded him. "I've taught you and them and everyone everything I can about first aid. But there's nothing I can do to give you my experience, and that's what you need out there. You need a field medic, pure and simple. So you've got Campollo and me, and Campollo is seventy-one with arthritic knees. This is one of those decisions that really kind of makes itself, don't you think?"

Connor closed his eyes.

"I don't want to lose you, Kate."

"I don't want to lose you, either," she said quietly. "That's why we need to be together. So that neither of us loses the other."

With her hand still on his cheek, she leaned forward and gave him a lingering kiss. Connor kissed her back, hungrily, craving the love and closeness and peace that had all but died so many years ago, when the missiles began falling to the earth.

They held the kiss for a long minute, and then Kate gently disengaged.

"Meanwhile," she said, giving him an impish smile, "you still have a Christmas present to open."

Connor smiled back.

"What in the world would I do without you?"

"Well, for one thing, you could have been asleep fifteen minutes ago," Kate said dryly. "Come on—open it."

Connor focused on the bag in his hand. It was one of the drawstring bags Kate packed emergency first-aid supplies in, turned inside out so that the smoother, silkier side was outward.

"I see you've been shopping at Macy's again," he commented as he carefully pulled it open.

"Actually, I just keep reusing their bags," Kate said. "Adds class to all my gift-giving. For heaven's sake—were you this slow on Christmas when you were a boy?"

Connor shrugged.

"Given that my mother's typical Christmas presents were new Browning semi-autos or C4 detonators, it didn't pay to open packages too quickly."

Kate's eyes widened.

"You *are* joking, aren't you?"

"Of course," Connor said with a straight face. "Christmas was survival gear; Fourth of *July* was munitions. Okay, here goes." He reached into the bag.

And to his surprise, pulled out a badly cracked jewel case with a slightly battered compact disc inside.

"What's this?" he asked, peering at it in the dim light.

"A little memory from your childhood," Kate said. "Or at least from simpler days. An album called *Use Your Illusion II.*"

Connor felt his eyes open. A memory from his childhood, indeed. "Thank you," he said. "Where on earth did you find it?"

"One of Olsen's men had it with him last month when they came by to swap munitions," Kate said. "I remembered you talking about listening to it when you were younger, so I traded him a couple of extra bandage packs for it. You know, those packs we dug out of the treatment room at the Orange County Zoo."

"I just hope Tunney was able to get that CD player working," Connor commented, cradling the disk carefully in his hands. "I miss music. That and Italian food, I think, are what I miss most."

"For me, it's definitely music," Kate mused. "Vocals, especially—I used to love listening to a live choir in full four-part harmony." She smiled faintly. "Just a *bit* different from your taste in music."

"Differences are the spice of life," Connor reminded her. "And G'n'R is probably better music to kill machines by."

"Probably." Kate's smile faded. "Besides, nowadays what reason does anyone have to sing?"

"There's still life," Connor said, eyeing his wife closely. Kate didn't get depressed very often, but when she did it could be a deep and terrible pit. "And love, and friends."

"But mostly just life," Kate agreed. "I know. Sometimes we forget what's really important, don't we?"

"A constant problem throughout history," Connor said, breathing a quiet sigh of relief. So she wasn't going there, after all. Good. "Thanks again, Kate. This really makes my day. Probably even my *year*."

"You're welcome," she said. "Oh, and *rock on*. The man who gave me the disk told me to say that." She took a deep breath, and Connor could see her chasing the memories back to where they belonged. "Meanwhile, it's been a late night, and the world starts up again in about five hours. Come on, let's go to bed."

"Right." Standing up, Connor reached for his gunbelt. And paused. "Did you hear something?" he asked in a low voice.

"I don't know," Kate said, her head tilted in concentration.

Connor frowned, straining his ears. A whispery wind was blowing gently across the bunker roof, setting cat-purr vibrations through the piles of loose debris up there. Everything seemed all right.

But *something* had caught his attention. And something was still screaming wordlessly across his combat senses.

"Stay here," Connor told his wife, crossing back to the door. He listened at the panel for a moment, then cautiously opened it.

The earlier overcast sky had cleared somewhat, allowing a little starlight to filter in through the cracked shutters. Connor checked both directions down the empty corridor, then headed left toward the rear of the bunker and the sentry post situated between the living quarters and storage room.

Piccerno was on duty, seated on a tall stepladder with everything from his shoulders up snugged up inside the observation dome. Like everything else these days, the dome was a product of simplicity and ingenuity: an old plastic office wastebasket that had been fastened to the top of the bunker, equipped with a set of eye slits that permitted 360-degree surveillance, then covered from above with strategically placed rubble to disguise its true purpose.

"Report," Connor murmured as he stepped to the foot of the ladder.

There was no answer.

"Piccerno?" Connor murmured, the hair on the back of his neck tingling. "Piccerno?"

Still no answer. Getting a one-handed grip on the ladder, Connor headed up. He reached the top and pushed aside Piccerno's bunched-up parka collar.

One touch of the warm, sticky liquid that had soaked the upper surface of the collar was all he needed to know what had happened. He spent another precious second anyway, peering up into the narrow space between Piccerno's face and the rim of the dome, just to make sure there was nothing he could do.

There wasn't. Piccerno's eyes were open but unseeing, his forehead leaning against the dome, the blood from the hole in his left temple still trickling down his face.

Skynet had found them.

Quickly, Connor climbed back down the ladder, a kaleidoscope of Piccerno's life with the team flashing through his mind. Ruthlessly, he forced back the memories.

This was not the time.

Grabbing the Heckler & Koch MP5 submachine gun that was propped against the wall, he hurried back to the living quarters.

Kate was already dressed, her gun belt in hand. "What is it?" she asked tensely.

"Piccerno's dead," Connor told her grimly. "Long-range sniper, or else one hell of a silencer."

"Terminators?"

"I didn't check," Connor said. "Skynet's obviously trying the sneaky approach, and I didn't want to do anything that might alert it that we were onto the game. Get back to supply—I'll go roust everyone and send them back there. Make a quick sort of the equipment and load them with as much as you think they can handle."

"Right," Kate said as she finished strapping on her gun belt.

"And keep everyone as quiet as you can," Connor added. "The longer Skynet thinks we're all still asleep, the longer we'll have before the fireworks start."

Kate nodded.

"Be careful."

"You, too."

He continued along the corridor, ducking into each room as he passed and nudging or whispering the occupants awake, giving them a set of terse instructions, then moving on as they grabbed their clothing and weapons.

Finally, he reached the bunker's main entrance. There, to his complete lack of surprise, he found Barnes waiting, standing beside the bunker door with his eye pressed to one of the eyeslits, a 9mm Steyr in his holster and one of the group's few remaining grenade launchers clutched to his chest. A few feet away stood the young man who was supposed to be on sentry duty tonight, his throat working as he nervously fingered his rifle.

"We got eight T-600s on the way," Barnes reported as Connor came up beside him. "What's goin' on in back?"

"They took out Piccerno," Connor told him. "Quietly, and at least several minutes ago. Probably means Skynet's about to send in the heavy stuff—T-1s or maybe a tank or two—and was hoping to sneak up on us."

Barnes grunted and straightened up from the peepholes. His bald head glistened with a week's worth of sweat, his clenched teeth glinting through two weeks' worth of beard stubble.

"So what's the plan?"

"We run on our timetable, not Skynet's," Connor replied. "If we can buy a few minutes, I can—"

Barnes nodded.

"Got just the thing."

With that he pulled open the door, and fired.

There was a soft *chuff* as the grenade shot skyward

out of its tube. Biting down hard on his tongue—*I can get more men here before you engage*—Connor stepped quickly to the other side of the doorway and looked out.

In the faint starlight he could see eight towering, human-shaped figures picking their way carefully across the treacherous ground. One of the T-600s looked up at the sounds from the bunker, and Connor caught a glimpse of glowing red eyes.

And then, with a brilliant flash, Barnes's grenade exploded.

Not in the midst of the approaching Terminators, but in the doorway of the half-collapsed four-story building immediately to their right. There was a stutter as the grenade's shockwave set off a line of smaller charges embedded in the pockmarked masonry.

And with a horrendous crunch, the entire wall gave way, raining blocks of concrete and rebar and broken glass across the street, toppling and burying all eight of the Terminators.

"That how you wanted it?" Barnes called to Connor over the echoing roar.

"Pretty much," Connor said. So much for giving the group as much time as possible to make their escape.

On the other hand, if Barnes hadn't blown the building when he did, the eight Terminators would soon have passed that particular trap, and Connor's fighters would have had that many more enemies to deal with.

"I'll send you some backup," he added, moving away from the doorway. "Hold for ten minutes, or as long as you can, then pull back to the tunnel."

"I don't need no one else," Barnes growled, throwing a contemptuous glance at the shaking sentry. "You just get the people and stuff out."

"I'll send you some backup," Connor repeated, making it clear it was an order, and headed back down the corridor. Barnes was probably one of the best ground fighters in the entire Resistance, but this wasn't the time for lone-wolf tactics. If indeed there ever was such a time.

If anyone had needed extra incentive to get moving, Barnes's wake-up explosion had apparently done the trick. The whole bunker was alive with people, many of them still scrambling into their clothing as they ran toward the supply room and the emergency exit beyond.

A few of the faster dressers had taken up positions in doorways along the way, their weapons pointed toward the front of the bunker, ready to sacrifice themselves if necessary to slow down the machines once the outer defenses were breached. Connor grabbed two of them and sent them up to the entrance, gave everyone else the same ten-minute warning he'd given Barnes, then headed back to his room for anything he or Kate might have left behind.

He made especially sure that he grabbed his new G'n'R CD.

Most of the fifty-odd people of the team had made it to the supply room by the time he arrived, with only a few stragglers still coming in. Kate was in the center of the activity, coolly pointing each newcomer to the boxes, bags, and packs she'd selected for the must-save list.

"How are we doing?" Connor asked as he picked up two ammo satchels and slung one over each shoulder.

"Another ninety seconds and we'll have everything we can carry," Kate told him, threading a bungee cord between the satchels' straps and fastening them together across Connor's chest so that they wouldn't slip off his shoulders. "They took Piccerno's body down," she added more quietly.

Connor nodded. He'd noticed that on his way through.

"Have Blair and Yoshi been through? I didn't spot either of them, but it was pretty dark and I wasn't exactly taking roll."

"Blair's here," Kate said, waving to a pair of late-comers and pointing them to a stack of ration boxes. "She said she'll go out with the rest of us and make her way back to the hangar. Yoshi's already there, or at least he's supposed to be."

"We'll need to get the ground crew out, too," Connor said, grimacing as a low vibration tickled at the soles of his feet. "Here comes our company."

The words were barely out of his mouth when one of the younger women dashed in from the direction of the sentry post, nearly running down an eight-year-old boy in the process.

"T-1s," she announced breathlessly. "Coming in from all directions."

"Are they heading for the main door?" Connor asked.

"No, toward here. I saw them through the—" she faltered a little "—where Piccerno was. Maybe a hundred meters out."

Connor nodded. T-1s were heavy, splay-armed fighting machines mounted on heavy treads, slower than the humanoid T-600s but more heavily armed and even harder to take down. The plan was probably to roll them up onto the roof near Piccerno's sentry post in hopes of collapsing it by sheer weight and trapping the group in a pincer.

"Go to the front and tell Barnes and the others I said to pull out now," Connor told her. "They're to collect the rest of the backstops along the way."

The girl nodded and took off down the corridor at a dead run.

"Tunney?" Connor called, looking around at the heavily laden men and women.

"Here, sir," Tunney called from the side wall. He and the other lieutenant, David, were standing beside the dark opening that led into the bunker's emergency exit. Like Connor, each man was loaded with two shoulder bags of ammo or grenades, but instead of just a submachine gun each of them also carried a grenade launcher and flame thrower. "Time to go?" he asked.

"Almost," Connor said, squeezing Kate's shoulder briefly and then crossing to join them. "Now it is," he said. "I'll take point; keep a three-meter spacing between us."

"I believe it's my turn for point, sir," Tunney said, his voice low but firm.

Connor shook his head.

"My team; my job. Stay alert—if Skynet's found the far end, we'll have some unpleasant surprises waiting."

He looked back at the group, to find them silently watching him. Watching, and trusting.

"Stay as quiet as you can, and don't stop moving," he said, keeping his voice as calm as if this was just another training exercise. "Once you're through the tunnel, depending on what's waiting out there, we may decide to split into small groups of two or three. Everyone knows where Fallback One is?"

The room bobbed briefly with nodding heads.

"Then I'll see you all there," Connor said. "Good luck." Nodding for Tunney and David to follow, he headed into the tunnel.

The group referred to the emergency exit as a tunnel, but a real, hand-dug tunnel would have taken far more time and manpower than the group had had to spare over the past few months. The route was instead a mostly natural pathway consisting of half-crushed hallways, basements, and service corridors. Connor's people had cleared out the blockages, propped up the ceilings, and dug short connecting shafts where necessary until they'd created an exit route that could take them invisibly a good three blocks from the bunker.

But there was always the chance that one of Skynet's endlessly roving machines had spotted the route, and Connor felt his nerves tightening with each step as he made his way through the darkness.

There were dozens of places where the roof had eroded through to the outside world, allowing in some badly needed starlight but also precluding the use of any lights by the escapees. Worse, the longest straight-line segment anywhere in the tunnel was about six meters, with everything else being a collection of zigzags, right-angle turns, and occasional backtracks. A T-600 waiting in the darkness around any one of those corners could have Connor and his vanguard dead before they even knew what had hit them.

But each corner was clear, the starlight filtering through the fissures never blazed with HK floodlights, and he heard nothing of the telltale growl of T-1 treads. Gradually, Connor's hopes and pace began to pick up. They might make it. They just might make it.

He was about halfway through the tunnel when the

sounds of distant explosions and gunfire began to echo through the passageway from behind him.

He swore feelingly under his breath. The blasts could be nothing more ominous than Barnes setting off the last string of the bunker's booby traps. But they could also be the rear guard fighting desperately against T-1s that had succeeded in crashing through the bunker roof.

And Kate would be one of the last of the group to leave, probably just a couple of steps ahead of Barnes. If the Terminators had cut through...

If they had, there was nothing Connor could do to help. He could only trust to hope, and to the destiny that linked him and Kate to humanity's ultimate salvation.

He'd gone twenty meters more when a blast rolled through the tunnel, sending a wave of warm air across the back of his neck. The final booby trap had been triggered, bringing down the bunker's ceiling and burying any Terminators that had made it inside as it sealed off the end of the tunnel. Connor and his people were committed now, with nowhere to go but forward.

Still no sign that Skynet had noticed them. Connor kept going, the drifting air currents from the overhead gaps slowly becoming a single steady breeze in his face. He rounded one final blind corner, and with a suddenness that for some reason never failed to surprise him, he was at the end.

Cautiously, he looked out between the carefully positioned rotting two-by-fours that blocked the exit. The street beyond was cleaner than some he'd seen, with much of the masonry and wood having been scavenged over the years by the handful of civilians who still scratched out a tenuous existence in the ruined city.

More importantly, there was no sign of Terminators.

From the direction of the bunker came a short burst of gunfire from one of the remote-activated guns set up there and in nearby buildings. The burst was answered instantly by a longer, staccato roar from the T-600s' miniguns. Connor gestured Tunney forward, and the two men set to work clearing the exit.

The wooden barrier looked sturdier and more impassible than it actually was, and it took less than half a minute for them to silently move the boards out of the way. Connor started to step out.

And ducked back as an HK swooped past, just half a block away, heading toward the bunker. Connor waited a few seconds, then tried again.

Nothing jumped or swooped out at him, either metal or human. As the sporadic gunfire continued from the vicinity of the bunker, he did a quick three-sixty, then gestured to Tunney and David. The two men slipped past him, moved ten meters in opposite directions down the street, and did three-sixties of their own. They hand-signaled the all-clear, then hunkered down in the rubble with weapons ready.

Connor stepped back into the tunnel, went back around that final blind corner, and gestured to the line of people waiting tensely in the dark.

Blair Williams, her dark hair tied back in a ponytail, was the fifth one out. She spotted Connor and stepped out of line.

"I'm heading for the hangar," she announced softly. "Any special orders?"

"Yes; that you wait a minute," Connor told her, grabbing her arm and pulling her down into a crouch as another HK appeared to the west, weaving its way between the skeletal remains of two of the taller buildings.

"Why?" Blair countered.

"Just wait," Connor repeated.

Blair huffed something under her breath, but obedient-ly moved over to the stubby remains of a fire hydrant and squatted beside it, drawing her big .44 caliber Desert Eagle from its holster.

Two more HKs had swooped in to join the party at the bunker before everyone made it out of the tunnel. But none of the machines came close, and there was no indic-ation that they'd noticed anything amiss, especial-ly with all the gunfire masking any sounds the group might make.

Kate, as Connor had expected, was the last one out before the rear guard. At the very end of the line, also as expected, was Barnes.

"You seen my brother?" he asked Connor, hefting his grenade launcher as he looked around.

"Yes, he's already out," Connor assured him. Along with his launcher, Connor noted, Barnes had also picked up a Galil assault rifle somewhere along the way and had the weapon slung over his shoulder along with his gear bags. If all the extra weight was bother-ing him, it didn't show.

"Good," Barnes said. "We're splitting up, right? I'll get my squad and take point."

"David will handle your squad," Connor told him. "I want you to take Blair to the hangar."

Blair rose from her crouch, a look of outraged dis-belief on her face.

"Is *that* why you made me wait?" she demanded. "For *him*?"

"I don't want you trying to get to the hangar alone,"

Connor told her.

"I don't need him," Blair insisted.

"Right—she doesn't need me," Barnes seconded.

"More importantly, Wince and Inji are still in there," Connor explained patiently. "Once the planes are out, someone has to get them to safety."

Barnes bared his teeth, but reluctantly nodded.

"Fine. Come on, flygirl. Try to keep up."

He set off down the street, his head moving back and forth as he watched for trouble. Blair paused long enough to roll her eyes, then followed.

"I'm sure they're secretly very fond of each other," Kate offered dryly.

"As long as they dislike Skynet more, I'm happy," Connor said. "Come on, let's get these people out of here."

To read what happens next, pick up a copy of *Terminator Salvation: From the Ashes* from your nearest bookstore.

www.titanbooks.com

 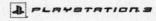

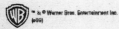